MW01244054

THE FLAWED LEGACY

THE FLAWED LEGACY

LEGACY OF THE SHADOW'S BLOOD™ BOOK 1

E.G. BATEMAN

MICHAEL ANDERLE

DISRUPTIVE IMAGINATION®

Copyright © 2020 LMBPN Publishing
Cover by Fantasy Book Design
Cover copyright © LMBPN Publishing
A Michael Anderle Production

LMBPN Publishing
PMB 196, 2540 South Maryland Pkwy
Las Vegas, NV 89109

First US edition, September 2020
(Originally published as a part of Legacy of the Shadow's Blood)
eBook ISBN: 978-1-64971-134-2
Print ISBN: 978-1-64971-135-9

THE FLAWED LEGACY TEAM

Thanks to our Beta Readers:

Erika Everest, Nicole Emens, Jim Caplan, Mary Morris, John Ashmore, Kelly O'Donnell, Larry Omans, Michael Baumann

Thanks to our JIT Team:

Dave Hicks
Deb Mader
Debi Sateren
Diane L. Smith
Dorothy Lloyd
Erika Everest
Jackey Hankard-Brodie
James Caplan
Jeff Eaton
Jeff Goode
John Ashmore
Lori Hendricks
Micky Cocker

Misty Roa
Paul Westman
Peter Manis
Rachel Beckford
Veronica Stephan-Miller

Editor
SkyHunter Editing Team

DEDICATIONS

Phil, for not only believing in me, but for hopping aboard this
crazy train.
Michael Anderle, for your support, mentorship and above all,
patience.
Craig Martelle, for being an inspiration and providing a place for
me and so many others to grow as authors.
Erika Everest, Kate Pickford, Anne Lown, Natalie Roberts and
Charles Tillman - For your support, time and kindness.
And... for the readers, always for you.

— *E.G. Bateman*

To Family, Friends and
Those Who Love
To Read.
May We All Enjoy Grace
To Live The Life We Are
Called.

— *Michael Anderle*

CHAPTER ONE

"Two Eighteen... Two Nineteen..."

Lexi walked along the balcony of the seedy Palm Springs motel and spun the room key around her finger as she counted off room numbers. She stopped, turned, and looked over the balcony and down toward the office.

Yep, the twerpy admin guy was checking out her leather-clad ass.

She gave him her best I-will-cut-you stare. He did a one-eighty and walked away from the window.

Smart man.

As she continued past the rooms, a car moved along slowly below her and matched her speed. She stopped at a door and raised her hand without bothering to look down, and the vehicle pulled into a parking space directly beneath the room.

When she'd opened the door, Lexi assessed the space. They usually stayed in shitty hotels but Dolores had outdone herself booking this one. It was super-shitty.

"Wow! This one's super-shitty." Scott materialized at her shoulder and voiced her thoughts.

Lexi jerked to the side and her head snapped toward him.

1

"Holy crap, can you *not* do that?"

He raised his arms. "What? You want me to walk up the stairs with these bags?" His wavy blond hair flopped into his eyes and he blew it away.

"Just…" She drew in a measured breath before she puffed it out. "Announce yourself." Her glance swept around. "And be more careful in public."

She could feel his shrug. "I *was* being careful. I waited until you scared the office guy away with your…you know, *face*."

He tried to shuffle past her to enter the room, but she blocked his path with an upraised arm.

"I have to check it's safe first." Lexi pulled a blade from…well, no one was ever quite sure where they came from, and that was how she liked it.

"Oh, right, of course." He vanished from beside her and appeared inside the room. He dropped the bags and reappeared beside her again, dusted his right sleeve, and picked distractedly at a thread. He looked up and made a shooing motion with his left hand. "Okay, go ahead." He returned his attention to the errant thread.

She stared at him, then closed her eyes. A succession of tiny jerks of her head coincided with the multitude of responses her brain flicked through and discarded. Most of them involved breaking bones. She opened her eyes, sighed, and moved inside.

Lexi walked through the room. There wasn't much to search. Two single beds stood on the left, a dresser and mirror on the right, and a door directly ahead. She opened it and stuck her head into the bathroom but pulled it back sharply and wondered, based on the overpowering smell of bleach, if she'd found a murder room.

Quickly closing the bathroom door, she turned to the motel room doorway to find it empty. A further turn revealed Scott lying on one of the beds and her eyes narrowed.

"It's safe, you can come in," she snarked.

His green eyes looked left, then right as if searching for a successful excuse, and he finally looked at her with a small grin. "Oh, sorry."

As he shifted, a spring pinged loudly. They looked at each other and simultaneously rolled their eyes. He opened the top drawer in the bedside table, pulled out a Gideon Bible, and felt around it. Finding nothing else, he returned the book and closed the drawer. "It smells funny in here. Kind of like vomit—if a dead person threw up."

"If we're lucky, we will get the job finished today and we won't have to be the main course in this revolting bugfest of a room tonight." Lexi lifted the rest of the bags onto the other bed.

"How do you want to handle it?" Scott swung his feet onto the floor and stood his duffel between his knees.

"Dolores is still gathering info, but the businesswoman being harassed for protection money wants it dealt with rapidly and quietly. I think this will be a quick in-and-out."

"She's a shifter, though, right? I don't understand why she doesn't get the pack to deal with it." Scott pulled underpants from his bag and sniffed them.

Lexi looked away with a shudder. "According to Dolores, the client doesn't want to involve the pack."

Scott raised an eyebrow. "In my experience, involving you won't necessarily make things any quieter."

"This is only our third job together. You don't have enough experience to make a judgment. Anyhow, this might simply require subtle negotiation." She pulled her cosmetics bag out and dropped it on the bed. Even with her back to him, she could still feel him staring at her. "What?" She turned to scowl at him. "I can be subtle."

He nodded as though he agreed. "So that's what you think will happen?"

"No. I'll find the gang, smack them around for a while, break some stuff, and make an example out of one or two of them, then

3

get the hell out of this shithole." She snatched her cosmetics bag up and took a step toward the bathroom.

"What about the local resource?" he asked.

She halted and turned. "What local resource?"

"Oh, I might have forgotten to mention we got an update." He grinned awkwardly.

Lexi stared at him while she counted in her head. "Perhaps you should fill me in." She could feel her eyebrow twitching.

"What would you like to know?" he asked, picked his cell phone up, and tapped in a code.

Rather than respond immediately, she gritted her teeth, then forced her jaw to relax. "You can start by telling me *who* our local resource is."

Scott scrolled through his phone. "I'm checking. It's a private investigator. Oh!"

She sent a prayer up. *Lord, give me patience, and I want it now.* "What?"

His mouth opened once, shut again, then opened a second time. "Well, you've worked with him before. He has a *great* track record."

Lexi took the few steps necessary to close the motel room's door. "I'm not playing Twenty Questions, Scott," she stated as she turned the paltry lock. "Who is it?"

"William Levin." He swallowed.

She spun to face him, a question written on her face. "William? I haven't worked with—" Her face lost the question. "Levin? *Dick* Levin?"

He ignored her as he read the file on the phone. "It says here he gets results."

"What else does it say?" She leaned against the dresser and folded her arms, waiting while he read.

"It says you tried to kill him six…" He looked up. "You tried to kill him six times? *How* is he not dead?"

"He is." She sighed and pushed away from the dresser. "What are Dolores's other notes?"

"She wrote that one at the top of the file. I think it was supposed to remind her to keep the two of you away from each other."

"Get her on the phone." Lexi shook her head.

Scott put a hand up. "I can't. There's no signal. Hang on, I'm still reading." He paused for a moment to decipher the hen scratches. "There's a note at the bottom. It says, 'Alexa, there's no one else. Suck it up, and don't try to kill him again.'" His gaze darted to her. "Hey, your name's Alexa? Like the music thing?"

She pointed at him. "You are never to call me that. I'll be talking to Dolores about this."

He continued reading as he asked his questions. "So, what's wrong with this Dick guy—and if his name's William, why do you call him 'Dick?'"

"It would be faster to ask what's right with him. He's rude, arrogant, dishonest, a monumental pain in the ass, and I'm sure you'll get the name eventually."

His finger pushed the display up to see more of the file information. "Yeah, but you can't kill a guy for that. And how come you keep *failing* to kill him?"

"He's a vamp. They're hard to kill." Lexi shook her head in disgust.

Scott sat up. "He is? I love vamps. They're so interesting. They know stuff from, like, the past." He could see she wasn't feeling the love, so he returned his focus to his cell.

"How many vamps have you met?" she asked as she sat on the corner of her bed.

"A few." He waved his hand in a vague manner.

She stared at him and held it relentlessly.

"Okay, one. I've met one vampire. But he was one of the old ones, hundreds of years old and really interesting. Anyway, I still don't understand why Dick's not dead. I haven't seen you fail to kill anything yet."

Lexi looked around and located a new remote that apparently went with the old-as-hell tv. She picked it up. It was light—no batteries, obviously. She returned it to the dresser and turned her attention to Scott again. "Well, this vamp doesn't know when to keep his mouth shut. At least you two will have that in common."

"It'll be fine. We probably won't even see much of him."

"I wonder what he's doing here? I thought he was based in Chicago." She spoke more to herself than to Scott.

"So, tell me more. You don't talk about yourself much."

She sighed. "My last partner died under horrible circumstances. I try not to get too close."

"Really? Wow! Because Dolores told me you didn't work with a partner before me." He smirked.

Thanks, Dolores.

"Well? What happened between the two of you?" Scott put his cell phone down, which signaled that he now gave her his undivided attention.

Lexi deliberated on how much to tell him and decided a fairly short version would be for the best. "After I left Kindred, they hired him to find me, which he did. At the time, I was beating the snot out of a nasty little witch. She'd cursed a girl with the misfortune of liking the same guy that she did. Then he—"

"What kind of curse?" he interrupted.

"The girl's hair and teeth had fallen out." She took a silver-tipped shuriken out and began to rotate the little four-bladed throwing star between her fingers like a fidget spinner.

"Gross." He screwed his face up in disgust.

"It wasn't only her looks. The curse had aged her from the inside out and her heart was failing. It was a death sentence."

"Did you make her reverse the spell?"

"She said it wasn't possible. Shouldn't you already know this stuff?" Lexi stopped spinning. She was genuinely surprised by Scott's question.

"You know witchcraft is different than the sorcery I practice. There are all kinds of magic and I don't know them all intimately. That's why I'm asking. If I had cast a spell to do that, I could undo it. I've no idea how she did it. It probably involved chicken guts and dirt or something." He shuddered.

"I told her to find a way to stop it or I'd come back and kill her. As I walked away, she threw something at me. I'd sensed something was coming and ducked out of the way, just as Dick appeared from nowhere and pulled me in the opposite direction. I almost took his head off, I was so pissed." She shook her head at the memory.

"What did she throw? Did it hit you?"

"It was a spell pouch. It hit Dick and burst on him with a poof." Her hands sprang open.

"Gross! What was in it? Did it do anything?" He took a book from his bag and put it on the dresser.

"It smelled like mouse droppings and it really messed his Gucci suit up. Otherwise, it did nothing. God knows what it would have done to me." She shuddered.

"What did you do to the witch?"

"I took her head off and dropped her into the river. Dick bitched about his suit all the way to the nearest bar. We sat, and he told me he'd been hired by Kindred to track me. I told him why I left them, and he agreed to give me a head start. Then he went straight back to them and told them where I was. It was close. They almost caught me, but that was the day I met Dolores. I still can't believe my luck. She got me out and I've worked for her ever since."

"What about Dick? You tried *six* times?" Scott leaned forward, engrossed in the story.

"After the dust settled, I spent a few days tracking him. I threw silver knives and tried to drop a silver net on him, but he's a slippery fucker, so I kept losing him. I finally managed to surprise him coming out of a jazz club, and I broke his neck and dragged him into an alley. I intended to finish him off, but I decided it would be worse for him to wake up in a dumpster."

"Worse than death?" He looked doubtful.

"You'll get it when you meet him. He's a real snob. I'm kind of surprised he's prepared to work with me. And I'm damned unhappy about working with him."

He picked the phone up and scrolled further. "Well, Dolores trusts him and I trust Dolores. It says here he'll meet us at sundown."

"What's the update on the job? Why do we need Dick the Douche?"

Scott read the details to her. "Kate. Shifter female. Owns a bar down the street from here. It says, 'further information is now being sought from a local contact.' We need to speak to Dick before we see the client. Then it confirms what Dolores already told us—that her business is being targeted by local thugs. That's funny, I thought shifters *were* the local thugs."

"Don't be a bigot. I've met some good shifters this last year." She turned her attention to his phone and raised an eyebrow. "How are you reading that if there's no signal?"

"I downloaded the file from the server, duh!" He spoke slowly as though it should have been apparent.

"You keep operational data on your cell phone? What if someone gets hold of that thing?"

He snickered. "No one will ever get hold of my cell phone," he assured her and tossed it on the bed. "I'll get the rest of the gear." He vanished.

Lexi walked to the bed and was tempted to pick the device up. As she closed her hand around it, though, it vanished. She strode to the window and stared at him as he waved it at her.

She rolled her eyes and turned to the room.

Her first decision was to claim the bed closest to the entrance.

When she looked at the distance between the door and Scott's bed, she confirmed that the only way someone would get to him while he slept would be through her. No one would complete that journey.

That settled, she looked around the room for the AC control and concluded that the hole in the wall near the door was where the switch should be. This would be an uncomfortable night.

Standing in front of the mirror, Lexi flicked her gaze to the door but there was no sign of Scott. She slipped a small glass vial from her pocket and placed it on the dresser before she turned her attention to the mirror. Quickly, she drew loose hairs back into her long, brown ponytail, which revealed a shaved undercut. Then, allowing her face to screw up in discomfort, she shuffled the girls around in her leather vest.

"If Dick won't appear before sundown, let's get something to eat," Scott said from his bed.

Lexi jerked from the mirror, turned, and gave him the evil eye, wondering how long he'd been there.

"Sorry." He blushed.

"We passed a barbecue place down the street. Let's hit that." Lexi swept the vial deftly into her pocket and headed to the door. "Can you sort the bags out?" she asked and turned to see there were no bags in the room and no Scott.

"Done. Let's eat," he called from beside the car.

She stepped to the empty bed and swept her fingers over the cover. While she knew the bags were there, she couldn't see or feel them.

"That will always be trippy," she murmured.

CHAPTER TWO

Still a little disbelieving, Lexi stared at the mountain of rib bones on the table in front of Scott.

While he gazed around the room, she looked at his torso. There didn't seem to be an ounce of extra fat on him. When she raised her gaze to his face, he was watching her with disturbingly green eyes.

"I can't work out where you put it all." She was embarrassed that she'd been caught staring but not sure why.

"I have a fast metabolism." He gave her a dimple-popping grin and leaned forward. "I messaged Dolores, asking her to let this Dick guy know where we are."

She looked at him with her eyebrows raised.

He gave a thumbs-up. "It's okay. No one can hear us."

"I wonder what Dick can provide that we can't get ourselves?" she mused aloud. She dipped the corner of a sugar cube into her coffee, and they both watched as the coffee rose and changed the color of the sugar. After a moment, she dropped the cube into the liquid and returned her gaze to her companion.

"I guess there's no other way to get the information Dolores mentioned. Maybe *the family* is involved."

"The what?" she asked pointedly. Her teaspoon had frozen in the air above her drink.

"Sorry. I mean Kindred—maybe *Kindred* is involved"

"And why don't we refer to them as 'family?'"

Scott rolled his eyes. "Because they're not family. Not anymore."

"They never were." Lexi stirred her coffee.

He leaned back and sighed. "Don't you miss it? Being part of an organization and fighting for justice?"

"No. You know why? Because it was all lies and now, working for Dolores, I *do* fight for justice. We rescued *you,* didn't we? From Kindred, as I recall."

"Don't you think it's weird that we're more like Kindred now than when we were with them?" He smiled. "Neither of us were blood-matched before we left, and now you've got access to my magic."

Lexi shrugged. "Your only choice for matching was a psycho, and I was considered a dud as a legacy. I feel bad that you're stuck with me. If we hadn't been in a bad situation, I wouldn't have done it. At the rate you keep having to top the magic up, we'll run into problems with that."

"You're not a dud. You're faster and stronger than any regular human and I've never seen fighting skills like yours. I think we're well matched."

"Yes, but for someone with the blood of the ancient supernaturals running through my veins, I'm somewhat of a disappointment, aren't I? I don't show a clear connection to any supe. I'm not as fast as a vamp, or as strong as a shifter, nothing. I don't think they'd ever have wasted a mage on a match with me. I suppose that's why I found it so easy to leave and not look back after I discovered the truth about them."

Scott leaned forward again and investigated the ribs for meat he might have missed. "I don't believe every individual cell can be bad. Why would the whole supernatural world agree to be policed by them if the entire organization was rotten?"

"That's the problem, isn't it? We all operated in little family units with no idea what was happening in the rest of the organization. We don't even know who the Kindred council are."

"Well, my family was definitely a problem, but I never really felt I was working on the Death Star."

"I'll tell you what is a problem. Your ability to turn every conversation around to Star Wars disturbs me."

"Yeah, I know." He laughed.

Scott looked at his watch. "I wonder when he'll turn up. If this guy's local, he might have a contact who can help." He shrugged.

"Then why can't he give us the name of the contact so I can throttle them until they tell me what I want to know?" Lexi gave him a tight smile.

"Which is precisely why you don't have my contact's name. Scoot over." When she looked up, it was into Dick Levin's smug, chiseled, irritatingly handsome face.

She didn't move and made her face as impassive as possible.

The newcomer turned his face to Scott. "You'll scoot over for a weary but stunningly attractive vampire, won't you, handsome?"

"Sure." Scott moved across the bench seat to make space.

Dick unfastened the buttons on his expensive-looking suit jacket, slid into the booth, and dropped his newspaper onto the seat next to him. He looked around. "I couldn't hear you as I entered. You must be shielded."

Lexi nodded.

"How's your earlobe, Dick?" she asked, with a staccato k at the end of his name.

"I should ask you that question since you were the one who ate it, dear," he replied with a smile as his hand moved involuntarily toward his left ear.

"I didn't keep it. I try to be discerning about what goes into my mouth."

"I suppose one of us should be," he replied with an infinitesimal twitch of one eyebrow.

"You look different." He glanced at her arm and his eyes widened. "You have the unhealing scar." He leaned forward for a better look.

She pulled the sleeve of her jacket down. Of course, a supernatural creature like him would be able to see the scar in its metaphysical form—a deep, angry red crevice the length of her forearm with white, shining energy running through it. To those with no magic, it merely looked like a healed pink-silver scar, but it would never truly close. It would always be raw and painful.

"It's a paper cut," she lied pointlessly.

Dick leaned back and gave her a perfunctory smile.

"Let's get down to it. Will you try to kill me again?" he asked, all business.

"I have to decide *now*?"

"If you want my help, yes."

"Will you crawl back to Kindred and tell them where I am again?"

He leaned forward and lowered his voice. "Last year, they hired me to find you and to be perfectly honest, I didn't put all that much effort into it. I don't like Kindred. No one likes them. They're the self-imposed bully boys of the supernatural world. So, I was trying *not* to find you. Hell, I was rooting for you. But you did a shitty job of running away. I simply followed the trail of dead supernatural bodies. Without those, I probably wouldn't have found you at all. That was on you."

"I didn't run away. I left. I chose to leave."

"No one leaves Kindred."

"Yeah, thanks. I'm getting that now. It's a shame that witch's pouch didn't give you eternally bushy eyebrows."

Dick recoiled in horror and automatically smoothed an eyebrow. "Anyway, I don't accept jobs from them anymore."

"Don't tell me you've suddenly grown a conscience?"

"Don't be ridiculous. They've adopted a ninety-day payment schedule. I can't wait that long for my invoices to be paid."

"There's the Dick I know and love." Lexi sneered.

"You got away—" he protested.

"No thanks to you," she cut in.

"*All* thanks to me. Who do you think sent Dolores your way?"

She froze. Dolores had never told her but at that moment, she knew it was true.

Dick continued, "I gave my word that I'd buy you time, so I called in a favor and asked her to get you out. I'll admit I was motivated. Kindred did something to me I considered inappropriate. I was ready to lie and tell them I hadn't seen you, but that mage girl picked the information out of my head. I tried to tell you at the time but you were hell-bent on trying to kill me." He pointed his finger at her but, she noticed, not so close that she could bite it off.

"If I had been trying to kill you, you'd be deader." She leaned forward as well. The two were now almost nose-to-nose across the table.

"Really? Because you seemed extremely bloodthirsty at the time."

Lexi looked away and straightened in her seat. His eyes narrowed and he seemed to sense he'd somehow struck a nerve. He leaned against the backrest.

"I tried to find a witch who could protect my mind, but no one would do it. Everyone's too scared of Kindred."

Lexi looked at him. She believed him and they had to work together. This hadn't gotten off well. She thought for a few moments. "I might have someone who can help you with that if you're serious."

Dick stared at her in surprise for a long moment. "Really? Sister, I am *so* serious."

"Then I won't kill you…for now."

"For now? If that changes, can you give a handsome vampire a head start?" He placed his elbows on the table, put his chin in his hands, and batted his annoyingly long eyelashes at her.

After a short silence, they smiled tentatively at each other.

Lexi chuffed a laugh and shook her head. "How've you been, you old bastard?" It was the closest she would get to making an apology and the atmosphere grew congenial.

"Bored. You?" He raised an eyebrow and smirked.

"Life's not boring,"

Dick swiveled toward Scott. "Which brings us to you, muscles. What glorious stone did she find you under?"

"Oh, I'm only—" her partner started.

"He's my traveling companion. A lady shouldn't travel alone these days."

Lexi could see that the vampire had recognized the opening for a cutting response. He opened his mouth but seemed to think better of it.

"Good for you. It's nice to travel with a friend." He sighed.

She was genuinely surprised by the apparent kindness in his voice.

"Excuse me?" A waitress appeared at the table.

The three of them turned to her as she bent much lower than she needed to place a tall drink in front of Dick, and she delivered a dazzling smile to go with the view of her cleavage.

"I didn't order this."

Lexi could see his gaze dipped no lower than her carotid.

"This is from the gentleman at the end of the bar." As she moved away, she nodded in the direction of a handsome, muscular young man with a square jaw and a varsity jacket. He smiled at Dick, stood, and headed to the bathroom. At the door, he turned and winked.

Scott looked from the man to her companion. "Do you know him?"

"Let's simply say my reputation precedes me. I don't come here anymore." The vampire raised the glass and smiled broadly at the young man while he muttered under his breath, "Not in a million years, jailbait."

"Why do they call you 'Dick?'" the other man asked. Lexi's lips twitched. He'd chosen that moment to voice the question.

"*They* don't. *She* does." Dick rolled his eyes. He turned to Lexi. "So, you need a document from my friend Leonard."

"Dolores told us you'd explain about that." She felt like she was a little behind the curve.

"There was a robbery at a bar a few days ago. The safe wasn't touched but the contents of the filing cabinet were all over the floor. It took a while for your client to discover important documents were missing."

"What documents?" Scott had his notes app open again.

"The whole block used to belong to Kate's father. He divided the land when she finished business school, and she opened the bar and sub-let the flower shop next door to a friend. The land ownership papers are missing," Dick explained.

"I thought she was being harassed for protection money." The other man used his cell phone to start making notes.

The vampire nodded. "Well, things are escalating."

"Shit! I hoped this would be a quick job. It looks like we'll have to stay longer than I had hoped." Lexi sighed. "So, how can your friend help?"

"Leonard is an investigator. We worked together for a while. He has a contact at the County Clerk's Office who can check the records and find the city's copy, if it's still there. If it's missing, you have a bigger problem than you thought."

"Have you already spoken to him?" she asked.

"I haven't discussed the particulars of the case but I've asked for his help. He might, he might not. He's probably angry with me."

Scott stopped typing. "I thought he was your friend?"

"He is, but he's so last-year. Or was it the year before that? One of those years that isn't this year." Dick waved his hand nonchalantly. "I'm meeting him for a date tonight, so I guess we'll find out. He was supposed to help me with…another job, but he's avoided me for months."

He noticed the plate of rib bones and looked at Scott.

"Did you eat *all* those?" He moved his gaze unnecessarily slowly down the other man's torso.

Scott moved his hands self-consciously into his lap.

Dick swiveled to Lexi. "Where does he put it all?"

"Excuse me?" The waitress had returned, this time with a low-ball glass containing amber liquid.

Dick stared at her with his bright topaz-blue eyes.

"This…er…" She faltered, and color bloomed in her cheeks.

"This?" he responded helpfully and gestured at the drink.

"Sorry, yes. This one's from the gentleman at the table in the corner." She indicated an impeccably dressed bald black gentleman who rose, winked at him, and headed through the door to the bathroom.

"Well, I'm sure they'll find each other," he muttered.

Another man walked past and smiled at him. "It looks like everyone around here knows you." Scott shook his head and smirked.

"Intimately." The vampire sighed.

"How about we go back to the room and talk business more privately?" Lexi signaled the waitress for the check

She brought over a folded piece of paper on a little plate and placed it in front of Dick with a smile before she turned away with a flick of her hair.

"Boy, is she barking up the wrong tree." He pushed the check across to her.

She read it, threw cash down to cover it, and passed the check to him. "I think that's for you."

He glanced at the waitress's number scribbled across the bill but made no move to pick it up.

Scott leaned closer and snagged it. Lexi looked at him with her eyebrows raised. "What? It's for our expenses." He pocketed the receipt.

Dick's gaze once again swiveled to the other man.

"Let's go then. Muscles and I can get better acquainted." He placed a hand on Scott's thigh and blue sparks erupted from the young man's skin to hurl the vampire out of the booth.

The bar went silent as people watched him skid across the floor.

Lexi smiled at Dick, who was on his butt several feet away.

He stood and dusted himself off. "I'm not averse to a little rough play but not when I'm wearing Versace."

"Sorry. It's kind of automatic." Scott didn't look even remotely sorry as he stood from the booth.

She did her best to hide a smile. "Don't take offense, Scott. He was only checking your credentials."

"Yeah, that was what it felt like he was doing." The man's face was aflame.

"So, you *are* her blood-match. Interesting. Sorry, handsome. You're cute but the surfer-dude thing really isn't my type. I'd rather take you for a good haircut." Dick picked his newspaper up and headed to the door.

———

They drove back to the motel and the vampire followed in his own car.

"You're quiet." Lexi glanced at her companion, who had sat with his head down.

"I revealed my ability. I shouldn't have done that. He knows you get magic from me now."

"He'd already guessed and was testing a hypothesis. Don't let it eat at you."

Scott pulled the visor down and looked at himself in the mirror.

"Seriously? You're offended because he said you're not his type?"

"No. Well, what's wrong with my hair?"

"Nothing. If you have what every other man has inside his pants, you're his type. He's merely trying to undermine your self-confidence. I told you, he's an absolute son-of-a-bitch."

"Do you call him 'Dick' because he likes—"

"No. That's purely a coincidence."

They pulled up and got out of the car.

Dick climbed out of his vehicle and walked toward them. "I couldn't believe it when you pulled into this shithole. This is the worst place in town. Even the guy with the meth lab in room twelve complained about the smell and moved out. Is Dolores punishing you for something?"

The three of them headed up the steps and entered the room.

The vampire appeared to try not to touch anything. "I heard about a man who woke up in one of the rooms here. He'd paced around it for two days before housekeeping came in and he finally realized he wasn't in the county lock-up." He gave Lexi a conspiratorial wink.

Scott looked at him. "That's not true." He didn't look completely convinced that it wasn't, though.

"No, but it could be," the vampire admitted as he looked around in disgust.

"I need to use the bathroom. I hope it's not too gross." Scott walked toward the door with obvious reluctance.

"It's really clean. This place isn't so bad," Lexi called as he entered. She sat on her bed and stared at the bathroom door while she waited.

Scott stepped out again and his face was white.

Lexi felt his sadness through their empathetic link. "Look, people get murdered every day. At least they scrubbed the tub with bleach after."

"It wasn't a murder."

"How does he—" Dick began.

Lexi shook her head to silence him.

"There's no fear, only sadness." Scott sat on the end of the bed in front of the mirror.

"Don't do this, Scott." Lexi knew what was coming.

"I'm curious." He muttered the words so softly that even Dick with his vampire hearing probably couldn't hear them.

The mirror reflecting the young man wavered and reversed everything that had happened in the room. It went back a few hours and revealed Lexi, her face twisted in obvious pain as she adjusted her breasts in the leather vest. The older man laughed and she face-palmed.

The image reversed faster. It showed a maid, the crime scene cleaners, the CSIs, the police, and the same maid backing away from the bathroom with horror on her face. Finally, a gaunt woman appeared surrounded by drug paraphernalia and looked like she'd simply had enough. He whispered a final word and the mirror returned to its natural state.

The three of them were silent. Scott stood, moved to sit at the top of the bed, and opened his new book—a sorcery tome Lexi assumed he'd probably picked up from a Seven-Eleven.

Dick went to the mirror and poked it with his index finger, and his manicured fingernail tapped the glass. "The moment I get home, I will smash every mirror in my house. Then I'll have them ground to dust." He paused, spun on his heel, and faced the others. "But she's in a better place now. Let's talk about me."

"I can see now why she calls you Dick. It's because you're a total dick, isn't it?"

"Good guess, but no." Lexi shook her head.

"It's not?" The vampire was clearly surprised by this revelation.

Scott looked from the mirror to her. "If that leather vest is so uncomfortable, why don't you wear a different one? You must have at least twenty of them."

"They're all uncomfortable. I hate them all."

"You hate leathers? But that's all you wear." His face was a mask of puzzlement.

Lexi stood before the mirror. "Hell, yes! They're tough, flexible, and they accentuate the curves. For the purpose of gathering information, there's nothing better." She slid her hand over the tight leather jeans and looked at him in the mirror. "But they make me sweat horribly since they don't breathe." She turned to Dick. "You don't breathe. I bet this would look good on you."

He glanced at her with one perfectly annoying—because it was perfect—eyebrow raised. "Why would you think I don't breathe? How do I speak?"

With a casual gesture, he flicked off some lint she couldn't see —and her eyesight was good enough to have seen it, she thought.

"Besides," he finished as he preened like a cat, "I make *everything* look good."

"Have you been told you can be an arrogant ass?" She pulled at her leather vest. The girls needed air. He raised that annoying eyebrow, so she clarified, "I mean, lately?"

Dick sighed and moved to stand at the door and waved his face with the newspaper. "I hate this town in the summer. It's too hot."

"It's Palm Springs. It's always hot." Silently, though, she agreed. "Why do you care? You're dead."

"Maintaining an undead body as good as mine careful balance. Too many degrees in the wrong direction and I could be standing in a puddle of fat bigger than your thighs." He cast an unimpressed glance at her legs.

"There's nothing wrong with my thighs." She smoothed the leather over her muscular legs.

His lip lifted into a smirk. "Do you ever see the skinny girls complain about sweat rash?"

"I've never seen a skinny girl clinically decapitate a smartass vamp with her thighs."

Dick cracked his neck and stepped into the room. "So, when do you plan to leave town?"

"Don't worry, we'll be gone as soon as the job's done. Aren't you late for your date?" she asked.

"You mean the date where I have dinner with Leonard? Where he'll be pissed at me at first, then hang on my every word? Then we go back to his house, screw each other's brains out for hours, and he'll profess his undying love for me...*again.* That date?"

"I guess." She wondered why he had a problem with that scenario.

"What's the point? As far as I'm concerned, it's done. We just did it, right there in my mind where it was probably better than, as I recall, it is in reality. Nauseatingly predictable." He rolled his eyes.

"I see. So, in this scenario in your mind, did he give you the information we need?"

"Oops. I forgot that part. I should probably get ready. I don't want to be late for my date. When did you last go on a date, Alexa?" He smirked when he looked at her.

Scott glanced up from his book at the mention of her full name. A flicker of a smile betrayed his intentions.

"Alexa, play 'All by Myself' by—" He stopped speaking as a spinning metal object shredded his book but was halted by the blue aura around his body.

"That joke got old already." She stood in a relaxed pose where she leaned against the dresser and enjoyed the confused look on his face. He hadn't even seen her move and she knew it.

He snatched the throwing star from the air and placed it on the bedside table. "This book was new."

"Where did it come from?" She tried to see the cover but he put it into his bag.

"Target."

"Do you think you should try to use a book of spells from Target? You know that shit will backfire, don't you?"

"It's not about the spell. It's the magic behind it." Scott's tone was prickly.

"If you want to make yourself useful, help me get out of these leathers." Lexi headed to the bathroom.

He bolted to his feet and took a step toward her.

"From out there." She closed the bathroom door. "I only need a second to..."

Scott muttered an incantation under his breath and moved his fingers as though to snap them, although they never met.

Metal clanged on tiles and reverberated around the walls as throwing stars, knives, and other trade tools fell to the bathroom floor. Lexi stood naked except for one gold ring on her hand and gazed at the weapons around her, then looked at her leathers, which were hung neatly over the chair.

"Sorry," Scott shouted. "But you know you shouldn't keep all that stuff in your pocket, right?"

Lexi, although naked, slipped her hand in and out of the magical pocket at her hip that appeared and disappeared at her command. He was right. This job could not be over fast enough.

She shook the thought off and stood at the mirror while she delved into her cosmetic bag. After a moment, she retrieved the dental floss and pulled off a length while shouting out to him. "I'll take the first opportunity to assassinate the person who decided 'Alexa' could be a name to call their artificial assistant. Hell, it doesn't even have to be for much money. Maybe like...five dollars and a burger." She thought for a moment. "I'll accept an IOU on the burger."

"That's a good life choice for those thighs, dear," Dick shouted through the door.

"Are you still here?" She toyed with the idea of trying to kill him again.

"I'm going, I'm going," he responded. "You kids have a great time and don't stay out too late." She gave him the finger through the closed bathroom door.

He laughed. "I saw that."

Five minutes later, Lexi emerged from the bathroom in gray sweatpants and a t-shirt. She crossed to the small round trash can and opened its swing lid to toss the used floss into it. With a startled exclamation, she leapt back as light burst from the can and a 3D projection beamed into the center of the room. The figure of a crouched woman stood before her. "Help me, Obi-Wan Kenobi. You're my only hope."

"Motherfucker! Scott, if you do that one more time..." She walked through the projection, which instantly disappeared.

Scott rolled on his bed, clutching his stomach as he laughed. "That was so funny."

Lexi glanced at her scar. The magic had almost dissipated again. She walked to him and held her hand out. He took it and transferred magic to her. As she walked to the door, she stretched her arm to reveal the raw, magical wound and hesitated. Because she hadn't been born with magic like Scott, they called Lexi's magic "borrowed." It was a curious term because she had paid dearly for it. She touched the scar.

This wasn't borrowed. It was bought.

Her companion had stopped laughing and now looked nervously at her.

All matched legacies had finite magic, hers more than most. She only used it in dire situations.

Oh, what the hell.

"You should shut up now, smart ass." She stroked the length of the scar and looked directly at him with a little smile.

Scott pawed at his mouth in horror as his top and bottom lips merged to form a seal.

"I'm going for a run." Lexi headed out with a broad grin.

She felt the sense of panic from him through their empathetic link and slowed on the stairs. On the bottom step, she waited for a few moments and had begun to return to the room when the feeling subsided. He had removed the spell. She set off at a leisurely pace.

Lexi ran in the direction of the client's bar, interested to see what kind of establishment it was. When she approached the corner and saw it was dark, she decided to do a lap of the block. She passed the bar, then a flower shop. Every other business was boarded up, seemingly closed forever. At the next turn, more buildings stood with boards covered in graffiti over the windows. The next street was bordered with a fence that warned of armed patrols. When she reached the entrance, a message read *Twenty-Four Hour Storage: Closed for remodel.*

She slowed as she reached the side of the bar and narrowed her eyes as a flashlight played along the wall behind the fence. She stopped and listened to men's whispered voices.

"Shh! I heard something."

"What was it?"

"It sounded like someone running."

"If someone in this neighborhood is running, they're running for their life. They've got their own shit going on."

"Hurry. Let's get this done. Throw it everywhere."

Something splashed, followed by the smell of gasoline. That was all she needed.

She retrieved a glass vial of vampire blood from her pocket, unstoppered it, and tipped it onto her finger. Quickly, she ran the finger down her tongue and felt the thrill as adrenaline flooded her system. Her senses went into overdrive. The darkness of the night lifted, and she heard two people breathing and smelled body odor, cheap deodorant, and gun oil. She knew she already had an edge, being faster and stronger than normal humans, but the extra boost helped enormously.

This is what it would be like if my abilities were as strong as they should be.

Unfortunately, the only sense that wasn't improved by the vamp blood was her sense of self-preservation.

She hopped the fence.

"Hi. I'm not interrupting anything, am I?" She gave them her best disarming smile. It was perhaps ambitious for the situation but sometimes, it worked. On the street, they would probably have been confident and at ease in her presence. These two were in the act of carrying out a crime so they were jumpy, a common failing.

The one with the gas can spun and spilled the contents on his friend. He dropped the container on the ground and immediately tripped over it. The other was faster, reached into the back of his jeans for his gun, and aimed it at her. She wondered if she should have taken a few moments to plan before she leapt in.

The die was cast, though, so she shrugged and ignored the weapon. "I only wondered what you were doing."

He looked at the building and then at the can of gasoline. "You need this explained to you?"

Lexi glanced at the gun and then at the man who held it. She needed to get him farther away from the building. "Don't shoot me or we'll all go up in flames."

His eyes narrowed and he sneered. "Statistically unlikely."

Not today, fuckwit.

"Good, then." She turned away and walked toward the fence while she activated the magic in her scar.

The men ran after her and, as expected, the gunman didn't shoot.

The first to reach her was the unarmed man and he grasped

her hair and yanked her back. She felt and heard hair rip from her scalp as she fell and noticed that the other put his gun away. Rather than struggle, she allowed her weight to take her completely to the ground before she rolled onto her shoulders and kicked upward with her heel under her captor's chin. His head snapped back and he fell. She flipped onto her feet, her focus on the second man. He drew the gun again, raised it, fired, and screamed when her magic caused the weapon to erupt in his hand.

Lexi was tempted to leave him burning but couldn't risk the building igniting. She attempted to douse the flame with magic but her scar was empty.

"Shit. It looks like we have to do this the old-fashioned way," she said to the shrieking, flailing man.

She kicked, felled him, and rolled him across the ground with her foot until the flames were out.

"I don't suppose you'd consider telling me who sent you?" she asked as she crouched beside his now unmoving form.

He sucked in a single breath, then died.

"I'll take that as a no." She stood and checked the vitals on the other man, who was also dead. Lexi hopped the fence and finished her run.

CHAPTER THREE

"Do you have to do that when I'm trying to sleep?" Scott turned his pillow over, punched it, and yanked the covers over his head to escape the morning sunlight flooding through the gossamer-thin curtains.

Lexi looked up from the whetstone she used to sharpen her katana, one eyebrow raised. "So you're speaking to me now?"

Her friend sat and pointed at her. "You left me in a vulnerable situation last night. What if someone had attacked me while you were on your run and I couldn't speak my protection spells?"

She rolled her eyes. "We both know you'd reversed the spell seconds after I left the room." With that, she lowered her head and her focus returned to the whetstone.

Unfortunately, he wasn't finished. "You used my own magic against me. Where did you even learn something like that?" He touched his mouth again and felt around his cheeks. "It was hideous."

"A great mage once said, 'It's not the spells, it's the magic behind them.'" She didn't look up.

His stuttering as he ranted threatened to crack her stoic

façade. "What a pile of crap!" His eyes narrowed a moment. "Who said that?"

Lexi focused on him with a gleam in her eye. "You—*yesterday*. You muppet." She smiled.

Satisfied with the sharpness of the blade, she stood and slid the katana into the magical dimensional pocket hidden within her tight leather pants.

When she drew her hand away, the sword had completely vanished. A moment later, she withdrew a shorter blade.

It came out with several candy wrappers stuck to it.

Scott looked at the sticky mess in disgust, his mouth open. "That's revolting."

"What?" she asked defensively as though she didn't know what his problem was.

"That!" He shook his head. "I give you access to a dimensional pocket for storing your weapons and you use it for candy. I use my magical energy to keep it accessible, so if you could not fill it with shit, that would be great." He laid down again. "And you smell like you've been in a fire." He covered his head once more.

Lexi wiped the sword clean, dried her whetstone, and slipped them both into the dimensional pocket. "Come on. It's six anyway. Let's get breakfast before we see the client."

He turned onto his side and away from her.

She eyed the ceiling as if asking the gods for patience. "If you stop sulking, I'll let you change the *Gideon Bible* into the *Ferrengi Rules of Acquisition* again."

No answer was forthcoming. Damn.

Resigned, she walked around and rested her chin on the edge of the bed to give him the best puppy face she could muster.

"What are you doing?" he asked and opened one eye.

Lexi smiled. "Thinking about steak, eggs, and hash, bacon, pancakes, maple syrup, and coffee. Why? What are you doing?"

A short pause followed before he sighed. "Well, now I'm thinking about food. All right, I'll get up."

Scott pushed off the bed and walked across the room in shorts and a t-shirt, yawning and scratching his back.

Dick had been right. With his tanned body and shoulder-length blond hair, he definitely rocked the surfer look. If he ever stopped behaving like a twelve-year-old, he'd be quite a catch for some girl one day. For now, he was infuriating.

Perhaps the Good Book will teach me patience, she thought. She opened the drawer and pulled out...*The Rules of Quidditch.* She laughed.

They parked across the street from the bar and walked toward it, but when she reached the other side, Lexi was alone. She turned to where Scott stood in the middle of the street with a faraway look on his face. The lights had changed but he didn't seem to be in any hurry to move. She stepped into the street, grasped his arm, and yanked him onto the sidewalk as a horn blasted.

Reflexively, she shook his shoulder. "What was that?"

He stared at her for a moment, his expression bewildered. "I'm sorry. Wow! I caught a really weird vibe."

"You almost caught the fender of that truck, dipshit. Wake up." She turned and strode toward the bar. Absently, she touched the unhealing scar, which had itched for a moment.

They found the business locked.

"Well, this is interesting." Scott held his hands cupped over his eyes against the glass.

Lexi looked in. "What?"

"You see that? Hanging from the ceiling?" He guided her by pointing.

Lexi noticed a rustic design of sticks bound together into a familiar shape. "Is that a rune?"

"Yes, it's Eolh. For protection from bad spirits."

"Or it's a decoration left from Halloween."

"Eight months ago?"

"Let's look around." She headed around the corner. They stopped at the side of the building.

"That must be from the robbery." Scott pointed to a boarded-up window.

They continued toward the rear and found the fenced area. Lexi sniffed. The smell of gasoline was still in the air and a pile of sand lay on the ground where the burned man had landed.

"Interesting. It smells like there's been a fire here." His gaze slid to her. She said nothing.

A man walked through a gate with a beer barrel on a dolly while another man stood at the back of a truck with a clipboard. He scribbled on the clipboard and clambered into the cab of the truck.

"Can I help you?" asked a voice from behind them.

They turned to see a young woman in the doorway of the flower shop, surrounded by tubs of blossoms.

"We're looking for Kate, the owner of the bar." Scott began to walk toward her.

"That's me." She looked at them suspiciously.

Lexi held her hand out. "Hi, Lexi and Scott. Dolores asked us to drop in."

The woman glanced quickly in the direction of the man moving the beer barrels. At that moment, he returned towing the empty dolly and looked at the two of them with a puzzled expression. He approached slowly.

"Shit," Kate muttered.

When he arrived, Scott looked at him and muttered a word, then touched his arm. "You know what? I have a mad craving for a McRib."

"Aww, man! McRibs are so good." The man dropped the dolly where he stood.

"I know, right?"

"What?" Kate, clearly confused, looked at her watch.

"I'll see you soon, sweetheart." He kissed her head and began to walk down the street.

"Tommy?" she called after him. "He'll be disappointed. They'll be on the breakfast menu for the next two hours." She stared at his back. "Did you do something to him?" she asked Scott.

"I made him think he had somewhere else to be. I'm sorry. It seemed you didn't want to speak with him here, and we were told you'd asked for discretion. We might need to be quick, though. How long it lasts depends entirely on how much he actually wants a McRib."

"He lives on that shit." The woman turned and picked up a tub of red roses.

"So, you work here too?" she looked at the front of the flower shop.

"No. I own the property but my friend Daisy runs this place. I haven't seen her for a couple of days. Her delivery arrived and I'm the emergency contact."

Lexi was immediately alert. "Is it unusual for her to go off like this?"

"She's somewhat flaky. Every now and then she disappears to LA to party or heads to the woods with her coven to do whatever they do there." Kate shrugged.

Scott began to move the tubs in.

The woman stepped out of the way, her expression surprised. "Thanks."

The two entered the building behind him.

"Can you tell us what's been happening?" Lexi asked.

"When I first called Dolores, I was being harassed by a local gang. They want me to pay protection money I can't afford. Then a couple of days ago, someone broke into the office. They smashed open the filing cabinet and scattered papers everywhere. It took me a day to realize important paperwork was missing. I called my lawyer to ask him if he could send a copy, but there was no response. I learned he's gone—left town. I think there's more going on than merely harassment from a group of thugs."

Lexi looked around the room. "Did the police get any prints from the robbery?"

"I didn't report it," the woman admitted and blushed.

"Why not?" Lexi asked.

"Tommy's uncle is the police chief and the alpha of his pack. I can't let this get back to our families." As Kate spoke, she moved pots from the front of the store to the back.

"I don't understand. If you're a shifter, why doesn't the local pack protect you?" Scott asked as he entered, having moved the last of the tubs.

"If they found out about this, there would be blood on my hands. I don't want that."

"How long have you been in business here?" Lexi asked.

"Seven years. I've never been bothered like this before. A businessman has been buying up the stores and properties on this block. He already owns most of them and closed them down. After the break-in, I can't help wondering if he might be behind the harassment. And something else happened last night. I came back to find the place stinking of gasoline and two dead guys out back. They must have intended to incinerate the bar. One looked like he had a broken neck and the other was badly burned. I think maybe one killed the other, then somehow set himself on fire instead of burning the building down."

"Yes, that must have been what happened." Scott looked directly at Lexi.

She turned to Kate. "So, where are the dead guys now?"

"I had to...uh, you know, dispose of them." She averted her eyes.

Lexi looked at the boarded window. "What did you tell your boyfriend about all this?"

"I said drunken college kids had smashed the window. I told

him they apologized and left money to fix it. This morning, I told him I'd reversed over a can of gasoline."

"Who's the businessman?" Scott asked.

"Caleb Linden. He was my dad's business partner and already owns the storage facility at the back of this building. When my dad died, the whole thing went to him. He wasn't very happy when he learned Dad had divided the property and given this part to me." Kate wiped her hands and passed the cloth to him.

"We'll ask Dolores to see what she can find out about him." He dried his hands and pulled his phone out to type.

"I can tell you exactly where he'll be tonight. He's holding a fundraiser for the mayor in Rancho Mirage. Everyone with money to throw at his campaign will be there."

Scott made notes.

Kate fidgeted and seemed to weigh the two of them. "Listen, there's something else—something I haven't told anyone. Walking home a couple of weeks ago through the park, I was attacked." She hugged herself as she spoke. "I've never seen the guy before. He dragged me into the bushes and I swear I thought he would kill me."

"Why didn't you shift?" Lexi asked. "You could have finished the guy."

She sighed. "I did shift. I bit him but the gun went off. It scared me, and I ran away." The woman shrugged.

"Are you saying there's a new shifter out there with no sire or alpha to control him?" Lexi asked.

"Not quite." Kate lowered her gaze and looked embarrassed. "Can I show you something?"

She locked the flower shop and they followed her to the bar. As they headed in through the rear door, they passed barrels piled up to virtually fill the back room. It was a tight squeeze. "Tommy thinks the storeroom downstairs is flooded. I told him the plumber's waiting for a part." She unlocked a door and they descended the stairway through a room filled with barrels attached to pipes. They stopped at a padlocked door. The three of them stood in silence as she unlocked it and led them along a hallway. She opened another locked door and they peered in to see a man chained at the far end of the room.

"He turned up a few days ago in wolf form, followed me down here, and simply sat there while I chained him."

Lexi walked halfway into the room for a closer look.

The young man woke up. "You bitch. Let me out of here." He ran at her. When he was about a foot away, she realized there were still a few feet on the chain so she punched him in the face. He dropped like a rock.

She looked around the room. In the other corner was a pile of bones.

Ahh! That's what happened to Crispy and Clumsy.

Lexi stepped out of the room. "I take it that's last night's visitors. What are you planning to do with this guy?

Kate sighed. "I don't know. I turned him so he's my responsibility. But he's a murdering thug."

"I suppose we could—" Scott started.

"I told you, Scott. No pets until you've proven you can be responsible."

"I didn't mean—"

"Do you want me to finish him?" Lexi began to withdraw a blade from her pocket.

"No, no. I need to think about it." The woman closed the door and locked it again.

"Well, the offer's there, but you'd have to clean up yourself. I don't do that."

The two friends looked at each other. This small job was getting bigger by the minute.

"Your boyfriend doesn't know about him?" Scott asked.

"No. He doesn't usually hang around here. He's angry about the window and is looking for any evidence that I can't handle this situation. That's mainly because he thinks I should sell to

Caleb. Tommy's usually a nice guy but he's been on edge lately. His whole pack has. Their latest gripe is that I should be popping baby wolves out instead of owning a business. We're supposed to be getting married soon, but I keep putting it off. His pack makes me nervous."

"Okay, you've given us a fair amount to go on. We'll keep in touch." Lexi turned to the cell. "It's good to see you're feeding him."

"I take care of that when I close the bar. As his sire, I can command him to turn and he's as pliant as a puppy. I feed and water him, and he goes on newspaper." Kate shrugged.

She simply stared at the woman. "That is too much information."

They stood on the sidewalk. Lexi glanced at a limousine with blackened windows parked at the curbside. She sensed that someone was watching from behind the wheel but couldn't see who it was.

"Where to now?" Scott asked.

"I could devour a McRib," she admitted.

"My God! Appalling! Those things are an absolute assault on the senses," said Dick's familiar voice.

"Oh! it's you." Lexi walked toward the car.

"Climb aboard and let's talk." The vampire released the locks on the rear doors.

They slid into the back seat and closed the doors. The locks clicked, and a dark glass partition between the front and back seats slid down.

As they pulled away, Lexi looked at her car, which was parked across the street. "What about my car?"

"Maybe you'll get lucky and someone will set fire to it." Dick smirked.

She let that slide. There was no denying it was a piece of shit.

"I assume you listened to our conversation with Kate?" she asked him.

"I didn't pull up close enough until the wolf left. Where did he go? He was in a hell of a hurry."

"He wanted a McRib too." The friends exchanged grins.

"This town is going to shit." Dick shook his head.

She leaned forward. "We need to crash a party tonight."

The vampire looked at her in the rearview mirror. "You don't need to crash it. I could use a date, though."

"You're invited?" Lexi couldn't keep the surprise out of her voice.

"I'm a fine, upstanding citizen. Of course, I'm invited. But Caleb Linden isn't someone to mess with. He's not a nice man."

Scott poked at the window control.

Dick flashed him a stern look. "What are you doing?"

"I'm trying to open the window but the button doesn't work." He continued to poke at it.

Lexi stared at him until he realized he was being watched.

"That's intentional. I have a mild sun allergy." The vampire regarded him calmly with one of his perfect eyebrows raised.

The penny dropped. "Oh, God, sorry." Scott yanked his finger away from the button and sat on his hands.

"I'm not taking this car to that shithole of a motel. We'll have to go to my place so I can actually get out of the car."

"Oh, great, a morning graveyard visit." Lexi's mouth twitched.

"You live in a—" Scott started.

"I do not live in a fucking graveyard. Seriously, where do you think I hang my designer clothes—in a crypt?"

The car slowed on an affluent-looking road and stopped in front of a gate. A gaunt man stood beside the barrier and stared at the vehicle as it slid through. Dick clicked his tongue.

"Who's that?" She stared at the man through the darkened glass.

The driver's shoulders drooped. "My fan club."

He idled on the other side of the gate and watched it close in the mirror.

"I love you," the man shouted as the gate closed in front of him.

"Don't ask." He continued up the drive and into one of three garages. They waited until the garage door had closed before the locks clicked to indicate they could climb out. An internal door took them into the hallway of a spacious home.

"*Mi casa es su casa.*" Dick dropped his keys into a little dish on a stand in the hallway. Lexi looked around and noted the retro decor. The huge windows and the glass doors leading to the garden and pool were darkened almost to complete blackness, but the lighting in the room was adequate.

"You live here?" Scott asked and gazed around the extravagant room.

"Darling, I don't *live* anywhere. But yes, it's mine. I stay here occasionally." Dick headed to the bar and poured himself a drink.

She peered around the room. "The furniture's quite retro." She wanted to say, "dated," but decided not to.

"Retro? Yes, you could say that. You could also say it's the original furniture that was present when Marilyn Monroe, Cary Grant, Frank Sinatra, and Marlon Brando attended parties here. I share this with the ghosts of the past." Dick spread his arms as though introducing them to those ghosts.

"I've heard of Marilyn Monroe but I'm not sure who the others were," Scott admitted.

"Philistine." The vampire turned away and gave his head a little shake.

"Hey, here's a picture of you with some dude." The other man pointed at the wall and looked at the picture.

Dick turned. "That 'dude' is Errol Flynn."

"Should I know who that is?" Scott squinted at the writing on the picture.

"Give me strength." The vampire pinched the bridge of his nose.

"It says November 1935. You're really *old*." The younger man was clearly impressed.

"I should have dropped you at that shitty motel," Dick muttered as he walked to where Lexi poured coffee for herself from a carafe.

Scott wandered the spacious living area and peered at the photographs on the walls. He looked from one picture to the corner of the room several times.

"James Dean sat on your thing?" he asked.

Lexi spat out a mouthful of coffee and coughed.

Dick smoothed his eyebrow. "I will neither confirm nor deny that James Dean sat on my thing."

"But there's a picture of it." The other man pointed at the wall again.

The vampire glanced at Lexi.

"Well, anything's possible," he admitted before he went to see what Scott was talking about. He looked at the picture and sighed.

"It's called a 'chaise lounge.'" Dick shook his head and returned to Lexi, who was spinning a shuriken again. He opened his mouth to speak to her but she tilted her head in the other man's direction and he followed her gaze.

They watched Scott as he walked around the chaise and attempted to sit on it. First, he sat on its edge, then he tried leaning to the side on one elbow, and finally, he reclined fully on his back.

"Comfortable?" Dick asked.

"I'm not sure." Scott wiggled around. "Do you find it comfortable?"

"I don't sit in it. It's a 1930 cowhide Le Corbusier, and it's insured for half a million dollars."

The man darted off it and stood nervously in the middle of the room, looking suspiciously at the furniture around him as though trying to work out where it might be safe to sit.

Lexi returned her focus to Dick. "So, what happened with your date last night?"

He rested his face in his hands and groaned. "He was still quite bitter that I'd stopped returning his calls when I got bored the first time. Although he didn't actually admit that, he ordered the Kobe steak and two bottles of the 1961 Haut-Brion at nine hundred dollars a bottle and drank all of it. I was quite tipsy by the end of the night."

"How did you get tipsy if he drank all—" Scott began.

Dick smiled at Scott and allowed his vampire teeth to descend while his eyes glittered.

"Okey-dokey. Forget I asked." The man made his way carefully to the kitchen counter and sat on a barstool next to Lexi.

"Did you remember to ask him about the case?" she asked pointedly.

"Oh, that. Yes. He'll find out what he can and try to get a copy of the documents from City Hall. I'm waiting for him to call back."

Scott leaned forward. "I didn't mean to insult you before— about your age. It's really cool that you've met interesting people and lived through those times. I think vampires are an important link to our history. I only ever met one vampire, but he told me stories from hundreds of years ago."

"Oh? Anyone I know?" Dick sounded more polite than interested.

"His name's Dimitri. I met him in Dallas."

"With long black hair, dresses like something from *Interview with a Vampire*?"

He nodded.

Dick and Lexi looked at each other and both rolled their eyes.

"What?" The young man looked from one to the other.

The vampire shook his head. "His name wasn't Dimitri, it was *Barry*, and he wasn't hundreds of years old, he was turned in the bathroom at a New Kids on The Block concert in 1989."

"Was? What happened to him?" Scott asked.

Lexi gave him a little finger wave. "Me. I happened to him. I killed him about a year ago. Just before I met you."

"You killed him? But he seemed like a nice enough guy." He looked disappointed.

"He developed a taste for toddlers that was unacceptable to my former employers."

"I thought you said vampires were 'hard to kill.'" He made air-quotes.

"I guess that depends on how hard you're trying. His predilections were also unacceptable to me. I took it personally."

"You take everything personally," Scott muttered.

Dick loosened his tie. "Barry's behavior was bad news for all of us. It brought unwanted attention."

"You have to be careful with vamps. No offense, Dick," Lexi added. "Whatever they were like in life is intensified."

"Take me, for example," Dick interrupted and spoke over his shoulder as he refreshed the water in a vase of flowers. "In life, I was fabulous and handsome, so I became even more fabulous and handsome." He appeared to be completely sincere.

She watched him as he pottered about the kitchen and smiled briefly at seeing him in a domestic setting before she continued her explanation. "Barry was an addict, always looking for his next hit. When you become a vampire, well, you know what the next hit is. Blood bags would never be enough," she finished.

"What happened?" Scott asked.

"The Kindred hierarchy put out a call for support. A kid had been found dead and it was a vamp kill. A five-year-old boy was still missing. To be honest, no one expected to find him alive but in the end, he turned up in Austin with the kid. We were asked to help. I found them and I killed Barry."

Dick looked at her. "You get around, don't you? Which reminds me, when was the last time you went to New Orleans?"

"I've never been." She shook her head.

"That's interesting. I suppose you should know that the other job Leonard was supposed to be working on is you."

"Me? I don't understand."

"He was trying to find out where you originally came from. Dolores asked me to find out. Obviously, I wasn't really feeling the love, so I passed the work on to Leonard because I know he has a contact in Kindred. Last night, he said he'd found evidence you'd spent some time in New Orleans."

"I don't remember it, but that doesn't mean it didn't happen. What was this evidence?"

"I guess we'll see when we meet up next. He'll leave a message for me today. I'll pick it up tonight and we'll catch up with him tonight or tomorrow night."

He rearranged the flowers in the vase, then yawned. "And that's the end of story time for me, kiddies. I need to get some sleep, and you need to go shopping."

"We do?" Lexi frowned in surprise.

"I'm not taking you to the fundraiser dressed like that. I have standards to maintain. My man will take you. I'll pick you up from the fleapit tonight."

"What about me?" Scott asked.

"You have homework." Dick went to a cabinet and selected several DVDs. He handed them to Scott one by one, reading the names as he did so. *The Wild One* with Marlon Brando, *Suspicion* with Cary Grant and *Robin Hood* with the *dude* in the photograph. Pay attention. I'll be asking questions."

"Jesús!" he shouted. A handsome young Mexican man appeared almost instantly. He was an interesting sight in a pair of tight short-shorts, a cropped t-shirt, a green scarf, no shoes, and a scrubbing brush.

"Yes, Mr. Levin?"

"Are we interrupting something?" Dick stared at the man.

Jesús waved the brush. "I was about to clean the pool."

"Wearing my Givenchy scarf?" he asked with a raised eyebrow.

"You have guests." He gestured awkwardly at the side of his neck, which was covered by the scarf.

Lexi assumed Dick had snacked on him for breakfast, something that would have been unacceptable to her when she was a member of Kindred. Now? Well, a guy had to eat and his friend didn't seem to mind.

The vampire picked the mail up from the end of the counter and leafed through it before he replaced the pile. "Any visitors or messages today?"

"Geoffrey's back." Jesús nodded in the direction of the front gate.

"Yes, I noticed that. Call the hospital and let them know they have one missing." He turned to Lexi, who was listening to the exchange with a smirk. "It's not funny. That man is the bane of my existence. Well, one of them."

His focus on Jesús again, he added, "You can do the pool later. Take my acquaintances shopping for an evening dress—you know the stores to go to—and drop them at their shitty car."

"Yes, Mr. Levin." He walked to the dish on the end of the counter and picked the car keys up.

"And put some shoes on."

"Yes, my flip-flops are there." Jesús pointed and rolled his eyes.

Dick shuddered. "I despise flip-flops. Those little toe posts are so invasive." Lexi grinned as his toes moved inside his deck shoes and she guessed he was curling them.

"Dude, you drink blood. That's way more gross." Scott screwed his face up.

"No, I'm very sure it's not." The vampire shuddered again.

"I'll pick you up later, Lexi. Please don't be dressed like Calamity Jane."

"I won't if you won't," she replied, her expression deadpan.

He stopped and scrutinized her for a moment. "My reputation will already be in tatters after I arrive with a woman. Let's not make it any worse."

His employee returned wearing sparkly flip-flops.

"Jesús, use my credit card. Is the gun in the car?" Dick asked.

"Yes, Mr. Levin."

"Good. If she tries to go to Walmart, shoot her in the face."

With that, he turned and left the room.

CHAPTER FOUR

"Say something. If you don't open your mouth and say something, I'll gut you." Lexi looked from the mirror to Jesús and back. She turned this way and that in *another* little black dress.

He sighed and looked up from his fingernails. "Too slutty."

She turned to face him fully. "You do understand I'm not kidding about gutting you? It's kind of my job."

"You asked me to say something, so I said something." He was unfazed.

"All you've said up to now is, too slutty, too slutty, too *Amish*, and too slutty." She twisted the ring around her middle finger, a nervous habit.

"They're all too short except the Amish one, and that was as ugly as sin." He screwed his face up and pointed. "This dress is nasty. You look like you'll start twerking like a girl from a rap video." He began to twerk in the middle of the Alexander McQueen store, while the younger store assistants giggled and the older ones looked horrified.

"The dress has to be short. I might need to fight."

Jesús narrowed his eyes. "You don't go to many parties, do you?"

Scott wandered over to join them. "How's it going here?"

"Horribly." Lexi sighed inwardly at the defeat in her voice. Her mind wandered to the little glass vial, which she'd stupidly left in the motel room. She frowned at the material slung over his arm. "What have you got there?"

"Another one for you to try. I think it might work." He handed it to her.

"It's long." She held the dress up.

"Give it a go anyway. I have a good feeling about it."

"If someone attacks me in this, I'll trip over my—" Her jaw dropped when she flipped the tag in her hand. "Have you seen the price of this?"

"Dick's credit card." Scott wiggled his eyebrows.

"Okay, I'll try it. I've never even had a car that cost this much." Lexi returned to the changing room.

She stepped out five minutes later, and Jesús whistled. "Holy shit! Tell my mama I'm going straight."

The assistants moved closer, oohing and ahhing.

In front of the mirror, Lexi admired the navy dress. Tied with spaghetti straps at the shoulders, it had a daring neckline. The garment hugged her curves all the way to her thighs, where a slit from there to the bottom of her right leg provided ample room for a face-high reverse roundhouse kick if required.

"Scott, my man, you have the eye. Hello?" Jesús waved his hand in front of the other man's face as he stared at Lexi with his mouth open.

"What's wrong?" She noticed him gaping.

"Erm…erm…gloves. You need to cover your arm." He walked away to speak to a sales assistant.

"What's wrong with your arm?" Jesús leaned in to stare at both her arms.

"I'm sensitive about this scar." She held her inner forearm out to him.

"But you can barely see it." He shrugged. "You need a clutch." He picked up a matching navy purse and passed it to her.

"What will I do with this?" She turned the small, sparkly purse over in her hands.

"I don't know. Maybe you could fill it with quarters and hit someone with it," he suggested with an exaggerated eye-roll.

Lexi tested the weight of it and nodded her approval.

Jesús touched the back of his hand to his forehead. "I'm getting a migraine."

By the time they reached the register, she had a dress, a purse, gloves, and shoes and Dick's credit card was over eight thousand dollars lighter.

It had been a good day, but she had begun to feel like she needed a little glass-vial-pick-me-up. Jesús dropped them at their car and drove away without a backward glance and they headed to the motel.

"Are you okay?" Scott asked as she drove. "You're feeling a little off."

"I think I need to eat." The one thing she hated most about their empathetic connection was that he could sense her emotional state.

"We can stop for something to eat on the way to the motel."

She cursed silently. Now, it would be even longer before she returned to the glass vial.

Lexi swung the car into the drive-thru and Scott looked at her. "We're not going in?"

"I won't leave those shopping bags in the car and I won't take them out in this neighborhood." She drew up to the window.

"Two McRibs, fries, and a Coke, please. What are you having, Scott?"

"Three Big Macs, large fries, and a vanilla shake,"

They parked with the food.

"You looked really nice in that dress." He stared at his food.

"I imagine anyone would look nice in a five-thousand-dollar dress." She shook her head. "I don't get it, you know? Dick owns that amazing place, so he's clearly rich. Why does he keep doing that shitty PI job?"

"Maybe he likes it. Eternity's a long time, so he might as well keep busy."

Lexi gazed out of the window. "I've never met a vamp who lived for eternity."

"I guess if *you're* rocking up at their front door, eternity probably won't happen for them."

"I have nothing against vamps, but if they hurt people…" She didn't need to finish the sentence.

"Like Dimitri? I mean, Barry," he asked through a mouthful of fries.

"Yes, like him."

"What happened to him?"

"When I found him with one of the kids, he tried to turn me so I killed him." She shrugged and bit into her burger.

"He tried to— Oh, yuk!" Scott pulled the slice of dill pickle from the bun and held it out of the window at arm's length.

She gulped her food. "Now, I *know* you're not about to drop that on the ground."

"The birds will eat it."

"The birds won't get a chance because you'll put it in the trash. It's roasting in here anyway." She pointed to a trash can ten feet ahead of the car. They both climbed out.

Lexi looked at the slice of pickle in his fingertips. "Why don't you ask them to hold the pickle?"

"I don't like the pickle itself but I like the taste of the burger where it *was*."

"You are too fucking weird." She sipped her Coke.

She leaned on the hood with her drink as Scott walked to the trash can and dropped the little slice of pickle in.

When he turned toward the car, his eyes widened and he dropped his burger. "Motherfucker!"

Lexi whirled to see that someone had crept to the back of the car and was taking the bags from the back seat. The kid looked up, realized he'd been seen, and bolted with their purchases. She put her cup carefully on the hood and stroked her finger down her scar.

Nothing.

Scott's magic had dissipated and she shrugged and ran after the thief.

She was fast, fortunately—unusually fast for a dud legacy.

"Lexi, just—" Scott started, but she had already set off in pursuit.

In five strides, she caught up with the thief and launched herself at his back in the same moment that she sensed a release of power from Scott. The boy tripped over his own feet and fell. Unable to stop herself, she sailed over him and met the asphalt face and arms first. She could hear her friend's sharp intake of breath from across the parking lot and raised her head as he winced at her hard fall.

Lexi staggered to her feet and walked to the young thief, who stared in disbelief at his feet. His laces were tied together. She picked the bags up and kicked him in the balls before she caught the young man by the back of his t-shirt and hauled him to the car.

Scott looked concerned. "What are you doing?"

"I'll tie him to the back of the car and drag him around the parking lot a few times. Maybe up and down the street." She passed the bags to her friend, who put them into the rear footwell.

"You can't do that. He's only a stupid kid." He didn't seem to know whether or not she was kidding.

"Hey!" the thief protested.

She flicked the wrist of her hand that held his collar, and his head bounced off the car's bumper.

"Ow!"

"I could get Dick to turn him. Then I could legitimately kill him."

"I thought we were trying to stay off Kindred's radar."

Lexi released a frustrated breath. She threw the thief down and kicked him in the balls again. The kid cried.

Scott walked around the car and made to open the door, but she had locked it. He looked at her.

"Where do you think you're going?" She pointed. "Your burger is lying on the ground."

He stamped to the front of the car, huffing like a grumpy teen, picked the burger up, and shoved it into the trash.

"I don't think I'd have liked explaining to Dick that we lost all that stuff he just paid for," he muttered as he climbed into the car.

Lexi assessed the damage to her face in the vanity mirror. She had grazes on her cheek, her elbows, and on the palms of her hands.

"Let's get back," he told her. "I can heal those for you but I want to clean them first."

She put the car into drive and they glided past the thief, who tried to undo his laces with one hand while he cradled his balls with the other.

For a while, they drove in silence. She was angry that she couldn't seem to maintain a hold on the magic and that he had interfered.

"So, what exactly happened then, with Barry?" Scott asked.

Lexi was glad of the opportunity to talk about something to distract her from the rage she felt. "We traced him to an old factory. I separated from my group and he jumped me and knocked me out. When I came to, he was dripping blood into my mouth. I realized the fucker was planning to turn me. Seconds after the blood went in, it was like someone had switched on a light and I could see the whole place like it was daylight. It was useful in that moment but not a good sign for going back to Kindred, even though I experienced for the first time what those enhanced senses were like for the other legacies. I had a shuriken in my sleeve. I slid it up his middle and ran while he tried to stop his guts from falling out."

"Was the kid okay? Or did you have to..." He left the sentence hanging.

"I ran to the next floor and toward the sound of crying. I heard the others coming in the front. If they had seen me then, they would have known I'd been exposed to vamp blood. I'd heard what happened to people who were contaminated. I had to get into the light, but the windows on that level were completely bricked up. I found the boy tied up and he looked unharmed. I was relieved that I might not have to kill him.

"I slapped an explosive charge on the bricks where the window had been, grabbed the kid, and ran into the hallway.

"After a hole was blown in the wall, I took him into the room. First, I forced my eyes open to the daylight. It was the hardest thing I've ever done and I wanted to scream. Inside, I *was* screaming. At first, it was like my eyes were on fire. After a few seconds, I blinked and the worst was over."

Scott stared out of the window. "So that's how it happened. I was taught tasting vampire blood meant you were lost forever. I thought that was true until I met you."

"That was what they told me too but I didn't feel lost. I merely felt like me."

He turned to her. "Did you get away with it? Or was that when you left?"

"When they came in, I held the boy's face to the hole in the wall and pretended to check *his* eyes. I felt them watching me as I turned the crying kid's face to me. His eyes were watering from the dust in the air after the explosion. I hoped mine looked the same—only irritated. I checked his neck, then cut the cable ties on his hands and feet. I took the kid to the doorway, passed him to my sister Maggie, and asked if anyone wanted to check me, but they said I looked okay. God, my heart was in my mouth." Lexi shook her head at the memory.

"So, they let you walk away?"

"Braxton, the father of the unit, wasn't convinced. My senses were heightened, remember. Honestly, I expected a silver dagger in my back as I walked down the hallway. As I reached the stairs, he spoke my name. I almost stopped before I realized he'd whispered. There was no way I'd have been able to hear that with human hearing. I kept walking and waited for it to wear off. So, any more questions?"

"Are you going to eat that last McRib?"

They parked at the motel and Scott stretched into the back to retrieve the bags.

"It's probably best no one sees those labels." He vanished.

Lexi sighed and trudged up the stairs, trying to keep her scraped palms from touching the rusty metal railing.

He was on the balcony and his cell was ringing when she reached the room.

"If I step in there, I'll lose the signal." He put it on speaker and placed it on the metal railing, then twirled his finger in a circle. Lexi knew by now that this meant no one else could hear them. She stood near the phone while he went into the room to pull his first aid kit from his bag.

"How's it going?" Dolores asked.

She conveyed her irritation in three words. "Well, hello, Dolores."

"Oh, dear. You didn't kill him, did you?"

Lexi paused long enough that she was certain Dolores would be perspiring. "No. We talked. He's still an asshole but we can work together."

"He's forgiven you? Just like that?" The woman sounded surprised.

"Excuse me? *He's* forgiven *me*?" Her voice was so high at the end, she squeaked.

"You did leave him with a broken neck, dear," Dolores admonished.

"He told me it was he who called you that night to get me out of Chicago."

"That's right. Did I never mention that?" She knew damn well she'd never mentioned it. Lexi remained silent.

"Did you know he's rich?" Scott jumped into the gap in the conversation.

"Well, he *was* one of the most famous movie actors in the forties. By *he*, I mean his grandfather, obviously!" The older woman chuckled.

"Did you know James Dean sat on his—" Scott began.

"We're not going through that again," Lexi interjected and held a hand up to silence him.

"Have you made contact with the client?" Dolores asked.

"Yes. She thinks a local businessman is behind all this."

The other end of the phone was silent.

"Dolores?" Scott checked the cell to see if they'd lost the connection.

"Yes, I'm here. Sorry. I was looking out of the window." She sounded distracted.

Lexi was immediately on the alert. "What's wrong?"

"It's probably nothing."

"But?" She drummed her fingers on the rail.

"You know when you see the same car too many times in too many different places?"

"That fucking cult. Why can't Kindred let it go?" She banged the metal rail with her fist.

Scott brought out the gauze and sterile water. "They could be looking for me."

She shooed him away.

"They think I'm stepping on their toes, dear, but yes, Kindred might have discovered one or both of you are with me." That the woman sounded so calm irked her even more.

"Is there anything we can do?" Scott leaned in the doorway.

"It sounds like it's time to move your office," Lexi suggested.

"I have a potential client coming in to speak to me about a job later. But yes, my Spidey sense is tingling. I'll pack after this appointment."

"Do me a favor, Dolores. Pack first." She was getting bad vibes about the situation.

"And if you need us, call," Scott added.

"I will, dear. Look after each other and Scott, make sure Lexi doesn't kill William."

"I'm right here," she retorted, but the woman had disconnected.

Scott took his cell and they entered the room. Lexi sat on her bed and he cleaned the scratches on her face.

"I don't like the sound of that." She bounced her leg up and down, a recent nervous trait.

"I hope she's careful," he muttered as he turned his attention to her palms.

"I could do this myself, you know." She didn't mean to sound sharp but being in close proximity to other people when she was injured made her nervous. Irritated with both herself and every-thing in general, she put her hand on her knee to force her leg to rest.

"I'd rather do it myself. I want to be sure I've removed all the dirt before I close the wounds. Plus, you're really jittery." He stood and threw the gauze into the R2D2-shaped can. "I'm sorry I interfered back there. I was anxious to show you that you have other methods at your disposal now that you have magic." He returned, placed a hand on the top of her head, and whispered something she didn't catch.

Lexi wondered, not for the first time, if he used real words or merely muttered nonsense to annoy her.

"Your way would have been more discreet, but I'd already committed to my action. That's not the time to butt in with a different plan." She looked at her hands and elbows and realized there were no scrapes. When she checked the mirror, her face was blemish-free. "Nice job. Thanks." She headed into the bathroom.

CHAPTER FIVE

Lexi didn't often feel like she was outside her comfort zone. Tonight, she thought she might need a map to find her way back. She jumped at a knock on the door. Scott stood to answer it while she tried to tuck a two-inch switchblade into her purse. It wouldn't fit with all the quarters.

Dick stepped in, wearing a dinner jacket and a bow tie. He stopped in his tracks. "Well, don't you scrub up nice!"

She smiled.

"Did you actually smile? Who are you, and what have you done with Lexi Braxton?"

"So, what's our story?" she asked. "Because no one will believe I'm your date."

"You're Bianca, an old friend from Chicago. We've known each other for years and you rarely try to murder me. Do you think you can follow the brief?"

"I don't know. That last part sounds tricky." She stuck her tongue out.

"Just a second." Scott took her hand and closed his own around it.

"Erm..." She glanced quickly at him.

He took his hand away, and in her palm was a shiny silver teardrop pendant on a silver chain.

"Scott, this is lovely. Can you put it on for me?" Lexi asked. She lifted her hair and he fastened it at the back of her neck as he muttered softly.

"This will cloak your magical ability from anyone who gets too curious." He stepped back and looked at her. "Okay, knock 'em dead."

"But please don't take that literally," Dick added. They left the room.

"Don't forget these." Scott passed the purse and gloves to Dick.

The vampire handed the purse to her. "What the hell's in this thing?" he asked as they reached the vehicle.

"Put it this way." She slid into the passenger seat. "If we stumble across a pinball machine, I got us covered." She winked.

He glanced sideways at the dress as he drove away. "I must say I'm surprised. You have exceptional taste."

Lexi smiled. "What's even more surprising is that Scott selected it."

"He's quite a dark horse." Dick laughed. "He seems like a good guy. How did you meet him?"

"Through Dolores. He went to her for help when his Kindred cell was forcing him to match with someone he didn't trust."

The vampire looked surprised. "It was my understanding that mages and legacies had the autonomy to choose who they were matched with."

"They usually do, but Kindred cells essentially run independently. Scott had watched this guy grow up and he was the kind of kid who tortured little animals. He hoped he'd grow out of it, but the guy only grew nastier. In the end, Scott flat-out refused to give him access to his powers. The head of the family was a bastard too. He tried to force him to comply. He didn't feel safe there."

"Couldn't they have matched the psycho with someone else?"

"He insisted on Scott. It's unsurprising. While we don't get to meet many other units, I have met other mages and Scott's abilities are beyond anything I've seen before."

"But he wound up matched with you."

"That was his idea and the situation we were in. Actually, I think it saved us both, but he wouldn't have been wasted on someone like me if we were still in Kindred." Lexi was ready to leave this conversation behind. "Have you heard from Leonard?"

"I haven't and I'm concerned. If I don't hear anything in the next couple of hours, I'll have to drop past his place tonight."

"I'll back you up, just in case."

"In that?" He indicated the dress.

"It's surprisingly versatile." She grinned.

They pulled up at the entrance and two valets opened the doors. Lexi took Dick's arm and they entered the grand foyer, where they were offered champagne. Both declined. Somewhere farther into the building, a soulful woman's voice sang "Summertime," accompanied by a live band.

"William, it's delightful to see you." An elderly woman in a long, beaded cream dress with an organza wrap approached him and air-kissed him with a *mwah*.

"Betsy, you look younger every time I see you." He kissed the woman's hand.

"Thank you, William. I've been bathing in the blood of virgins." Betsy winked.

"Good grief, the import fees must be exorbitant." He returned the wink.

"William!" The woman feigned shock. "Are you suggesting Palm Springs is completely without home-grown virgins?" She laughed and whispered conspiratorially, "Thank goodness you're here. We simply don't see enough of you. I thought I was in for another boring evening of trying to wrangle money out of my *frenemies*, as the kids say."

"So, is there any gossip?" he asked as they walked through the entrance hall.

"Well, the town's most handsome and eligible bachelor has arrived with a mysterious, stunning beauty. Let's start with that."

"Where are my manners? Betsy O'Donnell, this is Bianca Maybury, an old friend from Chicago."

Lexi shook the woman's hand.

"Are you by chance related to the New England Mayburys?" Betsy asked.

"Oh, we don't talk about the New England Mayburys," she replied smoothly.

"Really? How perfectly delicious. I look forward to hearing you not talk about them later after you've visited the gin bar." The woman grinned at her.

She grinned in response and decided she liked her irreverence.

"Save a dance for me, muffin. I'm still holding out hope." She patted Dick's behind and moved on to greet more guests.

"Let's mingle." He led them through the rooms and pointed out various paintings and pieces of furniture.

They stood before a huge painting depicting a War of Independence battle scene. He looked at her. "You're not very talkative."

"I thought you'd use your vamp hearing to listen in on the conversations around us."

"I can do both. Anyway, I have a question. If you weren't trying to kill me in Chicago, what *were* you trying to do?" They both continued to gaze at the painting.

He'd probably mulled over her reaction to him calling her "bloodthirsty" in the restaurant the night before. More than likely, he'd already guessed correctly.

"Can we not get into this now?" Lexi asked.

"As you wish, but it's something we need to talk about, isn't it?" Dick turned to look at her face as she stared resolutely at the painting. She nodded as though she agreed.

Not if I can avoid it.

As they wandered past a group of men talking about local business, she slowed to listen. "This is a beautiful"—she looked around for an excuse to have slowed—"vase."

The vampire glanced quickly at it. "I'd guess 1899."

"As old as that?" She was surprised and leaned in to look closer.

"Not the age, the price. It looks like it came from Home Depot." He sneered.

"Well, there's William," a raised voice said from the group of men, clearly intended to get his attention. "If you're looking for property, Caleb, you could see if he wants to sell."

"Stanley, how are you?" Dick asked and maneuvered them toward the group.

"I'm very well, William." A man in his fifties stuck his hand out, and they shook.

"This is Bianca, an old family friend. Bianca, this is Stanley Horton. He's the chief of police so you be good now." Lexi shook the man's hand.

"What are—" Another man stared wide-eyed at her. He turned to Dick. "You're in...surprising company this evening." Turning his attention to Lexi, he continued with an oily smile. "Well, you look too young to be anyone's *old* friend." He licked his lips.

"And this is Caleb Linden. He's in property and virtually everything else. Be careful of him. He's a rascal." Dick chuckled.

"William, my reputation—" Caleb started.

"Precedes you." The vampire laughed and the men all joined in.

Lexi understood exactly what he was saying and shook the man's hand as he continued to stare lasciviously down her neckline.

She smiled and giggled as she imagined thunking the Home Depot vase into his face.

"What's this about buying my property?" Dick asked.

"Don't worry, William. I know what the answer would be." Caleb sighed.

A handsome, slick-looking man with gray at his temples smiled to reveal perfect teeth. "Will, I absolutely forbid you to sell that beautiful piece of history to Caleb. If it became a ninety-nine-cent store, the voters would blame me and this election's already giving me an ulcer."

"Bianca, this is Todd O'Donnell, the current and future mayor," Dick told her.

Lexi shook hands dutifully. *This is useful. All the players together.*

"Are you local, Bianca?" asked Todd.

"He means, are you a voter?" Caleb Linden guffawed.

"I'm visiting with my fiancé, John. We're here looking at wedding venues, as recommended by Uncle William, and to get the paperwork arranged for our wedding."

"Oh, did you hear from the records office, dear?" the vampire asked.

"No, not a thing." She shrugged.

"Not to worry. We'll call again tomorrow." He patted her shoulder.

Lexi saw a brief flicker of a look pass between Caleb and Stanley.

"How do you pass your time when you're not at parties with gentlemen of questionable character, Bianca?" Caleb asked.

Dick put his hand over his heart as though wounded, then chuckled.

She smiled, but the man wasn't looking at her face.

My eyes are up here, douchebag.

"I'm a dental hygienist, and my fiancé John is a systems design consultant." She often used the dental hygienist line as no one ever wanted to know more. People usually glazed over at John's systems job too, but not today.

"Really? If you're looking to put roots down here, he should come see me. Where is he currently?" Caleb handed her a card. She took it, smiled, and handed it to Dick. Not even a sliver of card would fit into the tiny purse with all those quarters.

"He's been working with a small tech start-up. He'd be able to tell you more about it than I could." She shrugged and gave a vacuous giggle.

"Well, I'm always happy to help a friend of a friend." The man's eyes were still glued to her breasts.

"So, you're *Uncle Will* now," Todd said, and the men laughed.

"It's a term of endearment. I've been friends with Bianca's parents for years."

Betsy approached. "Darling."

"Hello, Mother." Todd put an arm around her. "You've done a wonderful job with the party, as always." He kissed her cheek.

The woman pouted. "I have a complaint for the mayor."

"Oh, dear. Never mind the voters. Now you're in trouble with your mother, Todd," Stanley added. The men laughed raucously again.

"I hear there's *another* Mexican restaurant opening in the area. Can't we have a French restaurant? Who even eats Mexican?" Betsy asked.

"I'm sure Uncle William had Mexican only this morning." Lexi smiled sweetly at Dick.

He returned it with a kind-uncle-like smile of his own and patted the back of her hand affectionately, but his eyes quite clearly said, "Do not fucking start."

"Mother, I thought you loved *huevos rancheros*," Todd replied.

"I do, but I love French food, too," Betsy assured him.

A loud laugh roared from behind Lexi, and she turned to see a group of young men around a billiard table in the room next door. She recognized Tommy, Kate's boyfriend, from their

E.G. BATEMAN & MICHAEL ANDERLE

morning visit to the bar. He was horsing around with the group. She turned away before he saw her.

"Stanley, dear, your…friends are quite exuberant." Betsy was clearly unhappy that the young men were getting rowdy.

"Of course, Betsy. I'll send them home. It's my fault they've been here all day. I thought they might be able to help," Stanley said and looked not at Betsy but at Caleb.

"They've been here all day?" The woman looked puzzled.

"They brought the produce this morning, remember? You haven't been at the gin, have you?" Caleb laughed.

"Of course I have. I paid for it. Well, they've been very well-behaved for most of the day. I haven't heard a peep." Betsy smiled and turned to her son. "People have given me envelopes all evening. It's going very well."

"That reminds me." Dick took an envelope from his breast pocket and handed it to her. "Here's another one for your collection."

"William, you are quite simply the most charming man alive." She took the envelope and it disappeared into her large purse.

"I'm sure nothing could be further from the truth," the vampire replied honestly.

"Please excuse me one moment." Stanley headed toward the billiards room.

"Your mayor thanks you for your support, Mr. Levin." Todd held his hand out.

Dick took the proffered hand. "The mayor can always count on my support."

Todd pointed an accusing finger at him. "Except on the golf course."

"Hey, I'm always there for bowling night."

The man looked at Lexi. "He's always late for bowling night."

"Fashionably so." The vampire glanced quickly at her.

"Do you wear the shirt? And holy sh…moke, the *shoes*?" She tried to picture it.

"His grandfather was an exceptional bowler, golfer, and tennis player." Betsy's eyes glittered at the memory.

Lexi heard the men leave the room behind her. They were laughing and chatting but suddenly stopped. She could feel their eyes on her back but realized their main attention was on Dick. She knew that being shifters, they would have smelled the vampire. If they had been in wolf form, their hackles would be raised at the sense of danger. In their human form, they might not have hackles but the atmosphere had definitely tensed. Lexi grasped the weighted little purse as her companion turned slowly and deliberately to face them.

"Gentlemen." He tilted his head.

She made to turn but he held her arm subtly. As this meant she would have to struggle to turn and that would draw attention, she remained as she was, facing away from the men.

"Move it," Stanley instructed quietly. They continued toward the exit.

"Have you done something to upset the locals, William?" Betsy asked in surprise.

"I believe my houseboy might have dinged someone's motorbike recently. I was under the impression the situation had been resolved."

"I'd guess from the looks those men gave you that the situation has not been resolved to their satisfaction. I will ask Stanley to ensure they don't return to the club any time soon." The woman looked suspiciously at the retreating men.

"Todd, may I borrow you for a moment?" Caleb asked with his hand on Todd's shoulder.

"Sure, Caleb." They walked away together.

"You boys promised no business tonight. You have five minutes," Betsy called after them before she returned her attention to the others.

"Uncle William, would you mind awfully if we head back

soon? John will work all night if I don't wrestle that computer away from him." Lexi wanted to follow the shifters.

"You promised me a dance, young lady, and a dance I shall have." Dick took her hand and wrapped it expertly around his arm.

"I did?" She was startled. "Are you sure I promised that? Because that doesn't sound like a thing I'd promise."

He led her through the room next door toward the ballroom.

"What are you doing?" she asked.

"Giving them a few minutes to leave. I'll be able to follow the smell of a wolfpack as well in ten minutes as I can now with the added advantage of not running into them. I don't think they like me."

"Have you had trouble with them before?" Lexi took a glass of champagne from a passing waiter as they moved through the rooms.

"No. I thought I had a good relationship with the Palm Springs pack. I mean, sure, some of the younger ones can be boisterous, but I can't remember the last time I met with such hostility." He seemed nonplussed.

"Stanley's the alpha, right? Can you talk to him?" She sipped the champagne.

"It seems I will have to. Are you sure you should drink that? We might need you to fire on all cylinders later."

"This is only to get me through the dancing." She knocked the drink back and handed the glass to a different waiter on the way to the dance floor.

The band played "Blue Moon," and the two glided across the floor.

She caught bemused stares from many young men in the room. "I'm guessing you've pretty much done this town."

"Repeatedly, over the years. To the point where it's beginning to feel a little uncomfortable. It's déjà vu all over again," Dick admitted with a twitch of his lip.

"Have you never considered settling down with one person?" she asked, genuinely curious.

"Attachments bring vulnerability. I've lived a long time, Lexi, and I've gained many enemies. Some come and go but some have long memories." He twirled her. "You dance surprisingly well."

"Kindred taught me to slip seamlessly into any situation. It's funny since I was clumsy as a child."

He stopped dancing and stared at her. "You recall your life before Kindred?" He remembered where they were and their purpose and continued to dance.

"Flashes." She knew she had confirmed what he already suspected.

"So, I wasn't wrong when I accused you of being bloodthirsty. You were literally after my blood. You should have merely asked. My prices are very competitive."

"I'm not a blood whore." Lexi felt her face flame. "When Barry tried to turn me, the enhanced speed, strength, and senses were all great, although I was already very strong and fast for a human. That night, however, memories began to surface. I thought I'd never been counseled before—that's what they call it when they wipe your memories after a particularly difficult mission—but I realized they'd done it to me many times and the memories were surfacing. That was why I left. I knew I couldn't trust them and I knew that as soon as they discovered my memories were returning, they'd kill me."

"I assume the blood-hit didn't take your memories back as far as you needed?"

"Not nearly. So far, I've remembered to my late teens and the occasional flash of life before."

Dick stopped again but she forced him to continue. "How many times have you done it?"

Lexi paused, then decided she'd told him enough of the truth so might as well finish it. "Only three times. Barry, then you, then a blood den in Portland."

"You know you can't keep doing it, don't you?"

"I'm careful. Look, I'm sorry about the whole neck-breaking thing. Don't get me wrong. I still think you're an arrogant jerk." She smiled and he laughed.

"Well, you'll have to go to the back of an extraordinarily long line of people who think that." Dick glanced at the pendant Scott had given her. "What's happened to your pendant?"

She looked down and realized that the shiny silver had turned black. "I don't know. How strange." The song finished and they started to leave the dance floor. He glanced across the room at Betsy, who had watched him dance but turned quickly to speak to a group of women. He hesitated.

"Go on." Lexi gestured toward the dance floor.

"I'm sorry?" He looked blankly at her.

"She wants to dance with you." She shooed him away.

The band was playing "Unforgettable." "How apt," he said. He walked across the floor and offered his arm to Betsy, who took it with a dazzling smile on her face. They danced and spoke but Lexi couldn't hear the conversation. At the end of the song, the woman delivered him to her side.

"You dance beautifully, exactly as your grandfather did. It's like being transported back and I could turn and find Harvey standing right there with a grin on his face. Do you remember how he hated to dance, William?" Betsy looked into the distance and into another time.

Dick smiled warmly, no doubt remembering too. "You've told me."

"The fun we all had." She grasped the younger woman's arm exuberantly.

"They must be wonderful memories," Lexi said politely.

"I'm a silly old woman." Betsy wiped a tear from the corner of her eye. "You look so much like him. It's the eyes, I suppose."

He kissed the back of her hand. "Everyone says that, so it must be true."

"Harvey spoke of him often. When he never returned from Europe, it broke his heart. We never forgot our William. Well, off you go, then. Don't let it be so long next time. It was lovely to meet you, dear." She turned to the party.

The vampire watched her walk away. "Let's get out of here."

While they stood outside and waited for the valet to arrive with the car, a voice spoke from directly behind them.

"It was good to see you again, William. Perhaps we'll run into each other again soon." Lexi jumped slightly at Caleb's voice. No one approached her from behind without her being aware of them. No one.

The vampire paused for a moment. "I'm sure we shall." He sounded absolutely certain of it.

They headed down the drive in silence and didn't speak again until they had left the property.

"He gives me the willies," Lexi admitted the moment they were through the gate.

"Yes. I've felt uncomfortable around him for as long as I've known him. And when a vampire says that, it shouldn't be ignored."

She stared into the darkness. "I have the feeling we didn't pull the wool over his eyes at all."

Dick glanced at her as he drove. "What do you think about tonight?"

"I think Kate's problem is coming from much closer than she thinks it is. You?"

He nodded. "I agree. Also, I'm concerned it's only the tip of the iceberg. Something bad happened today. I think those young shifters did it and Caleb gave them an alibi."

"Telling Betsy they were hanging around at the club all day." She nodded.

"I think we need to drop in on Leonard. I shouldn't have involved him and have a very bad feeling about this."

"Agreed. We can find the shifters later."

"I don't think that's an option. We have a bogey on our six." Dick frowned into his rearview mirror.

"A what on our what?"

"Someone's tailing us. I thought all you Kindred types spoke like the military."

"No. What on earth gave you that idea? Can you lose them?"

"I'll give it a try." He accelerated and the vehicle behind matched their speed.

They rounded a bend to find a truck parked across the street. Dick skidded the car onto a side road.

"What's up here?" she asked, then twisted sideways in her seat to look out of the back and front.

"It's residential. We might be able to lose them on one of these roads."

A truck suddenly hurtled from a side road. He was able to speed up to avoid a T-bone, but it impacted with the rear of the car, which fishtailed. Dick pressed the accelerator to the floor.

"These guys aren't messing around." Lexi turned to kneel on her seat. She dug in her pocket and drew a rifle. Dick looked at her as she adjusted the scope.

"Where the actual fuck did that come from?"

"A lady never tells." She slipped a magazine into the weapon and slid into the back seat, banging her head as the car went through a pothole. "Ow!"

He made eye contact through the rearview mirror. "Complain to the mayor."

She turned to steady the rifle on the back of the seat. "I'm afraid you'll lose your back window."

"Just do it."

With a nod, she leveled the rifle as best she could. "Do we have a straight road?"

"We're coming up on a bend now. I think they'll attempt to herd us over the canyon wall. There aren't many places where that's possible, but we're heading toward one."

"Shit."

He skidded around the bend. "Okay, straight for twenty seconds."

Lexi leveled the rifle again and took two shots in quick succession. The first was intended to shatter the window and the second the driver of the truck, but the first one took the driver and the second simply compounded the damage. The truck went out of control and off the road. It was replaced by the two others. The one closest turned on a row of four spotlights above its cabin, intending to blind them. The large vehicle behind also had its high beams on and created a silhouette of a man who stood out of the sunroof in the first truck and tried to aim a rifle.

"Amateurs," she muttered, aimed at the man, and fired a single round as Dick swerved. With a grimace, she returned her aim to the gunman and killed him.

"I'm turning," the vampire told her. "This road leads to a hiking-trail parking lot. The moment I stop, find somewhere to hide."

He skidded into the parking lot and vanished. Lexi had a moment of indecision. She didn't need to look at the scar to know the magic had completely dissipated. Her first instinct was to retrieve the vial from her pocket, knowing it would help her in the fight to come. The moment she'd used to think was all the time she had. Before she could get out of the car, one of the trucks plowed into it and shoved Dick's vehicle several feet.

It's a good thing I wasn't hiding behind this fucking car.

A man jumped out of the other vehicle and walked closer. She put the rifle into her pocket and climbed out with her hands up. The guy she'd shot still dangled from the sunroof. He'd been a little too round in the middle for that maneuver.

"Where's your friend?" The man walked toward her with his weapon raised.

"He ran off." She tried to sound pissed about it.

When he pushed her back with the end of his rifle, she

E.G. BATEMAN & MICHAEL ANDERLE

complied and noticed that these were not shifters. He ducked his head quickly into the car and returned his attention to her.

"Where's the gun?" He poked her again with his rifle.

"He took it." She maintained a blank expression as he shifted his gaze around the darkness.

"The guy's armed," he shouted to his friends. Two of them had joined him and now stood a few feet behind, which left two more near the back truck. "What's your friend's name?"

"Dick."

As she faced them, she saw the one at the very back disappear quickly and silently in the dark.

The guy before her lifted his semi-automatic weapon and called to the others. "Get the lights on and shine them around the area. We're looking for Dick."

"Aren't we all?" Lexi agreed to the men's amusement.

The next man vanished.

"To be honest, he's not usually this hard to get," she added. "If you simply stay in one place for any length of time, he'll probably get around to you." The remaining men all laughed now except the one who returned the aim of his gun to her.

"Come on, smart mouth. You can come with me." They walked to the edge of the trail and a spotlight followed them.

"Oh, good. With all this light, he's unlikely to hit me," she commented.

"Don't point it at us, you idiot. Point it ahead of us." The dark settled around them when the light was redirected.

She spun, disarmed him in three seconds, and swept her leg out to drop him while she twisted the gun out of his hold. He had other ideas and head-butted her in the face, and she stumbled back. In the darkness, she hadn't seen it coming.

Lexi struck him on the ear with her quarter-filled purse, and he fell to his knees.

I'll have to thank Jesús for that idea.

As she delivered a kick to his head with her right foot, he

lashed out, and she stumbled and toppled. He was on top of her immediately with his rifle across her throat.

She had stretched her hands closer to pop his eyeballs with her thumbs when Dick's face appeared from the darkness behind him, barely visible except for his teeth. It was a truly terrifying sight—the stuff of nightmares, but not hers. The man made a choking sound, and the vampire whisked him away. She scrambled to her feet, sprinted through the darkness, and settled behind the car with the rifle.

"Should we keep moving the light?" asked a voice from the truck. Receiving no reply, the light moved in the opposite direction until it illuminated the man lying on the ground.

"He's down! Go get him," a voice shouted. There was no response. "Chad? Mike?"

"I'm afraid they're rather indisposed," said Dick's chillingly cold voice from the darkness.

The man scrambled from the vehicle and ran directly into his adversary.

Lexi stood. In the light from the truck, she saw the trail of blood from the vampire's mouth to his white shirt. With none of their attackers remaining, they climbed into his car and drove away past the two trucks. The third vehicle, which had left the road and should have had a dead driver, had disappeared.

He leaned out and sniffed as he went past. "That one had shifters in it. I'll want to speak to them after we've been to see Leonard."

"Let's pick Scott up first," Lexi suggested.

She felt his eyes on her. "You should have sensed that headbutt coming. The more you rely on that stuff, the less you can depend on your natural ability."

"I don't rely on it," she snapped, knowing she hadn't fooled him.

"Of course not." He returned his gaze to the road.

CHAPTER SIX

Dolores checked the time. As promised, she'd packed everything in her Denver, Colorado office. The only things visible were the desk, two chairs, the filing cabinet, and the clock she now watched.

The client was expected to arrive on the hour. He had sounded desperate on the phone and in her experience, the more desperate a client was, the earlier they arrived. She considered the possibility that he might not be as desperate as he had intimated.

To distract herself from the wait, she stood and went to the window. The car was there again. A coincidence? Probably not.

When she glanced at the clock, she saw a fly walking across its face. She approached it slowly and smacked it with her yellow legal pad, then took it down and wiped the brown stain from its face with a tissue. As she polished the glass front, she considered returning it to its place, but the sound of footsteps on the stairs made her lean it against the wall on top of the filing cabinet. She returned to her chair.

The man knocked and opened the door. Three deep, angry scratches raked his face. One went through his left eye, which was half brown and half milky-white. He looked nervously around the office.

"Are you Dolores? I'm Eric. We spoke on the phone."

"Come in, Eric." She looked at the clock. "You're exactly on time."

He glanced at the clock as well and smiled nervously at her.

"Take a seat. Tell me how we can help."

"You deal with unusual situations involving unusual…people, yes?"

"That's correct." She leaned forward.

The man looked around the room. "I'm sorry, but have you just arrived or are you moving out?"

"We're preparing to decorate. So, your problem?"

"I'm sorry, I didn't mean to be intrusive but I don't want to hire you and have you disappear on me."

"Eric. I'd like to save you the effort of bullshitting me. Why don't you tell me what Kindred wants?" Dolores asked.

Eric ceased wringing his hands and straightened in his chair.

"Thank you, Dolores. I respect expediency." As he spoke, the scratches vanished from his face but the half-white eye remained. "You were involved in taking something of ours."

"As you can see, Eric, I don't have much." She gestured to the sparse room. "Do you see your property in here?"

"I thought we weren't going to bullshit." He was unsmiling.

"Under US law, it's no longer legal to keep people as property."

"*People*, quite," he agreed as though she had proven his point for him.

The door opened to admit an angry-looking young man and a pale, thin girl. She remained at the back of the room and leaned against the wall, while her companion walked to Dolores's side of the desk and sat on it to stare belligerently at her. The older woman glanced at Eric with a raised eyebrow that asked why he hadn't taught the boy any manners. His eyes flicked in irritation at the young man.

"Our asset's disappearance has caused friction for his family. They merely want him back. We know you were hired to assist with his removal. I'd like to hire you to find him again—unless you still know where he is?"

"I'm afraid I don't have your...asset." She would never think of Scott as her or anyone else's property.

The young man jumped from the desk and back-handed her across the face. She saw it coming and winced as she tried to turn her face away.

The room wavered and flickered slightly and they all saw it.

"Lucy, what was that?" Eric turned in his chair to face the girl.

"There's a glamor on the room." The girl closed her eyes, held a hand up, and muttered.

Dolores turned to the young man. "I see you favor the fae. Personally, I never approved of the unseelie fae blood being used in the legacy ritual. They are too...unpredictable, or perhaps I mean predictable." She wiped blood from the corner of her mouth.

Lucy's face tensed and eventually, she sighed. "I can't get through the glamor."

"I can." The young man drew his hand back.

"Warren!" Eric snapped.

Warren glanced briefly at the man and curled his hand into a fist. Dolores tried to get out of the chair but he struck her on the side of the head and she fell beside the filing cabinet. The room wobbled, and a door appeared in the rear wall. The three of them turned to face it while she lay unmoving on the floor.

"It's a portal." The girl walked toward it.

"Let's see what the bitch was hiding." Her assailant barged past the others, caught hold of the handle, and opened the door.

CHAPTER SEVEN

Dick and Lexi reached the motel and she ran up to the room with her stilettos in her hand. Scott was watching the Cary Grant movie while playing cat's cradle absently with a luminescent blue-white light. She observed that he was fully dressed and had his sneakers on.

"Were you planning to go somewhere?" she asked.

"Only staying ready. It felt like you would need me." He dissolved the ethereal string instantly.

She snatched her leathers up and hurried into the bathroom.

"Dick's waiting in the car." She closed the door.

Seated on the end of the tub, she retrieved the vial, pulled the stopper, and shook it with her finger over the end. She stroked her fingertip over her tongue and sighed as the strength returned to her extremities and her mind cleared. These things were great and she told herself that wasn't why she took the vamp blood but sometimes, she wondered if she was simply fooling herself. She stood quickly. No, it was to help her find the memories buried by Kindred. With her eyes closed, she sought those memories and returned to her oldest ones—brief flashes of a stolen childhood—

but nothing new surfaced. She replaced the stopper and put the vial into her pocket.

Within three minutes, she was in her familiar leathers. Removing the black pendant, she slipped it into her pocket. Scott still stood in the room. "I thought you'd be in the car."

"I won't leave you alone. Dolores told us to look after each other. Let me fix you."

He put his hand on her head. The pain in her nose and throat disappeared and her depleted magic re-energized.

Scott pulled his beanie on and waited at the door for her to walk through.

"What the hell happened to your car?" he asked as he stared at the dents in the bodywork, the bullet holes, and the missing back window.

"It drives okay. It's a little wobbly at the back, but otherwise fine." Dick sighed.

The young man looked around before he placed his hand on the vehicle. He closed his eyes and whispered. Dick gaped in surprise as the dents in the back buckled into their correct shape and the wheel straightened. When the process finished, the bullet holes weren't perfect but at least they wouldn't draw attention. He couldn't put the window back so he created a glamor of one instead.

The vampire gazed from the car to him several times. "If you'd consider a change in employment, I'm wondering if I could keep you on retainer."

"If this is a service you need regularly, I'd suggest *you* need a change of career." Scott opened the back door of the car, swept the glass off the seat with his beanie, and climbed in. As they drove to their next destination, they filled him in.

The neighborhood in Cathedral City was dark and quiet. Scott cloaked them when they parked a block from Leonard's house and prepared to walk to it. Lexi detected a curious odor but before she could step onto the street to follow it, Dick pulled her back. "This whole area smells of shifters. I'm sure they're still around."

"Ah, yes. That's what it is. So if we'd followed the shifters from the party, we'd have wound up here anyway." She looked into the darkness and although her senses were temporarily improved, she could neither see nor hear them.

"Why would they hang around if they've already—" Scott searched for the right words. "Uh, done something to your friend?"

"I don't like this. Simply walking in there could be a bad idea." She continued to scan the area all around them.

"I have to know if he's okay. I'll go alone." The vampire prepared to step onto the street.

"Wait, let me." She touched his arm. "Scott can keep me cloaked from a distance through our link."

"Are you sure?" He sounded doubtful.

"Yes. I...feel better now." She averted her face to avoid his stare.

Scott glanced at the other man. "Let's get to the car. It'll take a fair amount of energy. I should sit for this."

Lexi hopped the gate of the property that backed onto Leonard's house with ease. She walked through the garden to the wall at the rear and came face to face with a shifter in human form who hid in the bushes. She assumed a defensive posture and prepared to fight. He looked up, sniffed the air, then settled into his hiding place.

Well, I know the spell works.

She jumped the wall and hurried to Leonard's house. The patio door hung open on a single hinge, and the home had been ransacked.

83

When she entered, someone she assumed was Leonard lay dead on the tiled floor. She studied the body and suspected she knew why the pack was still in the area. Her phone buzzed in her pocket. When she glanced at the caller ID, it was Dick.

"This isn't the best time."

"Is he?"

"Someone is. I'm sorry. The place is a mess. It appears they were looking for something."

"Are there a couple of silver birch logs in the fireplace?" he asked.

"Yes, but I need to get out of here." She glanced at the logs.

"One of them is hollow. The end pops out. If he found anything, it'll be in there."

"Surely he'd have told them." Lexi didn't want Dick to know the condition of the body.

If he knew anything, she was *sure* he'd have told them.

"Dear God. I was there last night so my prints will be all over that place," he whispered as she disconnected.

Lexi stepped over the body to the fireplace. The second log she lifted was as heavy as the first, but when she moved it, she heard something shift inside. She puzzled for a few moments about how to open it and finally pushed the end. It clicked and came away to reveal a metallic lining, which explained the weight of the hollow log. She shook it until an envelope fell out, followed by a wad of cash. Hastily, she pocketed both items, stood, and returned to the door. She looked into the room and stroked the length of the scar.

Ablaze.

Little flames ignited all over the room. She started to leave, then turned again and stroked the scar again, "Oh, jeez, and definitely the bedroom." A loud whoosh sounded farther inside the house. It was time to go. She was about to turn away again when a high-pitched squeal issued from inside the house. Uncertain, she stood still and listened. It came again. She looked at the flames that now rose quickly, turned away, then spun back again.

"Shit," she muttered and raced into the house and through to the hallway. She stopped and listened but heard nothing. There were several doors, but only one was closed. Cautiously, she placed her right hand on it and pulled it away quickly. It was already hot. That would be the bedroom. She ran up the hall and glanced into the other rooms, but they were all empty.

Of course, It would have to be this room.

Reluctantly, she returned to the hot door and moved her hand over the surface. It was still cool at the bottom, so she crouched and pulled the handle down quickly as she shoved the door. Flames surged across the ceiling of the hallway in a whoosh. The room was black with toxic smoke but luckily, she didn't have to look far. A little ball of fur lay curled and still near the entrance.

Lexi picked it up and ran. The fire in the living room was well underway now. While she needed to conserve the little magic she had remaining, she would have to create a path to protect her from the flames. She used the magic, held the unresponsive creature to her, and bolted along the edge of the room to the exit. In the last moments, the flames licked at her left side, and the sharp smell of burning hair caught her nose.

She sprinted through the garden, hopped the wall as best she could with her bundle, and hurried through the neighbor's yard. Halfway across the lawn, she became aware of a snorting sound behind her. She turned to where the shifter sniffed the air where she had come over the wall. The spell was wearing off. She wasn't sure if he'd be susceptible to a spell in his wolf form, but she stroked the unhealing scar and whispered, "Sleep."

Instead of falling asleep as had happened when she'd used this spell previously, the young man staggered and shook his head as though trying to shake off a dizzy spell. Protecting herself from the flames had used the magic reserves. When she realized this moment of distraction was all she would get, she ran to the shifter, who was still unaware of her, and launched a kick to the side of his head. He dropped like a stone. She hopped over the gate and ran to the car.

"Move it." She leapt in.

Dick complied and they accelerated away. His face was like thunder.

"Maybe that wasn't him." Lexi patted the face of what appeared to be a French bulldog puppy.

"A mole on his face here?" Dick asked and pointed to the lower jaw on the right side of his face. She looked at him and nodded.

His gaze moved to the dog. "Marcel doesn't look good."

She fixed him with a horrified look. "Tell me he didn't have any more pets."

"No, Marcel's the only one."

"Why didn't the shifters leave after they killed him?" His gaze moved from her to the rearview mirror.

"It wasn't shifters who killed him. He was murdered by a vampire," she told him.

"He was *what*?" He almost lost control of the car in his surprise but regained it quickly.

"That's why they were there. The guys in the trucks were simply to delay us so they could get into position around the house and catch *you*. I think it was a trap."

"The deeper into this mess we get, the less sense it makes." Dick glanced at the puppy.

"That means Kindred either is or will soon be in town. Scott, I'm out. Can you help me?" She looked into the back of the car and frowned when she realized her friend was sprawled unconscious across the back seat.

"He's okay, isn't he? He only slumped a minute or so before you appeared."

"He'll be fine. What he did takes a ton of energy. He needs to recoup but I need help." Lexi stretched awkwardly and touched Scott's knee for a few moments.

She put her hand on the little dog's chest and whispered, "Breathe."

The animal lay still for another two seconds before he coughed and barked feebly several times. He whimpered, wobbled to his feet, turned in her lap, and flopped again.

"Oh." She wasn't sure what to do and shook him gently.

"He's okay. His heart's beating stronger now." Dick stroked the dog briefly. "Poor little guy."

They reached the vampire's house and Lexi shook Scott awake. "Are you okay?"

"I'm fine." He yawned and climbed out of the car, although he wobbled slightly and leaned against the car. "Mostly."

"Great. Hold this." She thrust the puppy at him and his face lit up.

"Can we—" he began.

"No, we can't keep it." She shook her head as they walked into the house.

The three of them gathered in the hallway and watched Jesús, who had his back to them and was mopping the floor. He had EarPods in and danced as he worked, singing "The Girl From Ipanema."

"Jesús," Dick shouted.

The man uttered a little scream and spun as he yanked his earplugs out. "Oh, my God! What happened to your dress?"

"It's fine. A little dusty but it lived. I changed after we left the party."

He walked toward them. "You smell of smoke. Please tell me you didn't burn the clubhouse down." He looked at Marcel in Scott's arms. "You got a puppy." He squealed.

Scott handed the animal to Lexi, and Jesús stepped closer to stroke the sleeping puppy. Scott moved behind him and whispered, "Sleep." The Mexican man slumped where he stood, and Scott caught him and carried him to a sofa.

Dick's jaw dropped. "That was amazing. If you could put that into an app, you'd be a billionaire."

She headed to the coffee pot and Dick followed, picking up a throw pillow on the way. They congregated around the breakfast bar. He placed the large pillow on the countertop and she placed the sleeping puppy on it.

"Right! What do we know?" she asked.

"I got Leonard killed." The vampire poured himself a large Jack Daniels. He offered the bottle to Lexi, who pushed her black coffee toward him. Once he'd topped it up, he offered the bottle to Scott, who shook his head.

"*We* got him killed." The young man took a glass and held it to the water dispenser on the refrigerator.

"Oh, I wouldn't—" Dick' protest cut off abruptly.

Thick red liquid ran into Scott's glass.

"What the fuck?" He put it on the counter.

"Waste not want not." Dick tipped his bourbon into the blood and swirled the glass. He knocked the drink back and looked at the horrified Scott. "You seem a little naive for a Kindred mage."

"They don't let mages go out on the dangerous jobs until they're matched with a legacy," Lexi explained.

"Surely they're more than capable of handling themselves." The vampire waved his fingers in a pseudo-magical fashion.

"It's complicated." She didn't want to discuss it any further.

The vampire opened the refrigerator and passed a bottle of water to the other man, who took it, nodded his thanks, and sat at the counter.

"How are your reserves?" she asked her friend as she stared at the gaping indent on her arm.

He paused to assess how he felt. "Building up. I feel like I'm at about twenty percent. I'll be fully restored in an hour."

"Halfsies?" She placed her open hand onto the counter.

He put his hand into hers, and all three of them stared at the unhealing scar as light surged into it.

Dick shook his head as if to clear it. "That's quite mesmerizing."

Lexi retrieved the envelope and the wad of money, which she passed to the vampire. "That was in the log. I don't know if he supported any charities."

"You're the worst charity case I know. Get a decent hotel." He pushed the money to her.

"I'll drop it at a dog shelter." Scott put it in his pocket and looked at Marcel. "What about him?"

"He's not going to a shelter. He'll be torn to shreds by a rottweiler." Dick was horrified. He folded his arms on the counter and rested his chin on them to stare at Marcel's sleeping face.

"You want to keep him?" The young man looked astonished.

"It's the least I can do." He stroked the puppy's silky ear gently.

She looked around the room. "What about your expensive furniture?"

Dick waved a hand. "It can go into storage." He didn't look away from the animal.

Scott removed his hand from hers. "What's in the envelope?"

Lexi removed two sheets of paper and a flash drive slid out with them. "Looking at the date in the corner, this is a copy of a page from an old desk diary. It's mostly full of meetings. Do you recognize any names?" She passed it to Dick.

He scanned the sheet. "I don't think it's the names. Look at this entry—it's the registration of a property transfer. The address is where the bar and flower shop are."

The other man read the second sheet. "This is interesting. He emailed someone at an offsite data storage facility asking for all the files from an industrial scanner created the same week as that diary page. It looks like they used a scanner with its own backup drive. That must mean the documentation was removed from everywhere else. Most people wouldn't know about this process. It's lucky for us that Leonard's contact did."

"Not so lucky for Leonard." Dick walked to a cupboard, pulled out a notebook computer, and activated it.

"Okay, what do we know?" Lexi asked.

Scott stepped into the middle of the kitchen like a teacher at the front of the classroom. "They knew about Leonard."

"But *how* could they have known?" she asked.

"Perhaps he—or most likely his contact—did something to draw attention to himself," he suggested. He wrote fiery words in the air.

Leonard, discovered how?

"When you received a call from Dolores, were you alone? How did the conversation go?" she asked Dick.

"I was alone. She told me she'd been asked to help with a situation in town. Then she said she was sending you, and I said, 'no fucking way.' She told me the situation had gotten complicated and suggested that if I could help, you'd be out of town faster. Obviously, I was *all* for that."

"No offense."

"She asked if I knew someone who could help us to get information from the clerk's office. I told her I'd call her back. I called ten minutes later and asked if she was absolutely positive you wouldn't try to kill me or break my neck again because that shit hurts. And as an aside, Lexi, we haven't even begun to visit the issue of the dumpster." He refilled his glass before he spoke again.

"I said I had a friend with a contact in the clerk's office and I'd try to contact him. We talked about the documents being stolen from the flower shop, and that was what I asked Leonard to look for—discreetly, obviously."

"I don't understand this case." Lexi scratched her head. "First, it was a gang bothering a business-owning shifter. Then–"

Scott put up his hand to interrupt. "Could this be connected to her being a shifter?"

"What?" She stared at him, puzzled.

"We've assumed Kate's being bothered because she's a business owner, not because she's a shifter. Tommy and his family clearly don't want her running a business, and now you've seen that Tommy is somehow connected to Caleb and possibly involved in Leonard's death," he explained.

"But what does that have to do with Leonard? Why was that worth murdering him?" Dick asked.

"Do you have the pendant?" Scott asked.

"That's weird too. It went black. Why would it do that?" She pulled it out of her pocket and placed it on the counter.

"It's tarnished." He stretched to pick it up and a spark spat from it onto his hand. "Fucker!"

Lexi moved quickly to stand between him and the pendant, but nothing else happened.

"Someone else's magic has touched that." He shook his hand out. "Dick, do you have any silver cleaner?"

"Silver cleaner? Sure, I use it to clean my silver daggers. It's in the solarium with the wooden stakes and everything else that can kill me." The vampire shook his head.

Scott tried again. "Baking soda and aluminum foil?"

"That I can do." Dick headed to the utility room.

Twenty minutes later, the young man had polished the silver pendant.

He cast a spell looking for magical or cursed objects and the pendant glowed green. Lexi looked around the room to see if anything else glowed. Fortunately, it didn't, and as Scott continued his work, the green glow around the pendant subsided.

"Will this be your mirror trick again? Isn't the pendant a little small for that?" Dick stared at the little piece of jewelry.

"Is it safe to ask if you have a mirror?" the other man asked.

"I moved them all to the spare room after seeing what you did with the one in your motel room yesterday. I planned to have them ground to dust." The vampire headed down the hall.

He returned with a framed wall mirror and propped it against the wall next to the countertop. Scott held the pendant before it and rolled his finger in the air. The reflection changed from the three of them to black. He continued to roll his finger until they saw the group of men around her at the party.

"There's Caleb staring at my breasts again. What a creep." She sneered.

Scott set it back a few minutes and let it play forward. "He's not looking at your breasts, he's looking at the pendant."

Lexi realized he was right. He was looking directly at it and seemingly at them through the mirror, which was even more creepy.

In the replay, Dick leaned forward on her right side to pass the envelope to Betsy. She remembered seeing that at the time. What she hadn't seen was Caleb using that moment's distraction to mutter a word. She watched his lips move, and the picture turned black.

"Caleb's a sorcerer? *Shut the front door!*" Dick's mouth was agape.

He picked the photocopy up and gazed at it with a sigh. Under it was the envelope. Scott took it, looked inside, and shook a photograph out.

The young man raised his eyebrows. "Of course, we could be jumping the gun assuming Leonard was murdered over Kate's case." He put the picture in front of Lexi, who glanced at it. To her surprise, she saw herself.

"I don't understand. I don't recognize this picture." She frowned as she stared at it.

Dick peered over her shoulder. "That's Jackson Square in New Orleans. You must have been there."

"It's not only that. I assumed this evidence would prove I'd been there when I was a child. This picture isn't that old."

The vampire tapped the photograph. "And you don't recognize the man you're with?"

"I have no idea who he is." She tried to force a memory—anything—but nothing came.

"What age would you say you are in that picture?" Scott looked from the image to her.

"Maybe fifteen or sixteen." She pinched the bridge of her nose and turned to Dick. "You asked Leonard to look into this months ago, right?"

"Yes."

"So why would it all blow up now?"

The vampire stood and tapped his chin in thought. "I think you're right. This is a distraction. Whatever happened to Leonard must have been related to the case."

"It's clear what we need to do next." Lexi finished her coffee and put the empty mug down.

"It is?" He swiveled to face her.

She smiled. "Whenever I have a question I can't answer, I find someone to help me think it through."

"Isn't that what we're doing here?" he asked.

"My method involves knuckle-dusters." She stretched and then curled her fingers.

He nodded. "I like it. It's expedient. Perhaps we should borrow one of those shifters."

"Yes. We need to find Tommy or one of his little friends." She cracked her knuckles.

"Preferably not Tommy. I don't think our client will be happy if we knock her boyfriend senseless," Scott added. He had his phone to his ear.

"By the time all this is over, she might pay us to do that." Lexi smirked.

I might do it for free.

"The pack tends to congregate at a bar off the highway." Dick picked his dinner jacket up and draped it across his arm.

"Not Kate's place?" She was surprised.

"Not for their pack meetings and until Kate's married, she's not part of Stan's pack. Also, the other place is out of the way. Jesús will take you to your motel. I'll meet you there." He untied his bow tie.

She looked at Scott, whose face was creased with worry. "What's up?"

"Dolores isn't picking up."

"Keep trying." The other two exchanged looks of concern.

Scott put his hand on the countertop while he redialed with the other, and she slipped hers into it. He flooded her with as much magic energy as she could tolerate and only stopped when her hair began to rise with static electricity.

The vampire waited until they had finished, then called Jesús' name.

"Huh? What?" The confused young man scrambled to his feet.

"Why are you sleeping on the job?" Dick frowned.

"I don't know. I'm so sorry, Mr. Levin." He looked mortified.

"Has everything been quiet here this evening? No guests or calls?"

"Nothing, sir."

"Drive my friends to their motel. Take the Jaguar and stop on the way back and pick up whatever the dog needs. Food, bed, bowls—whatever you think is appropriate." Dick looked at his watch and turned to Lexi. "It's midnight. I have about five hours."

CHAPTER EIGHT

"How are you?" Lexi asked Scott as they watched the shifter bar from their car at the back of the parking lot.

He stared ahead. "I'm fully recharged."

She repeated the question, demanding a better answer. "How are *you*?"

"I'm okay. You don't have to worry about me."

"If we were still in the cult, you might not even be active yet."

"I'm twenty-eight. I'd have been active long ago if I'd been able to match with someone I could trust." He sighed. "Well, I'm getting a crash course now. I'm not a liability, Lexi. Anyway, what happened to *you* out there earlier? I picked up some disturbing emotions." He turned in his seat to face her.

"Don't divert the issue. You can't ignore the possibility that your empathy might slow you in a confrontation."

"You mean, I might slow *you*." Color rose in his cheeks.

"Yes, that's what I mean." She smiled. "If you feel like you're losing it, cloak yourself. Give me one less thing to worry about. Promise?"

"I promise I won't get you killed." He looked at his hands in his lap and drew a deep breath. "I would never—"

The back door opened, and Dick hopped in. "Would it kill you to clean this thing?" He shoved takeout boxes across the back seat.

"What did you hear?" She knew he would have been hiding in the shadows before they arrived.

"Apart from you two bickering? There's something going on. I think there are two shifter packs in there. One group seems quite vexed with the other."

A window shattered at the front of the bar as a man careened through it. He landed, turned into a wolf before their eyes, and howled with rage.

Scott opened his mouth to say something and Lexi snapped her hand to his lips but Dick had beaten her to it. She looked her friend in the eyes and shook her head once. He nodded and removed Dick's hand. In wolf form, their hearing was exceptional. They'd hear a whisper in a car less than a hundred feet away.

The wolf shook his head and bounded in through the window.

More howls filled the air as shifters turned inside the bar.

"This—" Scott started before he paused and removed Dick's hand again. "I've cloaked us. They can't see, hear, or smell us. As I was saying, this doesn't look good."

The vampire nodded. "I agree. I'm really not feeling this. Walking into the middle of that would be suicide. No good joke ever started with 'a vampire walks into a shifter bar.' I think we need another plan."

The young man straightened and grinned. "I've got one. A vampire walks into a shifter bar and asks for a steak. Wait, no, you won't like that one."

Lexi tightened her lips, then sighed. "We'll meet you at your place."

Dick exited the vehicle and looked at the seat again. "Seriously, this makes your motel look like the Ritz." He disappeared into the night.

"Maybe we should go back to Kate. She might be able to suggest someone who can talk to us." Scott took the keys but was stopped by her upraised hand. A side door had opened, and a tall, dark-haired man with a walking stick stepped out, holding a cell-phone to his ear.

She stared at him. "Wow! They don't make them small, do they?"

"This isn't going well. They insist it wasn't them and it's getting quite heated," the man said into the phone. "Something's going on. When we got here, they were already fairly somber. It sounds like a couple of their pack members are missing or dead. Stan's not here, but they're all very evasive about where he might be."

"Maybe we should borrow this guy?" Scott suggested. Lexi nodded her agreement.

The man listened to his caller for a few more seconds. "Okay, I'll go in to see if I can make any sense out of this." He discon-nected, turned to step through the door, and instantly fell asleep.

Dick carried a chair into the garage. "What were you thinking? It was ill-advised to move one dog into the house. Now, I have two. Where is he?"

"He's in the trunk." Scott walked to the back of the car.

"Bad Marcel!" Jesús said from within.

The vampire's head spun to the open door. "What now?" He strode into the house and closed the door behind him.

Lexi and Scott puffed and groaned as they pulled the man out of the trunk and sat him in the chair.

"Hello. Come on, wake up." She tapped their guest's cheek.

His eyes snapped open and alarm filled his face when he real-ized he was unable to move.

"Don't panic. I have some questions and I don't want you to shift and rip me to pieces before I get the answers." She tried to sound more reasonable than she felt but itched to get the knuckle-dusters out.

He stared at her.

"Oh! Scott, he can't speak." She looked at her teammate, who waved his fingers in the air.

"My bad, sorry." She gave the man an apologetic grin.

Their captive sniffed. "This place smells of vampire."

"Well, we're in a vampire's garage and this is the vampire's fucked-up car. We were attacked by shifters and clueless human thugs tonight. We're trying to work out what the hell's going on. I'm guessing from the phone call we overheard it wasn't your pack, but you might be able to help us." She removed her jacket and the shifter's face went expressionless at the sight of her scar.

He glared at her. "You're Kindred? I don't smell much shifter *or* vampire in you."

"I'm ex-Kindred," Lexi explained.

"I've never heard of anyone being *ex*-Kindred."

"We're a dying breed. Literally." She leaned on a workbench.

"May I move my head?" he asked. His voice was slow and measured. He was well-spoken and didn't seem as hostile as she had expected.

She flicked a glance at her friend, who stood behind the man. Scott complied.

The man looked around. "This is William's place."

"What makes you think that?" This wasn't going at all as she had hoped.

"I'm sitting in an original 1956 Eames Lounger. That's his car, which appears to have been shot up. And hanging over there near the washer? Well, those are definitely his Burberry boxers. I hope he's okay."

"You have to be kidding me. Is there anyone he hasn't—" Lexi pinched the bridge of her nose.

Scott sighed. "We're like the world's worst kidnappers."

She caught the man's mouth twitching and rolled her eyes. "Dick," she shouted.

The vampire walked in wearing pink rubber gloves and carrying a pooper-scooper. "This dog's shitting every— Edward? Oh, dear God, Edward, I'm so sorry." He turned to her. "You kidnapped Edward? What's wrong with you?" He dropped the scooper and pulled off the gloves.

"It was your idea to kidnap a shifter," she replied.

"I didn't mean Edward. He's the Alpha of the San Bernardino pack and a very close friend. Edward, this is awful. Come into the house." Dick marched to the door and glanced back, confused that the man wasn't following.

"If I might move now?" Edward looked at Lexi.

Scott released him.

The shifter rose from the chair and turned to face Scott, who held the walking stick out. "Thank you." He followed the vampire into the house.

"Nothing seems to be going to plan." Her friend headed to the door.

"You are not wrong." Lexi slammed the trunk closed and, shaking her head, walked into the house behind him.

The other two men were talking as the friends stepped into the kitchen.

Edward chuckled. "It's okay, don't keep apologizing. To be honest, I'm kind of amused and I've been meaning to drop by anyway."

"Well, that's embarrassing." She flopped onto a bar stool.

The shifter took his cell phone out and held it to his ear. "It's me. I got a call and had to run. I'm dealing with something. How did the meeting turn out?"

She stood, went to the coffee machine, and pulled a mug out to pour herself one.

The man continued his phone conversation. "Oh. Well, that's

not surprising, is it? Okay, head back. I might have answers in the morning." He disconnected.

"Would you like coffee, Edward?" Dick asked.

"Thanks, Will."

The vampire snatched Lexi's filled mug as she returned the carafe to the machine and put it in front of Edward. She sighed and took down another.

"Who's the female shifter you mentioned, Will?" Edward asked.

"Her name's Kate. She owns a bar here in town."

"Dick. Client confidentiality." She rolled her eyes.

"Kate is from our pack. She agreed to mate with Tommy to end hostilities between our packs. Why hasn't she gone to Stanley about this? The Palm Springs pack is the largest in Riverside County and he's the alpha. They could resolve this mess in no time."

"She wanted to keep the pack out of it. When she first contacted us, she was being harassed for protection money by a gang of thugs in town." Lexi took a sip of her coffee and screwed her face up at the bitterness.

"But this kind of situation is what the pack's for." Edward shook his head.

"Well, there's another problem now. It looks like this whole thing might have been orchestrated by a local businessman—a nasty piece of work named Caleb Linden. Do you know him?" Dick asked.

"I know of Mr. Linden." The shifter took a sip of his coffee.

"Did you know he's a sorcerer?" Dick asked.

"Actually, that would explain a few things." The other man walked to the refrigerator and retrieved the cream for his coffee, then went to a cupboard on the wall, opened it, and withdrew a bowl of sugar. It wasn't lost on Lexi how familiar he was with the house.

He put the bowl in front of her, and she spooned sugar into her mug. "Thank you."

Edward turned to Scott. "A sorcerer and a mage are the same thing, right?"

The young man nodded. "Yes. Mage is a Kindred term to distinguish between a sorcerer who's part of Kindred and one who isn't."

The shifter sat on a stool and turned it to face Lexi. "So, what has Caleb been up to?"

"He's buying up the whole block where Kate's bar is. We think he's trying to get rid of the evidence of her ownership. Dick's friend got murdered for looking into it." She stirred her coffee. Her next sip was much more enjoyable.

"Was that the records clerk they fished out of the lake today?" Edward asked.

Dick's shoulders slumped. "I didn't even think for a moment about Leonard's source."

"Doesn't Kate have her own copy?" Edward nodded when Lexi passed the sugar.

"She had a break-in. Someone stole it from her office," Scott explained. "It's possibly connected to the person who tried to attack her on the street a couple of weeks ago."

He paused for a moment and light dawned in his face. "Did she by any chance bite the guy?"

"She...might have." Dick swiveled his gaze to Lexi, then shrugged.

Edward nodded. "Which answers our question. We have a new shifter running around out there who's killed a couple of transients. He hasn't been seen for a few days but it can only be a matter of time before he strikes again. That was why we were at the bar tonight— trying to find out who it is and who's responsible for turning them. Kate should have come to us or gone to Tommy's pack."

The vampire raised an eyebrow. "Apparently, they're quite

provincial. Her mate and his family aren't happy with her being a business owner. They're looking for an excuse to force her to give it up."

"Or creating an excuse," Lexi added.

"What? They never used to be like that. Tommy's uncle is the police chief and his mother was an attorney. She ran her own firm." Edward was clearly confused.

"I think Stanley has something to do with all this," Dick explained. "He and Caleb are close buddies."

Scott wandered around the room. "Dick, where's Marcel?"

"Jesús is walking him."

"William, why do they call you 'Dick?' Is it because they've seen your magnificent—"

"No," the two friends said together.

"Thank God," Lexi added under her breath.

"Come to think of it, Edward, it's been a while since—" Dick started but didn't manage to finish the sentence.

"Seriously? Someone should put a muzzle on you." She was exasperated.

"Now *that* brings back memories." The shifter's eyebrows raised speculatively at Dick.

"Oh, my God!" She put her palms up and stepped back.

"It's perfectly natural to want to have a life-affirming experience after having been in mortal danger. It wouldn't kill the two of you to—" The vampire swiveled his finger between Lexi and Scott.

"I think we should head to the motel," she interrupted.

"That's the spirit," he added.

"Not to— Oh, never mind. Come on, Scott." Lexi picked her jacket up, and they headed toward the garage door. She stopped and turned.

"Are you safe here?" she asked.

"You're asking a vampire and a shifter if they're safe?" Dick raised an eyebrow, and Edward's jaw dropped.

"Okay, but Caleb knows you're involved and he knows where you live. *And* he has his own packs of shifters and goons. Are you prepared to move quickly? Do you have a go-bag?" she asked.

"You don't live as long as I have without picking up a few tricks. Of course I have a go-bag. I'm not an amateur." The vampire turned away dramatically.

She nodded and they left.

They parked in their spot under the room and headed up the steps. Scott put his hand out to the door and Lexi shooed him away.

"What did I tell you? Me first." She walked into the room and was met by a punch in the forehead with a knuckle-duster.

When she roused, she realized that she was sprawled on the floor and slouched against the side of Scott's bed with her hands tied behind her back. She glanced to where her friend stood at the end of the bed, his face a mask of abject fear. When she attempted to move, the thug who lay on the bed slapped the back of her head with his gun. She grunted and glared at him.

"Thank God you're awake. Your stupid friend here is playing statues. He's very good at it but I was about to shoot him. We know you have the file. Our boss wants it back." He stroked the back of her head with the gun. "Your hair's pretty."

She struggled to respond. Her head was fuzzy from the punch, and her emotions were all over the place. That was probably because something was going on with Scott on an emotional level and it flooded her through their link. She looked at him and noted the bruises on his face. He did seem physically frozen like a statue.

"What have you done to him?" She tried to twist her hand to touch her scar but the ties bit into her too tightly.

"Not a thing. Well, barely a thing. But back to the question at hand."

"Maybe Mr. Linden should come and get it himself." She looked at her friend and then at the door, trying to somehow signal to him to get the hell out.

"I've never heard that name." The man conveyed with every word that he knew exactly who she was talking about. "And my colleague is outside, so I wouldn't try that."

"He doesn't know anything. Look at him—he's damaged. Let him go." Lexi indicated Scott with her head.

The man smacked her with the gun again. "We're reasonable people. If you hand it over, you can leave. We won't lay a finger on your pretty…" He stroked her neck slowly.

"You'll let us leave?" She tried to sound like she believed the lie. Of course, she knew the moment she produced what the thug was looking for, they'd be dead.

"Sure. Tell us where it is."

She paused and tried again to make eye contact with Scott. "It's in one of the bags." Against her instincts, she did her best to look defeated.

"And they are where?"

"He hid them." She indicated her teammate with her head.

The man sat at the headboard of the bed, crossed his legs, and pointed the gun at Scott. "Where are the bags?"

The young man merely stood motionless and stared into the middle distance.

"Scott! Snap out of it." Lexi knew they'd both be dead if he couldn't pull himself together.

He blinked and looked at her. "But–"

"He wants the bags." She said it very slowly and deliberately.

Scott muttered under his breath, and the bags appeared on the bed—exactly where they had always been and precisely where the thug lay. The young man spun instantly to face the wall, not wanting to see the result.

She shuffled out of the way as the man's right arm slid to the floor and heard its opposite drop on the other side. For a long moment, she stared at the thug on the bed. His body lay in several pieces between and around the bags. Scott's backpack was in the middle of his chest. His head had fallen forward against the side of the bag.

Lexi looked away from the gruesome scene. "Can you untie me? We still have to deal with the goon outside."

For a moment, the beginnings of a scream came from outside, followed by silence. The door opened and the bloody thug fell halfway into the room.

Dick appeared in the entrance. "Did someone call for a rescue? What the fuck happened to him?"

"I'll stand outside for a minute." Scott moved carefully toward the door without looking around. He met Edward, who moved back to let him step over the second dead thug and out.

"Are you okay?" The shifter crouched to cut Lexi's ties.

"They were after the evidence." She rubbed her wrists but didn't think she could trust her legs to support her.

"I assume they didn't get the USB." Dick stared in fascination at the body mostly on the bed. The legs had rolled so the feet now pointed out, which looked grotesquely comical.

"They wouldn't have found the flash drive. It's a good thing we didn't have the paper files on us." She touched her forehead gingerly.

"I have the papers here." He held them out. "I didn't want to leave them at the house."

She attempted to stand but swayed and sat heavily on the other bed. "Can you put them in the case, please? I'll get them to Kate."

He nodded and she stumbled to her feet and grasped the legs of the second thug to help Edward drag him fully into the room.

"I don't need the help, but thanks." The shifter took hold of the shoulders and pulled.

Lexi heard Dick unzip the small carry-on case. "What's this? Woah! Your case is full of junk."

"Seriously? You choose now to start critiquing my stuff?"

"No. It's junk," he repeated.

"Well, I highly doubt those shoes are really Versace but sometimes, we have to make do," she snipped in response.

"Okay. I'm going to give this another try. Lexi, I'm sorry about this, but this guy's junk is in your bag."

"What?" Lexi and Edward moved to stand beside the vampire, who held some gray pinstripe material in one hand and the bag's lid in the other. They stared at the place the thug's lower midsection had been lying before the bag materialized.

"Poor guy. He wasn't blessed, was he?" Dick said and shook his head. "Hey, what do you mean about my shoes?"

He started to put the papers into the bag.

"What are you doing?" she asked.

"You said you wanted the papers in here." He sounded annoyed.

"Close the lid. I don't want anything in that bag. I don't want anything *from* that bag." She stepped back.

"Are you sure? I know someone who could fashion you a great pair of earrings from his—"

"I'm sure."

Dick dropped the trouser material into the case and flipped it closed, then looked at the man again with a grimace. "We need to get rid of this."

"Don't worry, I have friends who will be only too happy to help." Edward took his cell out.

Dick and Edward shared a look. "The twins," they agreed.

The shifter stepped out to make a call.

"You have your own cleaners?" Lexi asked when he returned.

"Something like that." Dick wiggled his hand in a way that gave her an uneasy feeling.

"How did you know to come?" she asked.

"Seconds after you left, a car started and followed you. I threw my stuff in the car and drove out to follow them, and *another* car followed me. It was like the Palm Springs Pride parade all over again."

"They didn't know I was there, so they were very surprised when I mauled their faces at the traffic light. They're in the trunk," Edward explained as he entered the room.

"If we can get them up here, could your twins deal with them too?" Lexi asked.

"Maybe we'll get a quantity discount." Dick looked around. "Where's Scott?"

"I'm here." His voice came quietly from just outside the room.

"Can you help us get the other two up here?" the vampire asked.

Edward stuck his head out the room. "He's gone. Oh, he's down at the trunk. I should help. Wait, he's gone again."

"He'll be fine. Let him do it." Lexi knew there would be emotional fallout from this. She wondered if he'd be able to continue working with her.

"He should have been able to handle a couple of human thugs." Dick seemed to know what she was thinking.

"He's learning on the job." She hoped that was all it was—a blip.

Moments later, Scott reappeared on the balcony. "They're in the bath." He walked in and lifted his bag from the bed without looking at the carnage.

"You might want to check that. His lungs are probably in there," the vampire warned.

"It'll be okay. There's a protection spell on it." The young man held the bag up. It was completely clean.

"Maybe consider putting one of those on my bag in the future." Lexi glanced at her little case. She didn't really need it. It was mostly for show, but still.

Edward looked around the room. "I think this will be okay.

The mess is limited to one bed and the bathroom. They should be able to clean it fairly quickly."

"Well, well," a voice said from behind them. A third armed goon stood in the doorway. He saw his colleague on the bed. "What the fuck did you do to Tony?"

Scott held his arm out with the hand raised and muttered a single word. The man was obliterated and a fine spray of red drenched the door, the wall next to it, and the ceiling.

Dick, who had stood closest, looked at himself. "My...everything."

"Sorry." The young man waved his hand and drew the blood spray from the vampire to the floor.

"I'm glad you got that out of your system." Edward's eyes were wide.

Lexi looked at the carnage. "I'll pay for another night."

A car pulled up below and three doors slammed.

The shifter glanced over the balcony. "Collect whatever gear you're taking. It's time to move."

"Where to?" she asked.

Edward shrugged. "My place for now? We need to plan."

She went into the bathroom and came out with her cosmetic kit. They stepped out of the room as the strangers appeared. A man stepped to the side to allow two others into the room.

"Wow! So fresh. I could smell it from the car." The boy's white eyes glittered.

"So hungry." The girl stepped forward and licked the door.

Scott put his hand over his mouth, clearly trying not to gag.

Edward introduced the twins politely. "This is Adele and this is Sam."

Lexi's jaw dropped in shock. She looked at him. "Are they zombies?"

"Kind of." He seemed to sense where this might go.

"Kind of?" Her eyebrows raised.

"As in, yes." He indicated the room as if to say, "Well, what else could we do?"

Dick placed his hand on her shoulder. "You're not with Kindred now, Lexi. Remember that."

Lexi took a step back. Kindred's rule was that zombies were "kill on sight." No ifs, no buts, kill immediately. She was conflicted and she guessed it must have shown on her face because the two flaky white dead people in front of her looked terrified.

"Kindred?" Adele squeaked. Her eyes widened so the entire white irises showed.

Everyone was silent and all gazes settled on Lexi.

"*Bon appetit.*" She walked away without a backward glance.

Lexi and Scott followed Dick and Edward onto the road and toward San Bernardino. Before they reached the edge of town, they turned into the hills.

The vehicles stopped at a gate and they waited in their car while Edward slid out and opened it. She continued behind the other vehicle down a long driveway through the woods that ended at a two-story home nestled among the trees.

Dick walked around to the back of the Jaguar and opened it while Edward took Marcel into the house. He was followed by Scott, who hadn't spoken a word on the journey.

Lexi waited while Dick pulled luggage out of the trunk. "Your go-bag looks suspiciously like a garment bag."

"That's not my go-bag, silly. *This* is my go-bag." He removed a huge old trunk.

Her eyes bulged at the size of it. She guessed she wouldn't have been able to lift it an inch off the ground, but his vamp strength made it appear as light as a feather.

"I don't think you quite have the concept. It's supposed to be small and light with money and identification, a change of underwear, and something to hit bad people with."

"But I don't travel anywhere without my trunk. It's French,

and an antique. I've had this for almost a hundred years." He patted the trunk before he headed inside with it. "And this *is* something to hit bad people with."

Once she was settled in her room, Lexi walked through the house and found Dick deliberating between two shirts in front of his open trunk. It stood on end and contained drawers and hanging space. She'd never seen anything like it except in movies.

"Hello, Lexi. How can I help?"

"I'm worried about Kate…and Dolores, and Scott,"

"Edward has put some of his boys onto protecting Kate. I've tried Dolores a dozen times, so I'm concerned too. And Scott—I know what you mean. He's barely spoken since the motel. You suspect he's not ready for all this?"

"I more than suspect it. I can sense his feelings through our bond. I don't know how to help him."

"I think I do." He put the shirts down.

"Is everything okay in here?" Edward asked and popped his head around the door.

"Edward," the vampire said seriously, "we need to get Scott drunk."

Lexi rolled her eyes.

Later, she lay in bed, thinking back to her life with Kindred. She remembered the lessons about werewolves and other shifters. They were dangerous, they weren't to be trusted, and they only looked after their own pack. Nowhere in her studies did it say they were big fans of karaoke. Yet there she was, listening to a werewolf, a vampire, and a mage drunkenly belting out "Delilah." It was a good sign that Scott was singing along. She smiled.

Annoying, but good.

CHAPTER NINE

Lexi wandered through the house in search of coffee.
She found Scott unconscious on the sofa with a throw covering him. He hadn't even made it to bed.

Still yawning, she entered the kitchen and set about making coffee. As she sat at the old wooden table, she watched the beverage drip into the pot.

I wonder if I could magic it to go faster?

Looking at the almost empty scar, she decided it was still worth a try and was about to attempt it when Edward walked in, wearing tight hipster jeans and no shirt.

"Morning," he whispered.

After a moment, she shook her head and realized that she'd stared at his abs. "Good morning-almost-afternoon. How's your head?"

He raised his eyebrows. "It's been better."

In silence, he made his way around the kitchen and dropped suspicious leafy green items into a plastic beaker. She watched as he went through the process.

Outstanding pecs, and you could bounce a quarter off those abs.

When he'd finally blended his green concoction, he stood and drank it with his back to her. She took the opportunity to stare openly at the well-defined lats on his back and almost called Scott in to point the muscle groups out to him. The dedication it took to gain that level of physical fitness was itself impressive, and she couldn't fault Dick's taste in men, not at all.

Lexi's gaze wandered around the room and stopped on the refrigerator. There were kids' drawings on it. "You have kids?"

"These were painted by my granddaughter. They visit over the holidays." He opened the refrigerator and removed eggs, bacon, and steaks.

"Oh, I see. You don't look old enough to have a grandchild." She tried not to sound too appraising.

"She's five. I'm forty-five. They live in Monterey with my ex-wife."

"Nice part of the world." She watched as he took bowls and knives from cupboards. "Can I help?"

"Sure. Crack and whisk?" He handed her a carton of eggs, a bowl, and a whisk. "How's Scott looking?"

"He's on the sofa, dead to the world, figuratively speaking. Where's Dick?" She cracked eggs into the bowl and looked around the kitchen for condiments.

"In the basement, dead to the world. Literally speaking." He smiled, opened a cupboard, and passed her the salt and pepper.

After a few minutes, he placed a mug of coffee on the table in front of her and removed the bowl of whisked eggs.

"Thanks." She stretched for the sugar.

"Scott talked some last night. He's embarrassed about what happened." He took a frying pan out.

"I know. I feel it through the empathic link. I felt what he was going through at the motel last night too. He was paralyzed by fear, and it's possible that when I was knocked unconscious, part of his mind lost consciousness too. He has so much to learn but not much time to learn it in. I think he's done well until now." She stood and took her coffee to the counter. He passed her a chopping board and a large steak. When he began to dice small cubes of potato, she realized he was making hash. She chopped the steak into small pieces, followed by the bacon.

"How do you know he won't freeze up like that again?" Edward asked as he scraped the potatoes into the pan to sauté them.

"He won't. It was my fault. I've been a little off my game lately." She stopped speaking when she heard Scott walking up the hallway. "Afternoon, sleepyhead. Edward's frying up something good and greasy." She took a mug down.

"Ugh! Don't." He groaned, flopped into a chair, and buried his face in his arms on the table.

"Tell me about it," the shifter agreed with a sigh.

"Not hungry?" Lexi passed the coffee to him.

"I want food but I don't think I can talk about it."

The other man's cell rang. "Yeah? Just, erm…" He started to walk out of the room, then looked at the pan. Lexi took the spatula out of his hand and he continued down the hall.

"I'm so sorry. I don't know what happened." Scott's voice was muffled, given that his face was still hidden by his arms.

"You don't have to explain anything to me. I know, remember?" She pointed to her scar even though his face remained hidden.

"I know too. I felt your disappointment when you woke up on the floor. I couldn't think or move." He sounded choked.

"I was disappointed in myself. Let's go for a walk after breakfast." She moved the pan from the heat and put the food onto plates. "Food's up," she called.

Scott raised his head as Edward walked in. She was disappointed to note he now wore a t-shirt.

"So, how do you feel about tequila this afternoon?" The shifter grinned. Lexi assumed this was an inside joke.

"I never want to look at it, hear about it, taste it, and most definitely, smell it again." The young man dropped his head again, and Edward chuckled.

"Did you want this food on the back of your head?" She stood over him with a plate.

After a few moments, he raised his head. He accepted the plate and attempted a smile, although he was wan and bleary-eyed.

The shifter took a seat at the table. "That was my beta. I've asked her to come over."

"Her? How progressive of you," Scott said.

"That position wasn't given. It was earned. She's strong enough to go for Alpha. I don't think she will yet, but that's not a fight I look forward to."

Edward talked about his pack as they ate.

"I'm worried about a friend of ours," Lexi began after they had finished.

"Dolores, I know. Will gave me the number last night. I've tried it a few times this morning, but it goes straight to voicemail. Can you track her?" the shifter asked Scott.

"I'll give it a try but I can't do it with this hangover." He pushed his half-eaten breakfast away and leaned back.

"I'm sorry. We shouldn't have let you drink so much last night. When do you think you'll feel well enough?" The older man stood and took his and Lexi's empty plates to the sink.

Scott sat with his eyes closed and breathed deeply. She felt the surge of magic and he opened his eyes. They were bright and clear. "I'll finish this and get started." He pulled the plate closer and snarfed the rest of his breakfast.

Edward looked from one to the other and shook his head. "Well, that's not fair."

"Do you have a map of Colorado? Her office is in Denver. That's where she was yesterday," Scott told him.

"I have Satnav or a tablet with Google maps on it."

"I've tried that before. It doesn't work." He stood quickly. "Where can I buy a map around here?"

"We're a ways out. Any nearby place would only sell local maps. I'll ask Jess to pick one up." The shifter retrieved his cell and texted.

Lexi waited for him to finish. "How are things with Kate?"

"All quiet. She's at the bar, and the Palm Springs pack is keeping an eye on her too. At least, I assume that's why Tommy's there again. She's concerned about her friend—the girl from the flower shop, Daisy. Kate called another friend from the coven, and she hasn't been with them."

"Is Kate safe with Tommy? If he's under Caleb's influence too, could he harm her and be completely unaware of it?"

"We have someone in there too. She's safe."

"In the bar? Who?"

"Her mother. She could rip Tommy to pieces. He's a little soft around the middle."

"Must be all those McRibs." Scott smiled.

"Right. Jess will be here after work, and speaking of that, I'll wash the dishes, then I need to get some work done." Edward picked up a briefcase from the hallway.

"What do you do?" the other man asked.

"I'm a financial auditor. You can hate me now." He grinned.

"We'll get the dishes. You do whatever you need to do." The young man stood from the table and carried his empty plate to the sink.

"Are we okay to go for a walk, Edward?"

"Sure. I have a few acres of woods and chaparral here. It's relatively safe. I don't get bears or cougars anymore. They know better." He disappeared into his study.

Scott washed a plate and passed it to Lexi. "What are you thinking?"

"He does not look like an auditor." She dried the plate and put it on the shelf.

"No. I suppose he doesn't."

They finished the dishes and cleaned the kitchen.

She knew he wanted to talk so the moment they were done, she turned to him. "Do you want to go for that walk now?"

They headed past the stairs to the basement where Dick was passing the daytime hours and left through the back door. Within a few minutes, they could no longer see the house.

"I feel sick waiting like this. We should be out there looking for Dolores," Scott said as he scanned the ground ahead of them.

"It's two-thirty now. The maps will be here soon. We also need to work out what we'll do about Kate and Caleb. He needs to pay for what he did to Leonard."

Her companion stopped and she didn't notice until she'd taken a couple more steps. When she turned to face him, it was obvious he was ready to talk.

He looked down but after a moment, looked her in the eyes. "There's something you need to know. When—God, *if* we find Dolores, I'll ask her to get you another partner. Someone more reliable than me."

'What? But that's—"

"The right thing to do. We're not safe out there if I can't be relied upon. We'll still be matched and soon, you won't need to have a physical connection with me for the energy transfer. It means you'll be able to draw on my magic when you need it without me being a liability at your side."

Lexi picked a stick up and began to strip the bark from it. "You've really thought this through, haven't you?"

"Yes, and you can't talk me out of it, although I don't see why you'd want to. I almost got us killed last night."

"There's something I need to tell you that might change your perspective." She walked to a fallen tree and sat. "You didn't put us in that situation. I did. When we got into that room, there were two guys inside. I know, because it was the last thing I registered before I had my lights punched out. That means the third guy was out there watching us, and I didn't have a clue."

"He could have been—"

"I wasn't prepared for what might have been behind the door when we entered. I've been off my game and making excuses. I even struggled to catch that thief. I should have been able to react faster rather than leaving you to save my ass by using magic on him, and Dick had to rescue me when we were attacked. The fact is, I can't even rely on myself anymore."

"But you're the most lethal human I've ever met, and—"

"We both know that's not true."

"But your skills—"

"Don't make me as fast as a vamp or as strong as a shifter. I've never displayed fae or witch abilities or any other kind of supe."

Scott attempted to interrupt again but she silenced him. "Let me say this or I'll never get it out. I've been using vamp blood." She said it fast because admitting it to him was the single most humiliating thing she'd ever done. Her face flushed.

"I know. It helped you get your memories back. You've done it three times—you already told me that."

"It's been much more than three times. At first, it was about the memories. Then, it was because my speed and strength increased and it made me feel more like I'm supposed to be. Like I could be effective in my work like the others are." She stared at the ground. "I can barely function without it now and even with it, something's not right. I don't know what to do, and I honestly don't think I can deal with this without you." The last word was a whisper.

Scott joined her on the tree trunk. "I thought you might be happier working with someone else. Maybe Edward. Your heart rate elevates when you look at him."

Lexi looked at him like he was speaking a foreign language. "I'm jealous of his muscles. His lats are really well defined. I was going to ask him how he isolates them."

He laughed. "Oh, I can tell you that. It's the shifting. It impacts muscle groups other exercises can't touch."

She sighed. "Well, shit!"

As he slid his arm around her, he chuckled. "What a fucking pair we are—an incompetent and a junkie. I guess we're stuck with each other."

Lexi snorted a laugh.

"There's something else." She stood, walked a few steps away, and held her arm out. They both watched as the white energy filled the scar. "I've been able to do this without physical contact for a few weeks. I liked the hand-holding part. It's kind of comforting. Of course, I still can't keep the magic from dissipating." She opened her hand and stepped closer. He took it and stood.

Scott picked a long stick up and glamored it to look like a wizard's staff with a crystal ball at the top. He passed it to her. "I'll help you with the vamp blood issue."

"I won't need help. I can do this. I *won't* use it anymore and I'll flush it when we get back." Lexi was determined. She made sure he recognized the strength in her voice, and he nodded.

They continued to walk and talk for another few hours. When they returned, Edward was seated in the kitchen with an attractive woman who looked to be in her thirties. She glanced from Scott to Lexi, to her scar and back to Scott, then studied the young man from head to toe. He swallowed and Lexi wasn't surprised. She'd seen women stare at him like that before. Surprisingly, the woman then proceeded to examine her from her feet upward.

Okay, that's new.

Edward opened the map, a pair of glasses balanced on his head. He glanced up and said, "Jess, Lexi, Scott," by way of introduction, then lowered the glasses onto his nose.

"Hi." Scott proffered his hand and Jess looked at it with an eyebrow raised. Lexi thought she might turn away, but she tilted her head, grinned, and took it. After a moment's shaking, it became apparent that she had turned Scott's friendly gesture into a pissing contest and grasped his hand tightly.

He smiled, and Lexi felt the familiar surge of his magic.

The grin faded from the woman's lips, the first indication that she knew something was wrong. She looked down to see that rather than a hand, she now shook the head of an octopus and its tentacles had wound themselves around her arm.

With a scream, she yanked her arm back, ran behind Edward, shook her hand as though it were covered in slime.

The shifter looked over his glasses at her. "I think you might have deserved that. What do you think?"

"He did that to me the day we met. He thinks it's funny." Lexi fixed her gaze on the back of Scott's head.

"He's lucky I didn't shift and rip his head off."

"I don't think that would have ended well for anyone." She made eye contact with Jess to ensure that the threat had been received and understood.

Edward ignored the women. "Do you need anything else to do this, Scott?"

"I need something that belongs to Dolores. I have something in my bag." Scott headed to his room.

"How's Kate?" Lexi retrieved a mug and filled it from the coffee pot. "Anyone?"

"No, thanks." Jess shook her head.

"I'm good." Edward pointed to his full cup.

She pulled a second mug from the shelf for Scott. When she held the pot close to the mug, it made a rat-tat-tat noise as they jostled together. She didn't look up and merely drew them apart and poured.

Shit. I have the shakes. I've only been off the stuff for a day.

"Stanley called the pack in, so Tommy had to leave." Edward took a gulp of his drink.

"Isn't that Kate's pack too?" Scott entered the room.

"Not until they marry and something's come up about that too." Jess looked at Edward. She hadn't told him this yet.

Lexi made her way around the table and sat.

"Stanley insists the two of them get married, like, now." Her eyebrows had raised.

"That's unconventional, but as pack leader, he has the right to insist. But why?"

"I might know the answer to that." Scott took the coffee Lexi proffered. "We know Caleb's a sorcerer. If he has Stanley enthralled, that could extend to the whole pack. He wouldn't need to control them individually."

"So, once they're married, Kate will be in the pack and Caleb only has to say, 'Give me your land,' and she'll hand it over. We need to get her away from him." Lexi was outraged.

"Her mom's bringing her home for now, but this could cause a great deal of trouble between the packs." Jess looked deeply concerned.

"Perhaps they should come here," Edward suggested.

"We don't know if they're being followed or tracked. I don't think you want to lead them to your friends. Let's send them to Carl's place."

"That makes sense. Thanks, Jess."

The woman gave her a curt nod, then eyed Scott suspiciously before she turned to leave.

The young man took a teardrop pendant from his pocket and held it in his hands.

"Wait, is that mine?" Lexi asked.

"You'll get it back." He smiled and looked pleased that she liked it so much.

When he opened his hands, the pendant had changed shape. It was no longer a teardrop but was five-sided, wide at the top and narrowed into a point at the bottom.

She studied it and tried to decide if she liked this shape more.

Edward stood, looked at his watch, and moved to the

windows to pull the shades down. He left the room and returned a few minutes later, having closed the blinds throughout the ground floor of the house. The sun was low in the sky at the front of the house and the back, where they were, was in shadow. Lexi glanced at the time. It seemed a little early for a vampire to wake.

Scott dug into his pocket and retrieved a purple crystal. "Dolores loaned this to me to help with meditation."

Fascinated, she gazed at it. "I've never seen a stone so dazzling."

He held it up between finger and thumb to give her a better look. "It's a fae amethyst."

She had to blink to force herself to look away.

His expression focused, he dropped the stone into his left hand and swung the chain over the map with his right. It moved freely in all directions. "I don't pick her up anywhere."

Edward stepped back. "This side is Denver, but the other side is all of Colorado."

They turned the map over, and Scott moved the pendant over it from north to south. "Where could she be?"

The shifter sighed. "Give me a moment." He disappeared into his study and returned moments later with a large globe. "Would this work?"

Scott moved it in the center of the table and tried again. "Nothing."

Lexi put her hand on his arm. "So she's not on Earth? That doesn't mean she's—"

"No. I won't accept that." He rested the pendant on top of the globe and sat, his shoulders hunched.

She rubbed her face and and her leg began to bounce again. "I can't think straight."

He glanced up. "Sharpen something. That usually calms you."

"Good idea. I'll sharpen everything I've got." She slid her hand into her pocket, removed her whetstone, and was embarrassed to see the wrapping from a Hershey Kiss stuck to it. With a sigh, she was about to sweep it away when she noticed something small wriggling on it. She dropped it onto the table.

"Eww, gross." She drew her hand back to squash the bug, but on its downward journey, it came to an abrupt halt in mid-air. She turned to Dick, who stood beside her with his hand around her wrist. "Where did you come from?"

"I wouldn't do that if I were you." He released her hand.

Lexi looked at the wriggling black thing in disgust. "What is it?"

The four of them leaned closer. She squinted to see more clearly.

Edward straightened a moment. "I'd say that's a tiny, tiny woman."

"It's Dolores!" Scott's voice was full of joy.

"I think you're right." Lexi frowned at the miniscule being. "Oh, yes. She's wearing her black skirt suit and covering her tiny ears with her tiny hands."

"You're probably deafening her." Dick's voice had softened.

As they watched, the tiny creature leaned on the edge of the whetstone, and a miniscule spray of brown vomit issued from her onto the table.

"I'll get that," the vampire said and wiped the table with a kitchen towel. There was barely a visible spec on it and he threw it in the garbage.

"At least she did it when she was miniaturized," Edward whispered.

The woman began to grow. The larger she got, the more evident it was that she was in distress. She was perspiring, and her hair had come out of its bun and stuck out wildly. The four of them stepped back but continued to stare in fascination as she continued to expand. She seemed to stop, finally, and lay groaning on the dining table.

"Has she stopped?" Edward asked.

Scott looked at him, puzzled.

The shifter shrugged. "Well, I don't know how big she's meant to be."

Dolores rolled over and vomited brown liquid all over the floor.

"Jeez." Lexi jumped out of the way.

Dick walked around it. "I got the last one."

Edward lifted the woman and carried her into the living room, where he placed her on the couch with cushions to prop her back.

"The monsters. Have the monsters gone?" Her eyes were wild.

Dick brought her a glass of water.

She took the glass and gulped thirstily. "Did anything follow me out? How long have I been in there?"

Lexi crouched beside her. "We spoke yesterday."

"What? It's been a week, at least. Hiding from those…things. I thought I was going to die. I've survived on Hershey's chocolate. I hate that stuff. It smells like vomit."

"I agree." Scott's face appeared around the doorway. He was cleaning the floor.

Lexi took the glass into the kitchen to refill it but stopped on her way to the refrigerator when she heard a noise. She looked at the table to where the pendant vibrated on the globe over where California would be. "Oh, look. Your spell found her."

His face appeared above the counter. "I've still got it." He grinned and she smiled in response. They were relieved to have found Dolores alive.

He put the paper towels in the trash, and Edward ran a mop over the area.

They moved into the living room.

Scott placed his hand onto Dolores's head and spoke a word.

The woman blinked and seemed to have recovered, although her pupils were huge.

Dick sat on the edge of the sofa and held Dolores's hand. "Can you tell us what happened? How did you wind up in Lexi's dirty magic pocket?"

Lexi rolled her eyes.

"Was that where I was? There were things in there." She shuddered. "Do you remember when I was in my office?"

She decided not to remind her again since that had only been yesterday and merely nodded.

Dolores continued. "I had visitors. Eric, from Kindred." She looked from Scott to Lexi.

"Eric? The Grandfather of Colorado?" Lexi's mouth hung open.

The woman nodded. "He had two others with him. Warren and Lucy." She looked at Scott now.

"Warren. That explains the bruises on your face. So, they were there for me. I don't know who Lucy is, though." His mouth set into a grim line.

"She's your replacement—a slip of a girl with a haunted look in her eyes. I don't think she'll last long. They know I was involved in your escape but I don't believe they know you're working with me. We only spoke briefly. I realized I needed to get out of there. When he hit me, I created the illusion of a glamor breaking but I actually created the glamor. I distracted them by making a door appear at the back of the room. As soon as their attention was diverted, I shrank the files. Oh, Lexi, dear. My filing cabinet is in your pocket. Could you retrieve it, please? Be careful putting your hand in there—there's something…"

Lexi was beginning to wonder what the hell was in there to have terrified Dolores so much. She dug tentatively in her pocket, thought about the item she sought, and pulled out the minuscule filing cabinet. Carefully, she put it on the floor and it began to grow.

"I made a fae door in the bottom of the wall and slipped the cabinet through, then shrank myself and got the hell out."

"Couldn't you think of somewhere nicer to go than Lexi's

nasty pocket?" Dick shuddered. "I can't imagine what it must have been like." He crouched and embraced Dolores as though she'd spent five years in a Japanese prisoner of war camp. Lexi tried to ignore it.

"The trick to traveling through a fae door is to know exactly where you want to come out. Unfortunately, I wasn't thinking straight, having just had the snot knocked out of me."

Lexi felt in her pocket again and thought *monster*, but nothing came out.

The woman looked at her. "I could see weapons but they were so large, I thought I might have stumbled into a giant's closet. I couldn't get out, so I suppose the pocket has a restriction spell on it. I thought about getting a message to you. I tried to write *help* on a candy wrapper. It took me hours to get the stopper out of your giant bottle of ink.

"Ink?" She drew her brows together in puzzlement.

"Yes, dear. The red ink."

Lexi and Scott shared a look over Dolores's head before she closed her eyes and mouthed, "Oh, shit!"

"But that was when the monsters came and I had to hide. Why do you have monsters in your dimensional pocket?"

"I don't know but I'll deal with that immediately," she promised.

Dolores's eyes grew heavy, and she slumped and drifted into sleep.

Dick turned to Lexi. "That wasn't red ink, was it? She's as high as a kite."

Scott placed a throw pillow under the woman's head and glanced at his friend. "I thought you were going to flush that stuff."

"I haven't had time. We've been busy."

"We have to figure out what to do about Caleb and we can't have you shaking and jittering everywhere." Dick gestured at her.

"Hey, leave her alone. Lexi knows she has a problem and she's trying to deal with it the best way she can. She's the strongest person I know, and if she says she can do this the hard way, that's what she'll do."

The vampire startled. "Scott, I didn't mean to—"

"If it was me, I'd simply get rid of the problem with magic, but Lexi has integrity and stamina and–"

"Wait, what?" She stood with her mouth hanging open.

"I said you have integrity and—"

"Not that, you muppet. I can get rid of this with magic? Just like that?" She clicked her fingers.

"Yes. I offered to help."

"I thought you were offering to drive me to meetings." Lexi took his collar and marched him toward her room.

"You kids have fun," Dick called after them and repeated her words to her.

She didn't even turn as she frog-marched Scott down the hall, but her arm came up with the middle finger extended. The two men chuckled behind her.

"Laugh all you like. You two will get your brains gagged. There will be no more secrets dribbling out of your mouth, Dick," Lexi called before she closed the door.

CHAPTER TEN

"Good evening, Betsy." Caleb stepped into the mansion Betsy shared with her son.

"Why, Caleb, what a surprise. Todd's in his study. I'll tell him you're here." She closed the door behind him.

He stared at her and narrowed his eyes. "What the hell is that on your head?"

"It's my golfing sun visor. But this isn't my hair, it's fake. It merely looks like it's coming out of the hole on top." She shook her head and the beaded blonde dreadlocks danced with the movement. "It's fun."

"I see." He shook his head. "I think I can find the study myself." He stepped past Betsy and marched down the hallway.

You should kill her, purred a voice inside his mind.

Stop that. I can brainwash her if I need to, he replied to the relentless entity.

It would be a waste of time to brainwash that crazy old bat. There's not enough brain to wash. Azatoth laughed and the man shivered inwardly.

We're too close to screw this up. Stop it. He paused outside Todd's study door and patted his brow with his handkerchief. The voice was almost unending these days. He would be glad to get it out of his head. Soon, he promised himself.

"I'm making fresh lemonade, sourpuss," Betsy called after him.

"No need." He entered the study without knocking.

Todd was reaching for the phone when he entered. "Caleb. I'm due on a call in a few minutes. Would you like a drink while you wait? You could take it into the den."

Caleb looked from the partly open door to the little ante-room, which Todd referred to as "the den," to the bottle of whiskey on the side table.

Bushmills? If I'd wanted cough syrup, I'd have asked for it.

He muttered a word and the mayor's face became slack. "How's everything going with my construction license?"

The man leaned back, the phone forgotten. "The paperwork is ready to go but the final property is still a problem. The girl has refused to sell again, even after the attack and the robbery."

For a brief moment, he stood with his hands on the back of the chair on the other side of the desk and stared at Todd. "It won't be a problem for long. William's friend has been dealt with. Did you take care of William?"

"Stanley sent some of his boys out and I contacted the man you suggested. Stanley lost two of his and your man called me earlier today, complaining that none of his boys had returned, but...I didn't understand what he was talking about at the time." The man spoke like he was half-asleep.

"I don't know why William has involved himself in my business, but I need him taken care of. Don't let me down again. You don't want to lose your mother the same way you lost your father, do you?" Caleb's eyes were pinpricks as he focused on him.

"Of course not. I love my mother. What happened to my father?" Todd was confused.

The sorcerer walked around the desk, stopped behind the

chair, and leaned closer to his ear. "I told you, remember? I asked his heart to stop and it stopped."

"That's right. You told me that." He sounded distantly sad.

"Did you find out why the girl is here?" Caleb straightened and continued his walk around the desk.

"No, but she's not who she claims."

"I know that. She lied to us." He stood in front of the man again.

"That's bad," Todd said slowly.

"Send more men to William's place."

"William's not there. They've been watching all day."

His hands curled into fists before he stretched them again. "William's a vampire, remember? He won't be out in the daylight."

"William's a vampire?" Todd's eyebrows rose in surprise.

The problem with making people's minds malleable was that it also made their brains soft.

"Send them around when it gets dark."

He should burn. He's a loose end.

Briefly, he considered that. The demon might have a point. "Actually, no. Go yourself. When you're sure he's in there, burn it down. But before you leave, send the approvals for the construction work on the last property through. Then, when you burn the house, stay inside it. Sit on that garish cowhide chaise he loves so much and watch it all burn. It'll be like watching a movie."

Azatoth laughed again.

"A movie. Burn. Okay. What if he isn't there?" Todd's face looked like he had battled sleep to ask the question.

"Burn it anyway. You'll forget our chat now." He muttered a few words and life returned to the other man's face.

Caleb gave Todd an open, friendly smile. "No, no. I don't want to interrupt. I was merely passing and wondered how you were fixed for eighteen holes on the weekend."

"I think I can schedule that in." The mayor beamed. He looked at his clock. "Good Lord! My conference call should have started five minutes ago."

"I'll leave you to it, then. I'll say goodbye to Betsy before I leave."

He found her chopping lemons in the kitchen. At the sight of him, she put the knife and the lemon down and walked around the island toward him.

"Caleb, dear. That was a short visit." She wiped her hands on her apron.

Pick the knife up and gut her, Azatoth suggested with glee.

Caleb ignored it. "Sadly, the business doesn't run itself."

"I know. You should think about retiring. Don't make the same mistake Harv made and work yourself to death." She sighed.

"Perhaps you're right. I think of him every day. The business has never felt the same without him. Not one day of the last five years."

Tears came to her eyes. "That's very touching, Caleb. There you go, making an old woman cry."

"Never my intention, Betsy. Take care. I'll show myself out." He put his hand on her shoulder.

Snap her neck.

He kissed the side of her head and left.

You're getting quite persistent, Azatoth. You seem to forget who's in charge here.

Forgive me, lord. You will gain powers beyond your wildest dreams for freeing me. The sorcerer imagined Azatoth cowering at his feet, which he would be...soon.

He climbed into his Porsche. The engine gave a throaty roar before he pulled away down the drive and onto the street. He was pleased with himself. The girl would soon be beyond the protection of her pack and the meddling witches. The moment she married into Stanley's pack, she would sign the property over to him. He wondered about telling her new husband to throttle her.

After. The place of ritual must belong to you.

"I know that, Azatoth." He spoke aloud to the demon. "I'm merely planning ahead. She's been a nuisance."

I agree. Azatoth assaulted his mind with visions of Kate being hung from a roof by her entrails.

He shook his head. "Well, that's a little exotic for me."

You could give her to me as a little gift. But you will learn to take great pleasure in these things, his inner companion whispered seductively.

Caleb doubted it. He could be vicious but the demon was... well, *demonic.*

CHAPTER ELEVEN

L exi lay in the dark and wondered what had woken her barely after midnight.

She thought about the day. They'd gotten Dolores back and she'd lost her craving for vampire blood. She couldn't believe how healthy she felt, but she knew she'd miss the benefits of it.

Only until I've built up my natural strength and speed again.

All of that was encouraging, yet she was wide awake. Why? Irritated, she sat and pulled clothes on before she wandered down the hall to the kitchen. She stuck her head into the living room as she passed and saw the still-sleeping figure of Dolores on the couch. As her eyes grew accustomed to the dark, she realized Dick was seated in the armchair watching over her, as still as a dead guy.

"How is she?" she whispered.

"We talked for a while. She's sleeping now. I don't think she'll suffer any long-term ill effects." He tilted his head. "Maybe the munchies."

She face-palmed and shook her head. Choosing not to respond, she wandered to the refrigerator and took out a carton of milk.

"Can't sleep?" he asked from the doorway.

After a quick shake of her head, she found a glass and poured the milk into it. She swallowed half before she turned to him. "I didn't know what woke me up at first."

"Something's coming." He nodded. "I feel it too."

Lexi looked at him in surprise.

"I feel things. I'm undead, not dead." Dick went to the blinds and lifted one to peer out into the darkness.

"Sorry." She shrugged but he didn't see it.

He turned to her. "Think of it like an electric car. It runs on a different fuel but it's not any less of a car than a Trans Am."

She choked on her milk and placed her glass on the counter. "Yeah, it kinda is."

"You're right. That was a terrible analogy." He laughed.

"Could you pour one of those for me?" Edward sat at the table while she took another glass from the shelf and filled it with milk.

The shifter looked at her. "The calm before the storm?"

Rather than answer, she nodded.

"I've been watching wolves in the tree line. I hope they're yours." Dick indicated the window with his head.

"Yes. It's only a few of the pack."

Edward took the glass from her and nodded his thanks. "How's Dolores?"

"She seems okay." She moved to return the milk to the refrigerator.

He turned to Dick. "What exactly is she? The shrinking thing—I've never seen that before."

The vampire walked away from the window. "She's a sylph. It's an air sprite—fae."

"How did you meet her?" Lexi had been about to ask but Edward had beaten her to it.

"I've known Dolores for ninety years. She arranges my papers when it's time for a new ID."

"You must be coming to that time soon."

"Yes. I'll have to discover I have a son somewhere in Europe, rent the house out, and go live out the remainder of my days with my son and grandson William...again."

"Why not choose a different name?" She had wondered about this for the last couple of days.

Dick shrugged. "I don't want to."

"I'll be sorry to see you go." Edward turned from him to Lexi. "What's your story?"

"I don't know what you know about Kindred, but most of us don't really have stories. Some are born into the organization but mostly, we're runaways. Apparently, I was in the system—a foster kid. I ran away and met a kid from Kindred who introduced me and I joined."

"What could they possibly have said to you to make you join an organization like that?" He shook his head.

"My mind was wiped so I guess we'll never know."

"Oh, right. That's what the vamp blood was for. How do you feel about never knowing?"

"I'm already thinking about doing it maybe once a year. Not enough to get into the mess I was in but I still want to know."

"What if you find out something you wish you hadn't?" Dick asked.

"I'll ask Scott to melt my brain again." Lexi smiled.

Edward studied her curiously. "What made you leave them?"

"A vamp tried to turn me and that night, memories started coming back to me—missions I didn't remember being on. I realized they'd regularly hidden my memories. By the morning, I'd remembered too much for me to be safe." She stood and walked to the sink.

I'd remembered Bryan.

"You know they put us into family units, right? We live in regular homes in neighborhoods all over the world.

"I had a kind of brother called Bryan—a mage. He wasn't my

real brother, but when we were kids, he looked after me like one. Then, when we were about sixteen, he was bitten by a shifter. He shouldn't have even been there, but he was with us when we were called in on an emergency mission and wasn't supposed to get out of the car. Because he didn't want to get into trouble, he hid it from us. A couple of days later, he got ill and became delirious. He started talking about missions no one remembered. Then, people came from another Kindred unit.

"I wasn't supposed to go near him, but he was my favorite brother. I know you're not supposed to have favorites, but he was much like Scott. We did everything together. He gave me this." She indicated the gold ring she always wore. "I was in the room reading to him, trying to calm him as he thrashed around. They walked in, Braxton dragged me out, and they shot him. Then, they counseled me and I forgot he ever existed. So they took him away twice. For years, I had no idea where this ring even came from."

"'Counseled?'" Edward sounded puzzled.

"Counselling is what they call hiding our memories." Lexi stared into the middle distance. "Anyway, when I was given vampire blood and the memories started to come back, I realized that it must have been the same as him being bitten by a shifter. I knew I wasn't safe so I ran."

He shrugged. "But aren't all you legacies enhanced with blood from all the supe species anyway?"

"Yes, but that happens once, in the ritual." She didn't feel like dealing with where this conversation was heading—back to the fact she was a dud. "I think I'll see if I can get some sleep now."

Dick stood. "I'll go to check the house. I'll call if I can't get back."

"Are you sure it's safe?" she asked as she stood.

He put his hand on his heart. "Well, Lexi Braxton. You care."

"Let's not get ahead of ourselves. I merely don't want to be the one chasing that dog around with a pooper scooper." She shuddered.

"You care," he accused her retreating back.

"I'm going to bed. Don't get yourself killed…again."

CHAPTER TWELVE

Todd drew up outside the house. He couldn't remember why he had come to see his friend William, only that it was imperative he find him. It seemed impolite to ring someone's doorbell at one-thirty in the morning, yet he was doing it.

"Hello?" said an accented voice.

"I need to see William," was all he could think to say.

"Listen, you. I've called the hospital, so they'll come and drag you back, you crazy motherfucker. Leave Mr. Levin alone."

"I'm sorry? I don't quite understand."

A light came on over the gate.

"Oh. Who is it?" Jesús asked in a sing-song voice.

"Can you tell him it's Todd O'Donnell?"

"Mayor O'Donnell? Of course. Please come in." The man buzzed the gate and Todd drove up to the house.

He climbed out of the car and retrieved the tote bag from the trunk. While he couldn't remember why he'd brought a tote bag with him, he felt it was important.

A man opened the front door. He recognized him as William's houseboy, Jesús.

"Please come in, Mayor O'Donnell. Mr. Levin isn't home yet, but he texted earlier to let me know he's on his way."

"Thank you." He entered and walked straight to the cowhide chaise longue.

He was vaguely aware of Jesús staring in horror as he sat on the antique.

"I'm sure this is more comfortable." The man indicated the couch.

"This is perfect." Todd sat, straight-backed, on the seat's edge.

Jesús finally shrugged. "Well, you're the mayor, so I'm sure it's okay." Then, he said something else.

"What?" Todd shook his head to clear it. In the space of a few moments, he'd actually forgotten he was seated there.

"Can I offer you a drink while you wait?"

"No. Thank you."

He realized the man was staring at his tote bag and placed his hand on it. "Why are you staring at my bag?"

"Your— No reason. Would you like me to keep it for you?" Jesús spoke slowly. Perhaps the boy was dim.

"No, it's fine." He moved it closer.

He watched absently as Jesús went to the bar, poured a scotch, returned, and handed it to him.

Did I say yes? I must have.

He took it. "Thank you."

For some reason, he felt nervous, but he had no idea why he would feel that way. He'd been in this house several times. He knocked the whiskey back and coughed. "Would it trouble you to pour me another?"

As Jesús turned to refill the glass, Todd fidgeted with the lighter in his pocket.

CHAPTER THIRTEEN

It was nearly two am when Dick arrived at his home. He parked in a cul de sac leading to the property behind his own, moved quickly across their tennis court, and hopped the wall. He walked silently around his pool, slid the patio door open with almost no sound, and entered.

He was hyper-alert as he walked past the back of the couch toward the kitchen. He smelled sweat in the air. Not Jesús' but a familiar scent he couldn't place. He also detected the smell of whiskey—his Scottish Glenfiddich single malt—and gasoline. He froze and sensed the air move near him before the light went on.

In the two seconds between registering the smells and sensing movement, he moved to the middle of the room. When the light came on, he stood in front of Betsy.

The woman appeared confused for a moment and looked where she thought he had been and then where he now was. She climbed off the couch.

"I didn't know what else to do," she mumbled and burst into tears.

Dick hugged her. "It's all right, Betsy, dear, but first things first. Why is Todd passed out on my chaise?"

They moved to the dinner table.

She sat. "He's all right. Jesús roofied him."

"I didn't roofie him. I merely crushed a few Xanaxes and Ambiens." Jesús entered with a throw, which he draped around Betsy. She patted his hand as he continued, "Betsy brought the pills with her."

He raised an eyebrow.

"I'm sorry, William. Todd came here to kill you." She began to cry again.

"Todd? Are you sure?" He looked at the unconscious man. The mayor didn't have a mean bone in his body. Dick had always thought he was too nice for politics.

"I didn't believe it myself until he turned up a half-hour after his mamma with a gas can. It's in the garage. He kept calling it his 'tote bag.'" Jesús shook his head.

"I don't think he knows what he's doing. Caleb...did something to him when he came to the house this evening. I was taking lemonade to them through that little side room to the study. You remember? Where Harv used to keep that couch he called his daybed?"

Dick nodded.

"They were talking about you and Bianca, except they said she wasn't really Bianca. I didn't understand that but then he told Todd to come here and set fire to your home. He also told him to let himself die in the fire and Todd agreed, just like that."

The vampire tried to sound calm, but he needed to know what she knew. "Do you have any idea why he would suggest such a thing?"

"He asked Todd to send paperwork through about a property deal. Are you in business with him?" She took a handkerchief from her purse.

He shook his head. "You were very brave to not give yourself away."

"I wanted to kill him." Her hand scrunched the handkerchief.

"When he came to see me in the kitchen, I had to put the knife down. I couldn't trust myself."

"He must have used some kind of hypnosis on Todd." Dick tried to think of an explanation Betsy would believe.

"I always knew." She placed a hand on his arm.

Dick looked at her and opened his mouth to ask what she meant.

"I always knew that somehow, you were our William. I always felt silly for believing it, but it was my secret belief that I never shared with anyone." New tears appeared in her eyes. "He said you're a vampire. It's strange but it makes perfect sense."

This was the moment when he could have denied it. He should have denied it. Kindred could end him for telling the truth but he couldn't bring himself to open his mouth and deliver another lie to this woman. "You're not afraid?"

"Of you? Never. But William, I'm terribly afraid of Caleb." She pulled the throw around her as though she had suddenly felt cold.

"I intended to return. I wanted to be his best man, but this happened." He gestured vaguely at himself. "And I wasn't…civil at first. I couldn't be near people for a long time. I had to be sure I wouldn't hurt the people I loved. Can you understand that, Betsy?"

The woman stood and embraced him. "Welcome home, William."

Dick sobbed once, then sniffed and pulled away. "Did they say anything else?"

Betsy paused. He could see from the look on her face that he wouldn't like it.

She returned to her seat and he returned to his as though he knew he should be seated for this. Betsy leaned forward and placed her hand on his. "He told Todd that he murdered Harv."

He felt as though she had delivered a blow to his gut and froze.

"William, William." Harvey ran toward him. They had been playing tennis and stopped for martinis. He turned to watch his approach, thinking he was beautiful in his tennis whites. Not for the first time, he thought the man should have been the movie star, not him. Harv knew William was in love with him but he loved him like a brother so he accepted that was all they could ever be.

"What's up, pal? You look like you'll have a heart attack." William held a martini out.

His friend took the drink and knocked it back in one. "She said yes. I popped the question and Betsy said yes. I want you to be my best man."

"That's great news. Harv. I'm thrilled for you both." He shook the man's hand enthusiastically and smiled until his face hurt.

But it was too much for him. He needed time and distance so he went overseas a week later and never returned, not as himself. The next time he saw Harv and Betsy, it was as his grandson. They were elderly but he still loved Harv and he loved Betsy for the years of happiness she'd given the man he loved.

"William, William." Betsy's hand was on his arm and she shook him out of his reverie.

"I will destroy him." His voice was strangled with rage.

He left at vamp speed.

CHAPTER FOURTEEN

"Lexi." Edward spoke as he knocked on the door.

Her eyes snapped open. She felt like she had barely closed them, but a knife was already in her hand.

She yawned. "Edward?"

He stood on the other side of the door. "I think we have a problem."

Lexi opened the door quickly enough to make him jump. She stood in a t-shirt and panties and carried a knife and a gun as she looked left and right down the hallway.

He turned and hurried down the hall. "Get dressed. William's missing."

Sixty seconds later, she was in her leathers and on her way to the kitchen. As she walked past Scott's room, she looked in to see him hopping around as he tried to get into his jeans. She knew they'd probably been inside-out on the floor and rolled her eyes as she continued up the hall.

Edward looked up from his cell phone as she entered. "Jesús called. Dick's gone after Caleb."

"On his own? What's gotten into him?" She pulled her jacket on.

"I'll call someone in to watch Dolores." He stood at the window and stared out into the darkness. All she could see was his reflection in the glass.

"And why do I need to be watched?" The fae stood in the doorway with Marcel in her arms.

"Because you look awful. You're pale and weak and no one wants to die protecting you in a fight," Scott said from the hallway.

Everyone turned to stare at him.

"I see. You're learning." The woman turned to Lexi and nodded her approval. "Take care." She returned to the couch.

A knock at the back door drew their attention and a denim-clad man walked in and sat at the kitchen table. He'd clearly already received his instructions from Edward, because other than a brief nod, there was no communication between them.

Lexi looked at the clock. It was 3:15. "We don't have long."

They climbed into Edward's SUV and headed out. Along the road, she tried Dick's cell repeatedly. Finally, she sighed. "If he could answer, he would."

"There's something up ahead." The shifter slowed the car.

She stared at the flashing lights. "Is it an accident?"

"Roadblock." Edward shook his head. "Shit. I should have expected this. Stan will have his officers looking for you. I'll try telling them we're heading to Brawley."

He came to a halt and Lexi moved her hand to her pocket. Scott leaned forward and put his hand on her shoulder and she relaxed her arm.

The driver rolled his window down and an officer shone his flashlight around the inside of the car, back and front, then asked for ID. He took it slowly from where it was tucked under the visor. The officer pointed the light at it, then asked, "May I ask what you're doing out so late?"

Edward opened his mouth to tell his lie. "Of course you may, young man. It *is* rather late, isn't it? I've been to Riverside to play bingo with June and Margo. We've played bingo together for forty years." His mouth snapped shut. That was not his voice.

"Your bingo goes on a little late, doesn't it, ma'am?"

He opened his mouth again. "Well, now that I think about it, there were a few years we didn't play when June and Margo weren't speaking. Now, why was that? You know, I can't remember. Oh, of course. How could I have forgotten? Margo caught her husband in the pool house with June. Of course, he's been dead these past twenty years."

"Who did it? Margo or June?" the officer asked.

"I believe it was Mr. Jack Daniels. Don't tell Margo I said that. She tells everyone he was raptured."

The officer laughed. "Drive carefully, ma'am." He waved his flashlight and indicated that the other officers should move the barrier.

"Thank you, young man," Edward called.

After they had driven through, he turned in his seat. "What did he see?"

"A little old lady in a 1971 Austin America." Scott sounded exhausted.

Lexi twisted to look at her friend and noticed he was perspiring. "Are you okay?"

"I'll be fine in a minute. I had to do the voice, the face, the car, make the rest of us invisible, and try to think of things to say. It was like juggling fire."

They travelled on in silence.

"Scott, we're near Dick's." She stretched between the seats and shook his knee.

"Right." He muttered some words. "We're shielded."

She was about to touch her scar and open the gate when it opened before them. Startled, she glanced at him. "Was that you?"

Scott shook his head.

The gate closed behind them. They drove around an unfamiliar vehicle and directly into the garage. Lexi heard shouting the moment she climbed out of the car, and she drew her katana.

"I have to do it." The mayor was red-faced and yelled from the corner of the room.

"But William's not here, darling. Aren't you supposed to wait for William?" Betsy said, the stress in her voice palpable.

"I think we need more duct tape," Jesús said from one of the barstools. He glowered at Todd, who was secured to Dick's half-million-dollar chaise with an already sizeable amount of tape.

"Hello, Bianca dear." Betsy saw Lexi enter, and her shoulders sagged with relief. She looked at Scott. "And you must be John."

"I'm Scott."

Edward walked in behind them. The woman smiled. "I'm sorry, then *you* must be John."

"Edward."

Lexi put her katana on the counter. "There is no John. What the hell is going on, and where is Dick?"

"Who's Dick?" Betsy asked.

Jesús stood and moved to the center of the room. "Someone called Caleb messed with the mayor's head and now, he wants to kill Mr. Levin. The mayor's mamma came to warn Mr. Levin but he wasn't here, so we drugged him. His mamma says I won't go to jail for that. Then she told Mr. Levin that Caleb killed someone called Harv. I don't know who that is, but Mr. Levin got super-mad and disappeared real fast. I tried to call him, but there was no answer, so I called Mr. Edward." He turned to Betsy. "And Mr. Levin is Dick, but I don't know why that is."

Edward's jaw dropped. "I'm so sorry. I know your husband was a good friend of William's grandfather."

"Oh. She knows about the *thing* too." Jesús made pointy teeth with his fingers and held them up to his mouth.

"He has to die," Todd yelled from the corner.

Jesús screamed and ran to his barstool.

Scott walked to the chaise and extended a hand toward the air around the man.

Betsy took a few steps toward them, worry on her face. "What's he doing?"

Lexi went to stand beside her. "He's going to try to help Todd." She looked at Edward. "Can you find some items belonging to Dick? Things he has a good connection with?"

The shifter nodded. "I brought something from his trunk. It's in the car."

She sat beside Betsy. "Hi, I'm Lexi. I was asked to help a young woman in town with a gang problem. Things have escalated."

"I heard Caleb say you weren't really Bianca. So no gossip about the New England Mayburys, then?" Betsy asked while she watched Scott and Todd anxiously.

"I could make something up." She also watched them and picked her lip nervously.

The older woman put her hand on her arm. "Don't do that, dear." She left her hand there. "How could Caleb do this?"

"Caleb's a sorcerer. The bad kind." Lexi patted the woman's hand.

"And him?" Betsy turned to face her. "The good kind?"

"You're getting it." She smiled. They both turned to the men.

As Scott muttered something, a dark cloud drifted from Todd and spread across the floor.

"Whatever it is, it seems to be coming out of him," Lexi said.

"I've got this." Edward held a small leather-covered box out. They stood around it and peered in as he opened it.

"Does anything stand out to you?" Lexi asked Edward as he pushed gold jewelry around the box.

Edward pursed his lips. "Not really. He—"

"This." Betsy darted her fingers into the little box and pulled out a silver pin in the shape of a lion's head. She held it up. "It was a gift from Harv. What's that sticking to it?"

Lexi peered closely at the flaky substance and shook her head.

Edward squinted. "Skin. Vampires can't touch silver."

'Well, he's touched that," she stated.

Betsy turned to her son. "Is that normal?"

She frowned at the black smoke that built behind Scott as he stood with his eyes closed, concentrating on Todd. She opened her mouth to ask what it was when it coalesced into the vague shape of a man. Its ethereal arms slid around her friend's throat.

Scott's eyes flew open and bulged, and his face turned red. He clawed at his throat, but his hands merely went through the smoke.

Lexi threw a shuriken at the shape, but it glided through and stuck into the wall.

Edward shifted instantly, attempted to jump at the entity, but powered through it instead.

As they watched, the center of it became darker until it was almost black. Lexi felt strongly that something worse was about to happen.

She held her arm out and stroked the scar. "Freeze!" she shouted.

The black shape solidified. She grasped her katana and slashed through its arms. No longer attached to the rest of the body, they transformed to pieces of black glass and shattered on the floor, and Scott moved away.

Edward shifted to human form.

Betsy's hand was clutched to her chest. "Jesús, dear, I think I need a drink."

Jesús brought her a bottle of gin and a glass. As he turned to walk away, she caught his arm. "His clothes are still on. How strange."

"You think that's the strange thing?" The man shook his head. "Actually, I know this one. Shifters were made from a spell or a curse or something, so it's magic. It's best not to think about it. I don't have enough migraine pills for both of us."

Scott dropped to his knees, where he gasped and drew in

deep gulps of air. Lexi put her hand under his arm and dragged him away while Edward picked up Todd and the chair in one and moved them away from the ugly frozen shape.

"I need to carry on. I was almost there." The young man tried to stand but there was no strength in him.

A bottle of water appeared between them. She glanced at Betsy who regarded her with a worried face. "I'm sorry, Jesús says the water cooler isn't working."

Lexi flicked a look at the man and took the bottle. "Thank you."

She passed it to Scott and he downed it.

"Do you have anything left?" he asked.

"Yes, do you need it?" She held her hand out, and the energy trickled away to leave only a drop at the bottom of her scar.

"Can you help me up?" he asked.

Edward stepped forward and lifted him easily to his feet. The young sorcerer returned to his position behind Todd, closed his eyes, and extended his arms once more.

Lexi and Edward walked carefully to the frozen black smokeman and circled him.

"What's this?" The shifter pointed at its center.

She walked closer and crouched. Staring into the deep, inky blackness, the only light she saw was a reflection of the light in the room. "It's a knife. Why would there be a knife inside it? And it's tiny. Should I break it?" She raised her sword again.

"Not yet. I want to look at it." Scott leaned on the end of the chaise and looked like he might faint.

Betsy stepped beside him, took his arm, and put it around her to give him stability.

"I've broken Caleb's hold on Todd. He won't be able to control him with sorcery again." He wavered, and Edward tried to guide him to the couch. "No. I need to see that."

The two men moved to the black shape. Scott looked into its center.

"That's not a tiny knife. It's far away. This is a portal. If you hadn't frozen it when you did, that knife would be somewhere in me by now." He wobbled on his feet and lurched to the couch.

"Are you spent?" Lexi asked.

"I should have enough for a location spell for Dick. Jesús, do you have a local map?" The man walked away as Scott extended his hand for the pin, and she dropped it in his hand.

His eyes widened. "Wow! Yes. This is good. He's connected to this by love, loss, and grief." He blinked away the tears that had appeared in response to the emotions tied to the little pin, held it in the palm of his hand, and spoke to it like it was a pet. "Come on, little guy. Lead us to your master." He passed it to Lexi. "I need to text Dolores."

The moment the pin dropped into her hand, she felt it tug. Jesús hadn't returned with the map, so she began to walk through the room with her hand held in front of her. She asked the others, "What is this, east? He's east of us? She side-stepped the frozen black mass and continued walking.

"Oh!" Her arm was pulled sideways. "North. Could he be on the move?" Her arm jerked again. She once again stood in front of the smoke-man. Lexi circled the portal with her hand out in front of her. It pulled her from every angle.

Edward stood beside her. "It's the portal. Wherever they sent that knife from, that's where William is."

"I'm sorry. I need to recharge or I might not be much help when we arrive." Scott sighed.

"Mom?"

They all turned to look at Todd.

"Why am I taped to a chair?"

"Jesús," Edward called.

Jesús walked in with a sheet to cover the frozen portal before the mayor could see it. "Yes, Mr. Edward?"

"We need a box-cutter."

The man looked at Todd and tutted as though in disappointment. "Yes, we sure do." He walked away, shaking his head.

Edward set about releasing Todd while Betsy stumbled to find a rational explanation for his situation. "Well, goodness. Such a... a thing."

Jesús sat on the floor next to the chaise, picked at the tape, and rolled his eyes. "We think someone roofied you." He shared a quick glance with Betsy.

"What? Where?" Todd brought his freed hand to his mouth.

"At the party," Jesús said as he peeled the tape gently from Dick's prized chaise.

"What party?" Todd looked at the people around him.

Edward released him from the chair.

"Oh, my God. He doesn't even remember the party," Betsy said and walked toward her son. "Okay, dear. Let's get you home."

He pointed at the covered object. "What's that?"

"It's a statue of me naked. You want to see?" Jesús took hold of the sheet as though to sweep it away.

Todd looked at him. "No." He turned his face away. "Mother, let's go."

Edward helped him to his feet while Betsy crossed to Lexi.

She took her hand. "Call me as soon as you know anything, please."

They left and Lexi, Scott, and Edward stood around the frozen portal.

The shifter stood and waved his hand slowly through the air.

Lexi turned and stared at him. "What are you doing?"

"I'm trying to determine where that reflection's coming from." He tried to put his arm between one of the spotlights and the reflection.

Scott looked into it. "It's not a reflection. That is what they call 'the light at the end of the tunnel.'"

Edward lowered his arm. "I never thought of that."

"So, what? You unfreeze it and we simply walk in?" Lexi tapped on it.

"Honestly, I don't know. It could only be one way." The young man paused to think. "If we *can* get into it, I don't think we'll be able to use it to come back. Jesús? Do you have a hammer?"

Jesús went to a kitchen drawer and pulled out a heavy-looking meat tenderizer mallet. "Will this do?"

"Possibly. This is kind of a doorway. We'll go through it, and when we've gone, it will freeze again. I want you to count to ten, then smash the shit out of it."

"I can do that." The man tested the weight of the implement in his hand. "Hmm… Can't I just shoot it?"

Scott smiled. "That'll work, but seriously, wait until it's frozen."

"Then you need to get into Mr. Levin's day car and wait for a call. He might need safe transport." Edward cracked his neck. He seemed to be getting ready to turn.

"Wait." Lexi squinted at the far-away knife frozen in the portal. "What's that on the hilt?"

They all looked closer. "Oh!" Jesús exclaimed. She jumped. "It's like a hand. See the black shape behind it? That's a man—kind of, maybe." His finger drew the outline of the shadowy figure onto the blackened glass. It was indeed a man or some-thing resembling a man, trapped within the frozen portal.

"What'll happen when you reactivate this?"

"I expect he'll continue his attempt to kill me." Scott sounded so detached and clinical that she blinked in surprise.

"I'll go first, then—" she said quickly.

He interrupted her and held his hand up. "If he's traveling through it, we can't enter it until he breaks the surface at this end. We need to be sure he keeps coming. The moment he leaves it, the portal could vanish, so we have to remain in contact with it when he's out to keep it active."

Lexi stepped back. "You're right. He won't come out with us waiting for him. Can he see us?"

Scott thought for a moment. "He's frozen in there and probably unaware of the passage of time. He'll still see what he saw before it froze."

Edward looked at him. "Which is you, waiting to be stabbed in the back."

"Then that's what he needs to see when I reactivate it. I'll take a step farther away. He looks to be deep in there, but portals can be visually distorted. He could be much closer." The sorcerer took a step away from the portal and turned his back.

"I don't like this." Lexi stood at the side and sweat prickled her scalp. She heard the bone-cracking sounds of Edward shifting and watched as the wolf stretched his injured leg, then padded around the back of the portal to the other side.

Scott gave a quick nod before the portal shimmered and became almost solid smoke once more.

No sooner had the surface lost its rigidity than the blade appeared from its murky depths. Lexi swung her katana onto it and Edward leapt at the arm to clamp his jaws over it.

A hideous, inhuman screech issued as the assassin was dragged out.

They had expected a man, a sorcerer, a wolf, or a vampire. What they were faced with was none of those. It was vaguely bipedal in shape, but its skin was black and oily. The mouth was huge and fanged, and the top half of its face was full of black eyes. Its second arm emerged and tried to swipe at Lexi, followed by four more arms. Each had a pincer on the end.

Edward whimpered and retched, his mouth black as he pulled away from the creature and collapsed, writhing, on the floor. Her sword was dragged from her grasp by one of the pincers.

It still seemed determined to attack Scott and thrust with four of its arms to grasp his shoulders. He pulled away and fell forward, which made the creature fall with him. Once on the floor, it climbed onto his back, drew its head back, and opened its mouth. Yellow fangs glistened from black gums and began their descent to his exposed neck when it was halted by the sudden appearance of Lexi's knife protruding from its mouth.

It gurgled and burst into a huge splash of slime that caught her and totally covered her friend.

She realized they were farther from the mouth of the portal than she had intended.

"No," she cried and spun to see that the portal was still open. Standing beside it, his face turned away and eyes screwed shut, was Jesús. He had poked one finger into the swirling surface and waved the meat mallet in the air in front of him.

Lexi slid closer and stuck her foot into it. "You can stop that now, Jesús. You did great. Scott, are you okay?" She was concerned that he hadn't moved.

He didn't respond immediately, but after a few breaths, he said, "What the fuck is all over me?"

"Some kind of demon gunk. I think it must have liked you. How do you feel?"

"Pregnant." He shuddered.

"Not up for a second date, then?" She looked at Edward. He had shifted but lay unconscious on the floor. "Edward? Scott, can you help him? I don't want to take my foot out of the portal."

He placed a hand on the shifter and black slimy liquid ran from his mouth. There was a surprising amount of it. He coughed and brought up the last of it, then sat and leaned against the wall. "What the hell was that?"

"Precisely. That was a demon," Scott said.

Edward rubbed his face. "I might have nightmares for the rest of my life." He stood and looked into the portal. "That tunnel looks long. Will there be any more of those in there?"

"I hope not. Are we ready to go? It's nearly sunrise." Lexi asked, her foot still in place and her katana raised.

"I need a minute. I asked Dolores to send stuff through to

your pocket. Is it there?" She began to retrieve various items from her dimensional pocket, including several crystals and a couple of cell phone power packs. As they appeared, she passed them to Scott. He held each crystal for a few seconds to draw the stored magical energy from them and discarded them in turn. Finally, he picked up a power pack that had four blue lights along its edge.

"Ha! Dolores is a genius." As he held it, the lights blinked out one at a time. He held his hand out to Lexi and transferred energy to her, then picked up the second and half-drained it, leaving two blue lights. He picked his bag up and threw the power pack into it.

They looked at each other and nodded. She turned to Jesús. "Start counting."

In silence, they stepped through.

CHAPTER FIFTEEN

In the space of two steps, they were in a room that stank of abandonment and urine. Someone screamed, and they all looked up. The shriek had come from an upper floor.

Scott twirled his finger. "We're shielded, but I'll have to drop the shield when we get moving or I won't have the strength to fight whatever's coming. Was that Dick screaming?"

"I hope so. That means he's still alive." Lexi withdrew her flashlight from her pocket and played it around the room. A set of shuttered doors with small windows at the top stretched the full length of one side.

"Is this a garage?" he asked.

She shrugged. "I'll take point," she stated and took a step toward the door.

"Wait. Take this." He fumbled in his bag, brought out two earpieces, and passed one to her.

Lexi smiled. It was Kindred protocol to wear the communicators on a mission. "You can take the boy out of Kindred..." She placed it in her ear.

"We don't know what might be up there or how many. Be careful." Edward shifted and padded through the room, sniffing.

She followed him with the light while he examined dark corners and shook his head at the disgusting smells.

They moved carefully to the hallway. She gestured that the shifter should go left and scout the rest of the ground floor and he nodded and turned away. Lexi smiled briefly at the absurdity of a nodding wolf, then climbed the stairs a few steps ahead of Scott. She reached the door to the second floor and extended her hand toward the handle when a garbled message came through her communicator. The sound confused her and she couldn't understand why it only came only through the earpiece and not from directly behind her. She turned and gasped when she realized a black cloud was enveloping her and there was no sign of Scott. Lexi froze and waited for him to appear or to repeat what he'd said over the comm.

"For fuck's sake, Lexi. Move your ass *now!*" His voice came loud and clear and she guessed he must have boosted the signal with magic.

"Forward or backward?" She hesitated and waited for the response. Finally, she panicked and turned to retreat down steps she couldn't even see. Her assumption was if something was going wrong, it was probably behind her.

The door flew open and before she could turn again, she was yanked inside by the back of her jacket. It immediately slammed shut.

She found her feet in a second, slightly dizzy and with her blade out, but couldn't identify anyone to aim it at. The room was in complete darkness.

Whatever it is, it's really fast.

Lexi fumbled for her flashlight but she had lost it, probably on the stairs. A muffled yell issued from farther inside the building.

Her mind began to play tricks. She imagined being surrounded by demons with their teeth bared an arm's length away, and a cold drop of sweat trickled down her back.

Cautiously, her senses alert, she drew her second blade. The long, metallic ring seemed twice as loud in the dark.

She tried to breathe slowly to quiet the sound of blood rushing in her ears. It occurred to her that if she could hear her blood, so could a roomful of demons or vamps. Her heart pumped faster.

As she strained into the silent blackness, she realized she could still hear Scott and that his tiny, tinny voice came from somewhere ahead of her. She'd also lost her earpiece, obviously.

Knowing she had to move, her first instinct was to go toward the device, but she feared they'd be expecting that and block her exit. Instead, she backed up to the door. It had been reinforced and she couldn't feel a handle.

Well, shit!

From there, she inched along the wall to where the window should be. Wooden boards covered it, and she didn't dare to turn her back to the room to try to pry them loose. She continued around the room and kept the wall at her back while she waved her blades ahead and to the sides. As she moved, she tried to calculate the best use of the magic she had.

I could use it to fill the room with light. But if I do that and there are fifty demons in here, I'll need the magic to deal with them. What if I use it on whatever's in here but Scott's injured and I need it to heal him? What if I need it for Dick or Edward?

Life was so much easier with Scott beside her.

Lexi tried to recall if she'd seen any of the room before the door slammed but remembered nothing of any value. She'd heard something fall and roll when she landed and realized that would have been the flashlight. It could have rolled anywhere, though, so wasn't of much use to her.

The pained howl of a wolf broke the silence. Was that Edward? Where was Scott?

She wanted to use magic but because it was finite, it was the last option.

Her next step was taken with the thought that she hoped the floor was intact and that she wouldn't step into thin air. Scott's tinny voice hissed from the earwig again a second before a crunch cut it short, followed by silence.

The sound had pinpointed the location of something, though. She flung a silver-tipped star and was rewarded with a screech.

"You bitch! You'll die for that," said a voice from the darkness. It wasn't one of the demons, then, so probably a vampire. Maybe the one who killed Leonard. She now had the sense it was only the two of them in this room.

"I'll die for *that?* Surely you planned to kill me anyway." She hoped he might respond so she could throw another star.

A second later, he surged into an attack that hurled her face-first to the floor.

His knees dug into her back, and the swords were ripped from her hands. She lay helpless and grimaced as they clattered across the room. Instinctively, she stretched her hand forward in an effort to activate the magic in her unhealing scar, but her arms were wrenched apart.

I should have used the magic earlier.

Drips of liquid landed on her ear, and the metallic tang of blood filled her nostrils. She must have caught him in the face with her shuriken. The thought gave her some satisfaction, but she wasn't strong enough to struggle against him. She had run out of options.

Here we go again, she thought and twisted her head to let the blood drip onto her face. It ran in rivulets down to her nose, chin, and as anticipated, to the edge of her mouth. She licked her lips.

It has been zero days since I last took vamp blood.

Instantly, the darkness was gone and her attacker's face appeared in the corner of her vision. She flashed her gaze around the room. It was empty and dirty with graffiti on the walls and a perfectly round hole in the center of the floor.

Another scream from above dragged her attention away from the odd aperture.

"Poor William isn't faring too well. Caleb asked me to drag it out. It's been fun, but nature will take over shortly. My friends will take him to the east side of the building to meet the sun. Perhaps he's already there. I'm afraid you'll miss that part."

His face descended and she jerked her head back and drove it into his nose.

"*Bitch!*" He pulled away.

Lexi used his momentary withdrawal to shove him off and turn onto her back, but the vamp attacked again. She tried to push him away with her feet but he resisted her effort to force him back. When that failed, she hooked him around the neck with her thighs. He tried to twist his head, no doubt to sink his teeth into her femoral artery. Thanks to his blood coursing through her body, her hold was strong enough that he couldn't immediately extricate himself. By the time he realized his predicament, it was too late.

She flipped to the side and smirked at the satisfying crunch when his neck severed from his spine. He slumped and she rolled free and raced to the window. She jammed the blade of her knife into the corner of the wood and twisted to lever a nail out enough to squeeze her fingers into the gap. Hastily, she wrenched one of the boards off. The vampire, paralyzed on the floor, was unable to move out of the morning sunlight from the east-facing window and burst into flames.

While she was now able to see, she still couldn't work out how to get the door open. She knew she could accomplish it with magic, but it might bring more of them. Frustrated, she sheathed her weapons, turned into the room, and looked through the hole in the floor. Her gaze moved above her and she located the place where bolts had been set in the ceiling. They were in an abandoned fire station.

This was where the pole had stood.

Before she could change her mind, she sat on the edge and dropped to hang by her fingertips. It was a fair distance but she let go, landed with a jarring pain in her ankle, and drew her katana before she'd even caught her breath. She didn't think her ankle was broken, which was good. Her first choice was not to use magic on herself and she preferred to keep it for one of the others, if needed.

She hobbled across the floor and into the hallway. To the left was what had probably been a small kitchenette. A wolf lay dead on the floor. She staggered momentarily in shock until she saw it was brown. Edward's wolf form was white and gray. Its throat had been ripped out, so her teammate had been there. Quickly, she found the way to the stairs. The black smoke was gone and as she started her ascent, a string of expletives came from the hallway to the right. She knew the voice and hobbled around the corner to find Scott once again covered in slime.

"Is this becoming some kind of fetish?" She was relieved, and tight knots of muscle relaxed that she hadn't realized were tense.

"Just don't." He looked furious and she helped him up.

"Why didn't you fix that?" he asked and looked at her foot in the beam of a flashlight.

"Is that my flashlight?" She blinked in recognition.

"It's mine. It fell through a hole in the ceiling and hit me on the head so it's mine now."

He took her hand and whispered something that sounded like "heal."

The pain in her ankle disappeared.

When they reached the foot of the stairs, he shone the light ahead of her and up.

"It's okay, I can see. I've been at the hard stuff again." Lexi strode upward.

"I thought you threw that shit out." Scott sounded disappointed.

She stopped. "I did. I got it from the source this time. It was a situational requirement."

"That's disgusting."

"Yes. Yes, it is. Look." Edward, in human form, peered down at them from two floors above. He appeared to be in pain.

They hurried to where he was crouched and clinging to the railing.

Scott stooped to assess him. He had a bite on his shoulder and a hideous rake across his face and Lexi assumed the blood around his mouth wasn't his.

"Don't waste it on me. I'll heal. See to him." The shifter pointed through a doorway.

The sorcerer placed a hand on his head. "I'll hurry your healing along a little."

She entered the room, where a ripped white shirt lay on the floor with a pair of black pants next to it. At the other side, Dick sprawled in only his boxers and covered by a net of silver. The restraint became more difficult to see when it sank farther into him and hissed and sizzled. It was already deep in his flesh from his head to his feet. He shook violently as though in shock.

"Hey, Dick. Smoldering hot as always." She swallowed. He was difficult to look at but she did it. "There's a vamp downstairs who tried the Lexi Thigh-Ride. I'm afraid he didn't come out of it as well as you did."

He tried and failed to laugh. "I've met him. He doesn't have my sympathy." As he spoke, blood dribbled from his lips. She tried to move the netting from his side and a chunk of flesh lifted with it. He screamed and her stomach churned. Instinctively, she dropped the mesh and it hissed alarmingly.

"How do I look?" he asked through chattering teeth.

"Honestly? Like Pinhead, minus the pins. What happened?"

"I raced out of my front gate at vamp speed, straight through a fucking portal, and into a brick wall."

Scott entered the room and turned immediately to hold onto the door frame. "Jesus, fuck!"

"What can we do?" Lexi asked the vampire.

"Well, it's been on for a while and you can see how deep it is. I think this might be it," Dick said and gritted his teeth to stop them chattering.

"Scott?" Lexi turned to him for guidance.

The young man rubbed at his face. "I'm not sure. On a vamp, silver clings to the skin around it. Taking that off will tear him apart. I can't see how he'd survive it."

"Could you translocate it?"

"Translocation causes friction in the air around the object. It wouldn't be a...helpful result."

"What if we tarnish the silver like Caleb did?"

"That won't work. Tarnish is silver sulfide and water. It would like bathing him in liquid silver." Scott looked away again.

Dick dragged in a strangled breath as the net sank even deeper.

"There's something you can do." He followed his statement with a low keen from the back of his throat.

"What? Anything." Lexi felt defeated.

"You can tell me why you call me Dick. I might not get another chance to find out."

She barked a laugh and choked back tears simultaneously.

"This will be so disappointing," she warned him. "It's because you're a detective. A private dick."

"Are you shitting me?" He raised his head a little, then screamed. After a moment, he continued, "That is so anti-fuck-ing-climactic."

Edward entered the room. The bite marks and scratches were gone. "Can you at least make it so he can't feel it?" His voice broke. He sat beside his friend and slipped his hand under the edge of the net to cover Dick's hand, so far untouched by the net.

"I...uh, I might be able to try something else. I can't tarnish the silver but maybe I could gild it if we had something gold." He pulled his bag from his back, crouched, and began to yank everything out of it. "There must be something. I have to have something gold."

Lexi tapped his shoulder and when he turned, offered him her ring. "Is this enough?"

"The ring Bryan gave you?"

She could see he didn't want to take it. "I've got a new family now and I don't want to lose any of you."

Scott took the ring and turned it over in his fingers. He seemed to be planning how he should approach it. After a long moment, he drew in a deep breath and exhaled slowly. "All right."

He closed his eyes and muttered while sweat gathered on his face. Lexi studied him quickly, a little concerned as he seemed unusually pale. The three of them turned to the vampire and noticed that the visible parts of the silver net began to take on a golden hue from the head downward. The hissing sound it emitted reduced as it changed and finally stopped. When Scott had finished, the ring was completely gone and the net was gold.

"It's not over yet. We still need to get it off him, but it should come easier and his own healing should kick in." He sat on the floor, breathing like he'd run a marathon.

With the net now covered in gold, it slipped more easily out of the flesh but it was still a slow and tense process. It took Scott and Edward about twenty minutes to peel it slowly from Dick, inch by agonizing inch, while Lexi found flattened cardboard and covered the gaps in the windows.

Finally, footfalls on the stairs drew Edward to the door. "In here."

Jesús entered, carrying a length of rolled black plastic, which he dropped at the sight of Dick who was still covered in a bloody pattern. "Santa Maria!"

"He should be healing by now. Why isn't he healing?" Lexi asked.

The Mexican clicked his tongue and shook his head. He turned to the three of them. "Out, you get out now." He herded them out of the room.

"What was that about?" Scott asked.

"He'll feed Will. It will help him heal. I'm embarrassed that I didn't think of it," Edward explained as they sat on the floor in the hallway.

After a few minutes, Jesús appeared at the door. "We can move him now."

They walked in to find Dick zipped into a body bag.

Scott looked at it and tilted his head with a small smile. "I'm surprised he doesn't have a diamond-encrusted body bag."

"I'm right here," the vampire said from inside and his voice sounded like it had gained strength.

"Oh. Where's your earpiece?" Scott asked Lexi as he picked the net up.

She slung his bag over her shoulder. "The vamp stamped on it."

"He busted your communicator? What a bastard." He shook his head.

Startled, she stared at him with her mouth agape. "He also killed Leonard and tortured Dick. I know you like your tech but get some fucking perspective." She slapped him upside the head and walked out.

CHAPTER SIXTEEN

Caleb sat in his office the next morning and waited to receive the call informing him of Todd's death. He wondered if he should have called off his request to burn William's home after he'd set up the portal trap, but what was the point? The mayor had to be dealt with sooner or later and sooner was better.

For a few moments, he fantasized about the call. Would it come from Stanley? Betsy? He imagined feigning shock and horror, then he imagined telling Betsy the truth and watching her little old face crumble. The mental image made him chuckle. It no longer mattered, though. Tonight was the night. It had to be. He'd clear Kate out of that store, pull its magical wards down, and tear it to pieces.

He was distracted by visions of Todd burning, his hair aflame and face crackling. Irritated, he shook his head. *Not now.*

Hahahahaha. Azatoth laughed in his mind.

The telephone in the outer office rang, then his personal line. "Yes,"

His secretary spoke. "It's Mr. Hughes."

His lawyer would no doubt have called to confirm that everything was ready to go ahead. "Put him through... Donald. How are things?"

"Hello, Caleb. I haven't received the paperwork from the mayor's office."

"You haven't? That's strange. Todd was going to send it last night." He hung up.

Caleb tried to recall if he had told Todd to send it or bring it. Conflicting orders—such as "Bring this to me after you've killed yourself"—didn't always raise the flags it should. He was sure he'd told him to send it. If the news of his death had reached his staff, they might have failed to forward it. He'd have to find out. The next mayor might not be as malleable as Todd had proven to be. He picked the phone up. "Get me the mayor's office."

The call was answered without delay. "Mayor's office."

"It's Caleb Linden. Put me through to the mayor."

"I'm sorry, Mr. Linden. The office is in disarray at the moment. We don't currently have a mayor."

"My condolences." He stifled a giggle that wasn't his own.

"I'm sorry?" The voice sounded puzzled.

"I...sorry, I automatically assumed..." He left the sentence incomplete and experienced a niggling feeling of doubt.

"The mayor has taken an extended break."

"He's...are you sure?"

"Yes. He called this morning and he's had a sudden family emergency. But he did ask me to send a package to you. It should be in your hands within the hour."

"I see. Thank you for your assistance."

Caleb disconnected and leaned back to consider what could have happened. Perhaps his brain had finally scrambled and he had been committed? It didn't matter. The paperwork was on its way.

He walked to the wall of bookcases, opened a drinks cabinet, and poured himself a whiskey.

Ten minutes later, the delivery arrived. His secretary placed it on his desk and left, and he smiled. Everything was turning out fine. A little last-minute, maybe, but that was okay. He opened the envelope and slid the documents out, and the smile froze on his face and slowly faded. The envelope contained several blank sheets, although the one on the front presented a clear message. It was a photocopy of two hands flipping the bird. He recognized Todd's class ring and Betsy's engagement ring.

How uncouth.

William was behind this. He knew it. Reluctantly, he came to the conclusion that things hadn't gone according to plan at the abandoned fire station either.

Caleb rocked thoughtfully in his chair. *I don't like this. There's too much interference. I think it's time to put my contingency plan into place.*

Azatoth spoke. *Dismember them.*

He rolled his eyes. *That might be overkill.* He looked at the telephone. *They won't like this.*

Azatoth hissed. *They don't have to like it. They serve...you.*

The man smiled again. William and his friends would have a nasty surprise if they interfered. He wadded the paper, dropped it into the trash, and snatched the phone.

CHAPTER SEVENTEEN

Lexi was awoken by the sound of Edward's telephone ringing. Having lost her favorite sweats in the junk-filled suitcase, she slipped quickly into shorts and a t-shirt. She headed past Scott's empty room and continued to the kitchen. Edward stood beside the kitchen door, speaking on the phone.

"I'm very well, Stanley. How are you? I hear we've got a wedding to attend."

He listened.

"Why would Tommy be worried? Marcia told me they were going to some spa or whatever it is women do these days."

The shifter glanced at her and raised an eyebrow. "Yes, I heard you'd requested that they hold the wedding immediately and it's about time, in my opinion. Those two have been pussyfooting around long enough. Marcia said that was why they were going to the spa—to get away from the menfolk and plan a wedd— You wanted it today? Is she pregnant? Well, I'll be honest, Stan. She's got a lot of family around here. I'm sure they'd be put out to miss Kate's wedding. Why not make it a month from now? Give me a chance to fit into my suit."

Edward held the phone away from his ear and Stan's tinny voice could be heard screeching through it. He rolled his eyes.

"You seem a little on edge there, Stanley. Is everything okay? Stanley? Stanley?" He hung up and smiled. "I think we were disconnected."

Lexi sat, picked up her low-tops, and slipped them on. "He sounded hysterical. Is he normally like that?"

"No." He tilted his head and drew his brows together in thought. "He sounds like the mayor did last night when he couldn't burn Dick like he was supposed to."

Lexi instinctively tried to twist her ring. When she realized her finger was empty, she placed her hands on the table in front of her. "So, the need to get them married is definitely part of the compulsion."

"I don't get it. Why now and why so fast? Caleb's been here for years. If he always planned to force this wedding through, he could have told Stan to demand it before now." Edward shook his head.

She stood and looked along the hall to the basement door. "How's Dick?"

"He's sleeping and healing. He'll be okay." Edward sat at the table and shuffled paper as she wandered away to locate the others.

Dolores sat at a table in the garden, watching as Scott threw a ball for Marcel. The puppy chased it and when it stopped rolling, he stood and barked at it.

"You're supposed to bring it back." The sorcerer explained Fetch to Marcel as though he were speaking to a human, then gave it another try with—unsurprisingly—the same result.

Lexi took a seat next to the woman. "How are you feeling?"

"I believe the kids would say I'm 'coming down.'"

She face-palmed. "I am so sorry."

"Well, I'm happy you don't actually have monsters living in your dimensional pocket. It needs a damn good cleaning in there, though, and I don't think I'll ever be able to look at chocolate again."

"It won't happen again—" she began.

Dolores leaned forward. "You need to train so you don't have to resort to such things."

Lexi spread her arms. "Well…you know, as soon as I can get to the gym."

"You don't need to wait for that." The woman turned toward the house. "Edward, dear?"

He came out through the patio doors. "Yes, Dolores?"

"Are you busy right now?"

"I've got my beta coming over in an hour. What do you need?"

"Lexi needs a little workout. If you manage to bite her, I'll give you this shiny dollar." She held a dollar coin out and put it on the table in front of her.

"What?" Lexi's jaw dropped.

The shifter grinned and flexed his leg.

"She's kidding." She turned to Dolores. "You're kidding, right?"

"I'll give you a three-minute head-start." Edward started to shift.

Lexi bolted into the woods. Knowing she couldn't outrun him, she tried to think strategically. Her performance was still enhanced a little from the diminishing vampire blood in her system, which was as well because she was now too far away from Scott to draw magic. She found a small grove of trees and ran around it. When she reached her starting place, she bounded as far as she could in another direction. She gauged that the jump took her almost thirty feet before she vaulted into the branches of a tree, hid behind the trunk, and peeked out.

As expected, she didn't have long to wait. A few seconds later, Edward appeared, padding along at a leisurely pace. He followed her scent around the grove and returned to the starting place. After a moment, he made another circuit, this time at a trot.

She watched from the tree with a smile.

When he reached the beginning again, he sat on his haunches and tilted his head but soon set off again at a run. She shuffled to turn and sit with her back against the tree while she held her hand over her mouth to silence her laugh. When she looked again, there was no sign of her pursuer.

Damn. I should have paid attention.

The grove was empty and she waited a few seconds to see if he would repeat his search, but he made no appearance. She climbed silently from the tree and she decided it was time to move on. Uncertain which direction to choose, she stood motionless behind the trunk and tried to make a decision when a long, wet, warm tongue licked the back of her leg from her ankle to the edge of her shorts.

Lexi shrieked. "Dude, that's gross."

Edward shifted. "That was for tricking me. First one back gets that shiny dollar." He began to shift again and she ran.

When she came out of the tree line, Edward was seated with Dolores, spinning the dollar, and looked like he hadn't even broken a sweat. He smirked and she stuck her tongue out at him as she strode past.

She showered, donned her familiar leathers, and joined the others again.

"Betsy called." Scott passed her a glass of juice. "Todd remembers everything."

"Everything? He knows what he tried to do?" She raised her eyebrows.

The shifter followed her into the house and stood for a moment while he tested the temperature of a bowlful of scrambled eggs. "He wants to know what Scott did to his mother." He put the bowl on the floor and scratched Marcel's neck as he descended on it. "Todd's upset because Betsy seems perfectly at ease with William being a vampire." The others joined them in the kitchen.

"What'll he do? Will he tell anyone?" For some reason, everyone absently watched Marcel snarf the food as if it were the most fascinating thing in the world.

Edward straightened. "You can ask him yourself. They're coming over."

Lexi looked at the others, who didn't seem concerned. "Is that safe? They might be followed."

"A few of the pack are waiting on the highway to deter anyone following."

An hour later, Betsy, Todd, and Jess joined them in Edward's kitchen.

"Is William here?" Betsy was fidgeting.

"William's catching up on his sleep. He's more of a night owl." Edward smiled.

"Oh, of course." The woman giggled. "Does he sleep in a coffin?"

The shifter laughed. "This is Will we're talking about. He sleeps in Ralph Lauren sheets and won't let anything with a thread count lower than six hundred touch his skin."

Betsy smiled. "Our William always did like to have the best."

Todd shook his head. "Well, we can't stay. We're on our way to the airport. I'm getting Mother the hell out of here. We're going to Europe."

"Oh, the vampire capital of the world." Dolores smiled.

The man froze.

She laughed. "Kidding."

Betsy joined her laughter and patted Todd's arm while he shook his head.

He held an envelope up. "I wanted to drop this off. Caleb asked me to post it last night. It was still in the outbound mail tray this morning." He put the envelope on the table. "It's my approval for further construction work to go ahead at various properties Caleb's been buying up on Palm Canyon Drive. I've voided it and requested a full investigation into his proposal."

Lexi turned to face his mother. "Can you tell me what you know about Caleb?"

The woman frowned. "He appeared nearly six years ago and came to the house a few times to meet with Harv. He seemed very pleasant. Then, out of nowhere, Harv announced he was taking Caleb on as a partner so he could expand the business. I was shocked. We'd been talking about selling the business. Within a year, Harvey died of what we thought was a heart attack and Caleb bought out Harv's half of the company."

"This sounds familiar. It's almost exactly what happened with Kate's father."

"The bastard." Todd clenched his jaw and fists simultaneously as though they were one muscle. "I still can't believe he killed Dad. What the hell is he? Mom says he's a sorcerer. Things like that don't even exist. And what did he want with our family business?"

"You were never interested in the company, Todd. I'd have sold it anyway."

"How are you taking this shit so well?" He looked exasperated but realized he'd cursed in his mother's presence. "Sorry, Mom."

"When you've lived as long as I have, you're never really surprised by anything. The good *or* the bad." Betsy stood, collected her bag, and took both of Lexi's hands. "Give William my love and tell him to be careful. You too, dear. I'll call William tomorrow. Oh! Tomorrow night."

The visitors left, followed by their wolfen motorcade.

"I've been looking into Caleb Linden too," Dolores announced. "I've only been able to trace that name back about ten years. He didn't exist before then."

Lexi "So who the hell is he?"

"He bought a mining operation in South Africa. There was

some kind of investigation because employees stopped going home after a while. Then, he simply abandoned it, sold up, and moved here. There was another purchase of land in England, but there doesn't seem to have been any activity at the site. So, what do we think?" Dolores asked.

The younger woman leaned against the counter and folded her arms. "I think I want to know what's so special about Kate's land."

"And why now?" Edward added. "We can assume the demand for Kate and Tommy to marry immediately has come from Caleb. What's so special about now?"

"Some supernatural group you are," Jess said from the doorway.

They looked up to where she stood at the patio doors.

Edward shrugged. "What are we missing?"

"It's the solstice." She entered and took an apple from a bowl on the countertop. Her movements casual, she pulled a chair out and turned it before she sat on it backward and took a bite from the fruit.

Dolores rolled her eyes. "I feel stupid for missing that."

The shifter's phone rang again, and he moved away to answer it.

"So, we've got a working theory for why now, but we still don't know what's at the heart of this." Lexi frowned in thought.

Scott turned to her. "Do you remember that weird vibe I got at the bar?"

"The one that nearly got you flattened by a truck? Yes, I remember it. And those Norse protection runes hanging from the ceiling."

Jess straightened. "Kira makes those. She and Daisy belong to the local coven."

The young man picked Marcel up and allowed the puppy to lick his nose. He turned to Jess. "Does Daisy sell them in her flower shop?"

"I don't think so. I don't remember them having price tags." The woman bit a piece of apple off and offered it to Marcel, who snapped it out of her fingers and dropped it immediately on the table and shook his head.

Dolores picked up the discarded fruit and placed it on the edge of her plate. "Jess, can you find out why Kate wanted the runes? She might simply have liked the look of them."

"I'll see what I can do." She stood and headed outside with her cell in her hand.

The woman sighed and her brow wrinkled as she thought. "Tell me about the demons."

Scott leaned forward. "Size of a man, black, jello-like skin, except for the pincers and claws on their arms and legs which were gray, huge mouths, and too many teeth."

"Poisonous skin," interrupted Edward with his hand over the mouthpiece of the phone.

"Way too many eyes. Like, all over its freaking head," Lexi added.

"They burst into goop when they die. It's gross." The young man shuddered.

Dolores nodded. "I know what you're describing. Did you notice its weaknesses?"

Lexi folded her arms. "My katana."

The other woman rolled her eyes. "Anything else?"

"Like what?" Now, she leaned forward too.

"These creatures don't have noses. They smell through their mouths and they don't have ears. They hear through soundwaves bouncing off their eyes. Loud noises can effectively blind them. They are vile lower-level creatures, have a hive mentality, and communicate by clicking their pincers. If they can't communicate, they can freak out but twice, you've met them acting alone, which is unusual."

"Good to know, but I hope to never see one of those things again." Scott shook his head in disgust.

"She what?" Edward pinched the bridge of his nose as he listened. "Okay. It looks like we've got a wedding to attend. Gather here as soon as you can and we'll travel together." He disconnected and turned to face them.

"That was Marcia, Kate's mom. Tommy turned up and spoke to Kate, and she went off on the back of his bike."

"Can we head them off?" Scott made to stand but stopped when Edward shook his head and spoke quickly into his cell phone.

"You think the wedding's going ahead today?" Lexi noted three of the wolf pack from the perimeter were walking out of the tree line.

Jess entered quickly. "It's definitely going ahead today. Kate took her wedding dress."

Edward moved the cell away from his ear. "How do you know?"

"Kira was squeezing into her bridesmaid dress when I called. She wasn't happy."

Edward returned to his call.

Scott looked up from Marcel. "Why?"

"She thought she had longer to lose weight and bought it a size too small." She rolled her eyes.

The shifter returned. "I hope you asked where the ceremony's taking place."

"It's at a private club—the same place the mayor's fundraiser was. I hear you're familiar with it." Jess had walked around the table and now put her hand on Scott's shoulder and leaned down to stroke Marcel, who dozed in his arms.

Lexi felt irked by the move and deliberately looked away. "We're dressing for a wedding, then."

Edward moved coffee mugs into the sink. "I am, you're not."

"Excuse me?" She raised her eyebrows.

"While Caleb's distracted by the wedding, you need to get to the bar and find out what's going on there. Jess, you go with them. Caleb's already got the rest of that block, which includes the storage warehouse at the back. I'd guess whatever's going on started there."

"Good call." She nodded her agreement and could see why this man was the pack leader.

"Dolores, you'll be safe here—" the shifter started.

"I'm coming to the wedding. I'd like to get a look at this Caleb Linden." She stood, headed to the family room, and returned seconds later dressed for a wedding.

Within five minutes, the two friends were in Jess's car and on the way to Palm Springs.

Scott leaned forward between the seats. "Did you learn anything more about the runes?"

Jess flicked her gaze to him in the rearview mirror. "The coven sells them at a farmer's market, along with other Wicca and witchcraft paraphernalia. She gave those particular ones to Daisy when she first moved into the store. Apparently, the flower shop is on a site that was owned or rented by a palm reader in the thirties—Princess Zoraida. She already had a good reputation when she arrived from doing a couple years at the World's Fair in New York, but when she moved into the store, her 'connection to the other side' became much stronger." She took her hands off the wheel to make air quotes, and he wriggled uncomfortably in the back.

"Scott, can you text Dick to see if he remembers this Princess Palm-Reader?"

"Zoraida," the other woman corrected.

"Yes, that. He'll get it when he wakes up. It shouldn't be long," she confirmed with a nod.

"I'll park near the entrance to the storage place." Jess glanced at Lexi, who nodded again.

They stood in front of the gate and studied the *Closed for remodel* sign.

"I thought these places were supposed to be accessible twenty-four seven?" Lexi raised her leg to kick the gate.

"Wait." Scott muttered a few words, and the barrier glowed. "Don't touch it. There's a protection spell on it. The rest of the fence looks okay." He walked along it and waggled a finger between the metal bars. The posts bent as though he'd hit them with a truck.

Jess clapped him on the shoulder and whistled. "Magneto!"

They jogged across the parking lot to the building's entrance.

With one last furtive look around them, they stepped inside. No one sat at the reception desk. Jess headed toward a set of double doors in a hallway behind the desk that led farther into the building. She pulled on the handles but they were locked and she scowled at the security pad beside the door. Lexi, who had come up beside her, glanced around and noticed there were several such doors.

The shifter turned to Scott. "Can you do your thing?" She wiggled her fingers.

"We need to be careful about using magic in here. Caleb's probably left a few surprises for intruders. Magic could set them off."

"We could take a door each and kick it in," Jess suggested.

Lexi shook her head. "We're not splitting up, not until we know what's going on in here." She looked at a map on the wall beside the door that showed the layout of the facility. Removing a shuriken from her pocket, she popped it onto the front of her leather vest. It stayed there, thanks to the magnet in the lining of the vest

A door down the hall opened.

They froze.

A man walked toward them but he didn't seem particularly concerned about them. He wore a dirty shirt that had at some point been white, a lanyard, and a *My Name's Clyde, I'm happy to serve you* badge from a local pizzeria.

As he approached, Scott stepped into his path and he stopped.

"Hi, we're looking for a staff member. Can you—"

The newcomer walked around him without acknowledging him or even focusing on him, turned to the double doors, swiped the card, and walked through. Jess slipped her foot into the crack before it could close.

They followed My-Name's-Clyde-I'm-happy-to-serve-you down the hallway and past roller shutters on either side to another set of double doors. When he opened them, Lexi drew the shuriken, used it to slice through the sleepwalking man's lanyard, and caught the pass with her other hand as it fell. He turned unexpectedly, and the shuriken bit into his neck.

"Oops!" She stepped back to give herself clear fighting space, but he made no sound. He trailed blood as he continued to walk down the hallway. She popped the shuriken onto her vest and turned to the others to show them she had the lanyard. They stared beyond her with shock on their faces. When she spun again, her jaw dropped.

"What the fuck?" she whispered and drew her katana.

The hallway ended abruptly ahead of them at what, according to the map, would have been a junction with hallways leading forward, left, and right, each lined with storage units.

The roller-shuttered doors of the units were still present on one side of the hallway, but everything ahead of them was gone. The units and the rest of the facility had been replaced by a huge pit about two hundred feet across and God only knew how deep. It curved in sections toward the southeast and a mechanical grumbling came from its depths.

Scott appeared at her shoulder. "That's moving toward where the flower shop would be, isn't it?"

Lexi nodded. She looked to her left and where Clyde, with

blood dribbling freely down his dirty shirt, descended a ladder at the end of the hallway and vanished from sight.

Her eyes narrowed in focus, she peered across the chasm and located many such ladders between levels descending into the pit. She counted them. "This is insane. I see at least ten stories." As she stared in disbelief, the workers at the bottom smoothed the dirt into curved sections like spirals.

People traveled up and down ladders as though asleep. They wore work clothes, uniforms, and pajamas, and a woman in a wedding dress stumbled along in one high-heeled shoe as she dragged a length of wood.

"There! It's Daisy." Jess pointed across the chasm. Lexi tried to identify her but there were too many people. Having never seen her, she couldn't guess which one was the flower-seller.

"You see those curves? It's kind of a shell pattern. What is it?" she tilted her head in various different angles as she tried to make it out.

Scott peered at it, his expression focused. "It's a nautilus shell. We need to get out of here."

"Just a second." She stepped to the top of the ladder. Clyde, who was on the next level down, walked toward the top of the next ladder. The sudden movement of dark shapes against the dirt walls alerted her to the presence of something she really didn't want to see again, and she stepped back.

Several demons with their many eyes and arms scuttled along the wall toward the man and descended upon him.

It must have been the smell of blood. Sorry, Clyde.

She retreated out of the sight of the slaughter. "You're right. We need to go."

They turned quickly but found their retreat blocked by three demons that had crept up behind them. The closest was a few feet away from Jess. Scott jerked his arm toward it with a word. The beast glowed for a moment, then scuttled sideways onto a unit door between them and the exit and moved toward them. It used its legs and two arms to hold it securely in place and held four more arms and their talons poised to strike.

Scott shook. "It's shielded against magic."

"I bet the door isn't." Lexi drew her finger down the unhealing scar and the door burst and catapulted the creature out and over the pit, and it plummeted.

The other demons crept closer but seemed more hesitant now.

A low growl issued from Jess, who had shifted.

"Don't bite them, they're poisonous," she warned the woman.

The shifter moved forward and back several times, and Lexi realized she was distracting them.

Scott extended his open hand to her. She passed him the katana and he vanished.

When he reappeared behind the second of the remaining demons, he positioned himself to strike but saw too late that its black eyes also continued to the back of its head. The creature's six arms—which had been poised to strike forward—flicked toward him.

At the same moment, he disappeared again and appeared between the two demons with his back to one of them.

He delivered a mighty slash immediately to behead the creature and reappeared beside Lexi seconds before its body burst into slime.

The remaining demon had flipped its talons toward where he had stood a moment before.

Before it could right itself, she threw a shuriken into one of its eyes, and the creature uttered a high-pitched squeal.

She realized there was no hope of blinding it, though. "This thing must have fifty eyes. Screw this."

Jess darted forward, and she used the distraction provided by the shifter to plunge her *wakizashi* into its brain, then danced away to avoid its flailing talons. It fell and curled. She stepped forward to retrieve the blade and shuriken, but Scott held her back. A second later, it burst. She snatched her blade by the handle as it began to fall into the ooze. After a horrified moment in which she stared at the shuriken covered by the goop, she sighed and put her hands into the mess to retrieve it.

They stood in silence to regroup and something scuttled closer. The demon's squeal had drawn attention.

"Move." Lexi pushed Scott and Jess toward the entrance and ran behind them, looking over her shoulder every two seconds the whole way.

The sorcerer smacked the green buttons to release the doors but the scuttling sounds of the demons in pursuit grew louder.

CHAPTER EIGHTEEN

As Edward and Dolores approached the club, they were almost run off the driveway by a bus full of wedding guests coming in the opposite direction.

She clutched the door when he swerved to avoid them. "I hope we haven't missed the wedding."

They turned onto a side road leading to the parking lot and delivery entrance at the back of the building.

The woman withdrew a gift-wrapped box from her purse.

His eyes bulged. "A wedding gift? You like to be prepared."

"I was a Girl Scout." She rearranged the glittery bow.

Edward's brow creased. "In Fae?"

"In Wisconsin." Dolores released her seatbelt as the car drew to a halt.

They climbed out of the car and started to walk toward the entrance. He looked across to the playground, shouted, "Oh, my God!" and bolted.

When she caught up, he was crouched over two young children. They had been playing with nerf guns and the ground was littered with foam projectiles.

"Are they..." She didn't dare say it.

"No, they're only asleep but I can't wake them." He felt hurriedly for a pulse.

Dolores put her hand on his shoulder. "I guess he's keeping them out of the way. Leave them. They're probably safer asleep."

Edward stood and strode away from the children.

They passed through the kitchen, and no one batted an eyelid at their presence.

"The security in this place is shocking," she observed. "I mean, I'm not complaining or anything."

He approached a cook. "Excuse me, we seem to be—"

The man looked straight through him as he stirred a bowl.

She peered into the bowl. It was empty. "Caleb has enthralled them all."

The shifter looked more closely at the staff. "You're right." He studied a young man with a cheese grater. The cheese was long gone and he now grated his hand and seemed to have done so for some time. Edward winced and looked away.

"That's horrific." Dolores spun away.

He shook his head. "Do you have any fae magic that can make him stop?"

"Yes, I do." She looked around, found a rolling pin, and cracked the man on the back of the head. He fell into an ungainly heap.

Edward crouched to check the man's vitals. "If you ever feel inclined to work fae magic on me, don't bother."

"You wanted him to stop and he stopped." Dolores passed him a tea towel.

He bound the mangled hand, his expression both angry and a little confused. "Why would Caleb do this?"

"I don't think he'd do it intentionally. There's no point. I think he's merely stretched too thin. He's trying to control too much. It's easier for him if he simply puts them into a loop."

The shifter looked around the kitchen. "Well, I'm relieved to find he has limits."

They stood next to a cart with a wedding cake on it. Written in icing was *Chester and Jeanette.*

"I don't understand it. All this over a strip of land. He's hijacked someone else's wedding to force Kate and Tommy to marry so he can gain access to the bar? Why? Why didn't he simply walk in there and brainwash her months ago? We're missing something."

Dolores found a white apron and tied it around her waist, then gave the gift to him. "I need to get to work. You find Kate and see if we can get her out of here." She picked up a tray of champagne glasses and headed through a swinging door to the party.

Edward gave her thirty seconds before he followed her through the door. He walked along a hallway that opened into a large ballroom. A man stood on the stage in the corner of the room and held a microphone, and although his lips were moving, no sound came from his mouth. He'd probably been singing for hours. The shifter continued to the next room, which had been set up for the ceremony. People were seated in the chairs and simply stared ahead. He worked his way around to the foyer and headed up the stairs, then crept along the hallway and listened at doors as he passed. About halfway along the hall, he heard crying from a room near the end. He knocked quietly and walked in.

Kate was seated in her wedding dress with mascara running down her face.

"Kate?" He didn't know if she might be in the hypnotic cycle too.

"Edward!" She stared at him. "Are you...normal?"

"Not if you ask my ex-wife."

She bounded up and wrapped her arms around him. "I'm sorry. I know I shouldn't have left. Tommy told me Caleb would massacre my family if I didn't come and get married. I didn't know what else to do. But I got here and I don't know these people. There's something wrong with them. I think this has something to do with the bar, because last night—"

"Okay, calm down. I'm here to get you out. Less talking, more moving." He ushered her toward the door.

Edward opened the bedroom door a crack and peeked out.

He whispered, "Surely there are back stairs in a place this size. They must be at the other end of the hall. We need to move quickly."

They hurried down the hallway and reached an open landing leading to the stairs to the foyer. Edward saw the fire exit sign at the other end.

"We'll have to move quickly to that exit."

He took her hand, looked her in the eye, and nodded once. She nodded in response.

They stepped out and prepared to move when the band struck up. Both of them startled, paused, and gazed down the steps. The guests stood at the bottom and stared at them with huge, empty smiles and weariness behind their eyes. The Palm Springs pack were gathered—about thirty men and women and all unsmiling. He looked at the fire exit and considered their chances of sprinting to it when he felt a hand on his shoulder and turned.

"Stanley, good to see you." Edward noted that the man appeared to have stepped out of a room behind them. "I was worried I'd missed the main event. I've come to give the bride away on behalf of her mother." He offered his hand to Stan, who merely stared at it.

"That's awfully kind of you, Edward."

He jumped at the new voice. Caleb stood on the other side of Kate, sweating profusely. There was no room he could have hidden in. He had appeared as though from thin air.

The mental weight of the man immediately seemed to thrust down on him. He was confident that he wouldn't be able to pick any thoughts from his head, but he knew that was the least of his worries.

"Now that you're here, let's get started." The man's smile was cold.

They descended the stairs. Kate held onto him tightly and he felt her shaking.

The moment they reached the bottom of the staircase, several of Stan's pack launched at Edward. He managed a couple of good swings before they surrounded him. It took several men to hold his arms back and force him to his knees.

"Now, let's see what you're hiding." Caleb placed his hand on the shifter's head.

As the man strained, Edward saw Dolores in his peripheral vision. He dared not turn toward her.

Caleb removed his hand, having been unable to access the shifter's thoughts. "Unfortunate. No matter. I can still manipulate you and through you, your pack as well as Kate. As soon as Kate is under my control, I can get what I want from her."

"Not likely," the woman retorted before Stanley smacked her across the mouth.

Edward growled. Caleb looked at Kate and smiled, and the shifter took the chance to glance at Dolores. He could see she wanted to help him but knew that would destroy any chance of stopping their quarry in the long run.

"This might hurt a little." His captor placed his hand on his head again.

The shifter looked directly at him. "Don't mind me. You do what you've got to do." He wasn't speaking to him, though. Dolores stepped into the crowd.

Edward closed his eyes and released Jess and Kate from the pack, which was his right as alpha.

It's up to you now, Jess.

CHAPTER NINETEEN

The three teammates didn't stop running. Jess didn't shift into human form until they were on the other side of the fence at the car. They scrambled into the little vehicle.

"Fucking go in!" she shouted at her key as she tried to jam it into the ignition with a shaking hand.

Lexi leaned closer, placed a hand on top of the woman's, and made eye contact. The shifter's eyes were golden, an indication that she might turn again. "Breathe."

Jess leaned back, put her hands in her lap, and breathed slowly in and out. After a few seconds, she opened her brown eyes and nodded at her, then slid the key in and started the engine.

They rounded the corner and Scott shouted from the back of the car, "Wait. The door of the flower shop is ajar."

"Are you sure?" The shifter tried to glance at it as they passed.

"He's right." Lexi pulled a shuriken out and placed it on her vest. "Scott, can you shield us?"

"Done." He nodded once.

She looked up and down the road but didn't see anyone watching. Of course, they were dealing with a sorcerer so that didn't mean they weren't being watched by a dozen of Stanley's brainwashed wolves.

"Oh!" Jess stopped outside the store with her hand on her chest.

Lexi glanced at her.

Scott turned to face her. "That's being caused by whatever's going on underground. It got me the first time. Try to ignore it."

"I'm not usually sensitive to this kind of thing. It's weird, I feel…kind of lonely." Tears welled in her eyes and she blinked them away and looked embarrassed.

Lexi glanced at her. "Magic hits people in different ways, especially bad magic."

They crept into the store and found a young woman removing flowers from buckets. She stopped what she was doing and turned slowly. Her eyes and nose were red, and she appeared to have been crying. Looking around, she narrowed her swollen eyes and frowned.

She removed a short, nasty-looking knife from her pocket. "You seem to be trying quite hard to remain unseen. Should I start waving this around indiscriminately?"

"Would you unshield me, please, Scott?" Jess asked.

He did as he was asked.

"Hi, Kira." The shifter gave her a little finger wave.

"Holy shit, Jess!" The tension dropped from the other woman's shoulders.

"Sorry. We didn't know who was in here. Are you okay?"

"My allergies are playing merry hell in here. Speaking of 'we,' I know you didn't do that yourself. Perhaps I could meet your friend?"

Scott took the rest of the shield down.

"This is Scott and Lexi. Kate called them to help with the problems she's been having."

He peered at Kira in her bridesmaid's dress and glanced into the box she was filling with flowers. "I guess you're picking a bridal bouquet."

She nodded, then looked at Jess. "What's going on? I got a five-second call from Kate, then you called about my protection runes. It's all a little sudden." She pulled out the bodice of her dress and took a deep breath, then sneezed.

Lexi glanced at one of the runes, which seemed to move slightly as though there was a breeze. There was none, however, and she returned her gaze to the young woman.

Kira focused on it too. "Something bad's going on here. Those have been vibrating since I walked in."

"Yes, you might want to get out of here. A sorcerer is up to something awful underground. Do you know Caleb Linden?"

The girl shuddered. "I've met him. I knew he was something, but I get that vibe quite often from people who don't know they have latent abilities. I tend to ignore it. It's none of my business." She continued to pull flowers from buckets.

Scott rubbed the back of his neck. "The vibes here are incredibly strong."

"I know! I almost didn't come in. There's always been something here. Previously, it was residual and connected to Zoraida, but it's stronger today than I've ever felt it. There's supposed to be work going on at the storage place in back of here, but it feels as though it's right beneath my feet. I thought they might have disturbed something." Kira turned to her task.

Lexi walked around to face her. "Caleb has a group of brainwashed people there, and they're digging a giant pit. Daisy's there and some nasty lower-level demons. The pit's almost the size of the block."

The woman dropped the flowers in her hand. "Demons? What's he doing?"

Scott shrugged when his teammate looked at him. "He's opening a portal to hell."

Jess rubbed her forehead. "Hell isn't below us. That's bullshit. I've seen subways deeper than that."

He turned to her to explain. "There are different dimensions and certainly more than one hell dimension. They move in their own orbits and occasionally move through the earth, but it's very rare that one coincides with when the veil between the dimensions is thin."

"Like now, on the solstice." Kira nodded as the significance came to her.

"So Caleb has decided this is the best time and place for a breach." Lexi glanced at the runes again.

Scott turned to Kira. "Do you have much more to do? You shouldn't hang around. They're making a nautilus portal. That means something's coming through—something very bad.

The woman nodded. "Okay, I need a length of white ribbon, then I'm done. I'll have to contact the coven."

She yanked flowers out of various buckets while he walked to a reel of ribbon on the wall and tugged it. The ribbon cascaded from the reel, and he gathered it quickly. He looked on the surface of the desk, tried a drawer and found it locked, then stretched to the shuriken on Lexi's vest. He picked it off and sliced cleanly through the ribbon. It left a fine line of red blood on the fabric. "Oops." He turned it to a different blade and cut again.

Noticing Lexi's raised eyebrow, he said, "Thanks." He moved to replace the shuriken onto the vest, then seemed to think better of it and handed it to her.

"You're welcome." She rolled her eyes, took it, and returned it to its position.

With another smirk at her friend, she turned to thank Kira and leave when a loud crack drew everyone's attention.

One of the willow-twig runes had split down the middle. They remained silent and watched as half of it fell to the floor.

"I'm getting out of here." Kira picked her box of flowers up and headed to the door with Scott and Jess directly behind.

Lexi looked from the half-rune swinging in the air to the other one, which was also swaying. She followed the others through the door.

Kira looked into the box of flowers. "I hope these are okay. I can tell you the magical and healing properties of any herb but I don't know a thing about flowers. I have no interest, not with my allergies."

Jess stared at the store. "What happened to the rune?"

"A portal to hell would require very strong magic. It's encroaching on the store. I think it would be best if I forget the wedding and call the head of my coven." The woman shook her head and turned to the others.

She put the box on the ground, then found a tissue and blew her nose before she retrieved her cell phone.

Lexi touched Scott's arm. "Can you do anything to bolster the protection in the remaining rune?"

He shook his head. "I don't think that's a good idea. It would interfere with what's already active. The rune could end up useless."

"Have a look through the window at the bar. How do they look?"

In response, he jogged to the front of the bar and looked through the window. He gave a thumbs-up and ran back. "They're fine. Still hanging and not moving."

She looked at the flower shop again. "So, it looks like the portal will be directly under the flower shop. This might explain why it's all so last-minute with Kate's property. It's merely Caleb's bad luck. He dug up the rest of the block and the thinnest point is under the one piece of land he doesn't own."

Jess took her keys out. "You think ownership's a factor?"

"It's all guesswork, but yes." She nodded. "Did Edward get back to you yet?"

"Not yet." The shifter shook her head.

"Can you contact the pack and let them know what's happening?"

The beta gave a curt nod and stepped away.

"Shit!" Lexi rubbed her face.

"What?" Scott looked worried. He could probably sense her conflict.

"This is huge. Are we even equipped to deal with this? We might need to call Kindred."

His jaw dropped.

"We've got a low-level demonic invasion going on down there. Something must have already aligned enough to let them through, and it looks like these are nothing compared to what's coming."

Jess began to cross to the other side of the street.

Kira put her cell away and turned to her. "The coven is coming here. We'll shore up the defenses in the store. They'll start getting here within ten minutes. The farthest is half an hour away. I assume you'll go to the wedding." She picked the box of flowers up. "Here's your invitation."

Scott opened the trunk and moved aside for her to put the box into it.

"Thanks." The woman smiled at him but looked away when his teammate closed the trunk much louder than necessary.

The two women glared at each other.

Lexi rolled her eyes. "Portal to hell?" she reminded them and headed to the front of Jess's car.

Scott followed her, completely oblivious to the interaction.

Jess joined them again. "I can't reach Edward or anyone through the pack link."

He thought for a moment. "Caleb might be blocking your communication with magic."

Kira was standing across the street from the flower shop when Ulla, a coven member, arrived. She parked and joined her on the pavement.

"I'm here. I had to lie to get out of work. If this is some kind of joke, I'll sue you for an hour's pay."

"Let's cross. I didn't want to go back alone." She led the newcomer across the street but Ulla froze halfway, obviously feeling it.

The woman took a step backward. "What *is* that?"

"It's why we're here. Come on, we need to get started." She tried to encourage her to move forward but she wouldn't budge.

Ulla shook her head. "I'm not going there, just the two of us. What the hell is it?"

"We need to strengthen the protections to counteract some very dark magic."

The woman's eyebrows raised in alarm. "No shit, there's dark magic."

Kira nodded. "Okay, let's wait for the others."

"Are you two trying to get yourselves killed? Get out of the street," called a voice from the sidewalk.

They looked up as Demeter, the leader of their coven, locked her car door and began to walk toward them. She stopped abruptly. "Oh!"

Standing in the middle of the street, she yanked her cell phone out and typed. Kira felt her phone vibrate and heard Ulla's do the same.

"Come on, girls, we've got work to do." Demeter ushered them to the sidewalk outside the flower shop.

Kira retrieved her cell to find a WhatsApp from their leader to the coven. *THIS IS NOT A DRILL.*

Ulla scratched her arms as though the creepy feeling could be removed.

The three of them were silent for a few moments, then Demeter took their hands and began to sing.

"The earth, the air, the fire, the water,
Return, return, return, return,
The earth, the air, the fire, the water,
Return, return, return, return."

Over and over, they sang the chant. Three voices, then four, then seven, then ten crowded into the little store and everyone held hands in a circle.

The door opened and another witch entered. Gaia had a five-pound bag of salt and began to pour a circle around them on the floor.

Kira stared at her and decided the woman had watched way too much *Supernatural.*

She noticed a tub containing willow branches intended for floral displays. Quickly, she grasped it and a reel of twine and moved to the center of the circle. As the women continued to chant, she fashioned a new protection rune.

CHAPTER TWENTY

Dolores moved out of sight but continued to watch.

"Edward, call your pack in. I want them here." Caleb sounded tired and she wondered what was keeping him going.

"I've called them." The shifter sounded like he was in a dream state.

"Finally! Edward, tell Kate to sign her land over to me."

Obediently, he turned to the woman. "Kate, sign your land over to Caleb."

"Screw you!" she shouted.

The sorcerer was furious. "Hit her."

She tried to duck out of the way of Stan's hand but the slap came from Edward.

"That should have worked." Caleb's eyes were wild. He stepped forward, grasped her head, and muttered a few words. His face was strained as if he tried to break through a psychic wall.

"Those witches! I'll kill the lot of them." He paused as though listening to something. "Yes, if you like. Entrails, the works." He stepped back and took a breath to compose himself.

Dolores wondered who he had been talking to.

"Edward, since I can't read your memories, we'll have to go the long way around. Where's William?"

The shifter responded with no emotion in his voice. "He's at my house."

Caleb's eyes lit up. "Splendid! Are any of your pack members with him?"

"Yes."

"Tell them to kill him."

Edward paused for a moment, then nodded. The command had been sent.

"Okay, boys and girls. On with this charade, then. Edward, you wanted to walk the bride down the aisle. Go ahead."

He took Kate's arm and pulled her roughly into the room set up for the wedding. The minister stood at the end of the aisle with Tommy. The shifter dragged her down the aisle and stood behind her.

The minister began, "Dearly Beloved—"

"I don't think so. Skip to the necessary parts," Caleb snapped.

Dolores ducked out and walked into the foyer. She stood for a moment before she felt eyes on her and knew instantly who it was. She strode to the nearest table, picked up champagne glasses, and placed them on her tray.

"I haven't seen you before," the sorcerer said to her back and his voice dripped with suspicion. She ignored him and moved to another table and more glasses.

Suddenly the pull on her mind was strong and the glasses fell, rolled from the tray, and shattered on the floor. He turned her without laying a finger on her.

"I was talking to *you*. What's your name?"

The compulsion to tell the truth was so strong, there was nothing else she could do. "My name is Dolores, sir. May I get you a drink?" She managed to recover a little and smiled in the same vacuous way the hypnotized people had.

"What are you doing here?"

"I'm doing my job, sir. May I get you a drink?"

"Why haven't I seen you before?"

"I'm from the agency, sir. May I get you a drink?

He turned to the other room. "Are they married yet?"

Dolores took the opportunity to sidle away and pick glasses up until she was sure he was no longer watching her. She sighed. All her answers had been truthful. He'd merely asked the wrong questions. She headed down the hallway and darted into the billiard room, then closed the door behind her and tried not to hyperventilate. When she turned her back to the door, her gaze was met by a scene of pure horror.

Todd was seated in an armchair in the corner of the room, covered with blood. He inflicted tiny cuts all over his body with a razor. Betsy stood in front of the chair between her son and one of the demon creatures and brandished a billiard cue menacingly. To her credit, a pile of goop with another cue laid in the middle of the table. She'd already eliminated one of the beasts.

This woman is in her eighties.

The fae was impressed but noted that the old woman had cuts on her face and arms and looked like she was on her last legs.

"That's enough of that." She approached the demon from behind. With its many eyes, it saw her coming and flipped one of its arms toward her. She put her hand up. The moment its claw touched her palm, the creature shrank to the size of a bug and she stamped on it and ground the goop into the carpet.

Betsy darted instantly to Todd and wrestled the razor from his hand.

Dolores rushed to help her. "What happened? I thought you had left."

"Edward's friends escorted us all the way to Ontario airport. We parked the car, and I don't remember anything after that." The woman broke down. "They said Caleb wouldn't be able to do this again."

"Scott protected him from sorcery but I don't think that's all

Caleb is using." She thought for a moment. "I need to get the two of you out of here." She gestured with her arm and a door appeared in the wall.

Betsy hesitated. "Those monsters came out of a door like this."

"This is a fae door. It will take us to safety."

They each took one of Todd's arms and walked him slowly toward the portal.

The handle on the door to the hallway turned.

CHAPTER TWENTY-ONE

Dick's eyes sprang open. He wasn't usually a late sleeper, but he was still recovering from the silver attack.

He listened for the sound again—a wolf padded along the basement hallway and he knew immediately it wasn't Edward. He knew his gait as man and wolf. The door opened and the wolf entered, its hackles raised. Although he recognized it, he could see this was no friend.

Instantly, he knew something had gone horribly wrong.

The wolf didn't rely on sight and instead, sniffed the air. Instinctively knowing where the threat would come from, it looked up a fraction of a second too late. Dick descended from the corner of the room above the door and bit into its neck. The wolf threw him off and he pounded into the bedside table. The creature tore at him. A fraction of an inch from his throat, it yelped and spun to where Marcel had sunk his teeth into its tail.

The second's distraction was all the vampire needed. Before his assailant could attack the puppy, he yanked its head back and sank his teeth into its throat. The wolf whined and sagged.

Dick pulled his clothes on at lightning speed and reached for his cell when he heard several growls. He managed to read one word on the screen before Marcel rocketed under the bed. When he turned, three more wolves snarled in the doorway.

CHAPTER TWENTY-TWO

Scott touched Lexi's shoulder from the back seat in the car. "What are you thinking?"

She put her hand over his and drew energy. They'd only done it a few minutes previously so she didn't need to do it again, but she wanted Jess to witness the intimacy.

What am I doing?

Hastily, she removed her hand. "Honestly? I'm wondering what the collective noun is for demons because I've got one. *Fuck No!* A 'fuckno' of demons."

The shifter slid her gaze to her. "Works for me."

Scott laughed. "I think 'legion' is the name for a group of demons."

"Not anymore. It's a fuckno. What is it?"

"A fuckno." Scott saluted. "I meant, though, what do you think we should do now?"

"Oh, that. Find Caleb, decapitate him, go back and destroy the fuckno of demons, then try that Korean place we just drove past."

Jess's gaze slid back to the road. "Their barbecue is amazing, but we've got a better place in San Bernardino. If we're still alive by the end of the day, I'll treat you both." After a moment, she added, "Would you really do that? Chop the guy's head off in front of a roomful of ordinaries?"

"Yes. They can be made to forget." Lexi shrugged and focused on the road ahead.

Anyone can be made to forget.

They headed up the drive to the clubhouse.

She turned to the back seat of the car. "We're not exactly dressed for a wedding."

"Are you sure?" Scott smiled.

A glance at Jess revealed that she wore her Alexander McQueen dress. When she opened her mouth to complain, she realized she wore one too. Startled, she gaped as both turned dark burgundy, the same color as Kira's bridesmaid's dress.

Lexi turned to Scott, who was now in a dark gray suit with a burgundy tie.

"What the..." The shifter darted confused glances at her attire.

"They're waiting." Lexi indicated the valets, and the car inched forward.

One of the men approached the window. "Invitation?"

"We're bridesmaids. Do we need one?" She indicated her dress.

"I've got it." Scott leaned forward and muttered a word as he held out a supermarket receipt for tampons he'd found in the back of the car.

Jess's eyes bulged and her cheeks flushed. She beamed a rictus grin at the valet as he nodded and opened the door.

Lexi approached the man. "Isn't it quite late for a wedding? It's nearly seven."

He smiled in an unfocused way and climbed into the car.

The shifter frowned. "I'm not thrilled about a sleepwalker driving my car."

Lexi shrugged as he moved the car around to the back of the building, apparently without problems. "Is Edward here?"

"No, and neither is the rest of the pack. If they were, I'd sense it." Jess seemed troubled.

They entered the foyer, and the shifter looked around. "Oh! The pack *is* here." They approached a group of people who stood with glasses of champagne in their hands.

"Rose. Where's Edward?"

"The bride looks beautiful," Rose said with a vacuous smile.

Jess's eyes narrowed. "Caleb must have brainwashed Edward."

"How do you know he's not…" Lexi didn't finish the sentence.

"Because I'd be the alpha."

Lexi took a glass from the waiter and sniffed it. "But you're still you." She passed the glass to Scott.

He muttered a word over it and nothing happened, so he knocked the drink back. "I wonder whose wedding this was supposed to be?" He snagged the invitation from a guest's hand. "Chester and Jeanette were supposed to be getting married at 3pm this afternoon. I'm guessing most of these guests were here to attend that wedding."

"I think we know where Chester and Jeanette are." Lexi thought of the bride working in the pit.

The three of them went into a side room and closed the door.

"We need to find Edward and Dolores," Scott said. "Caleb must have gotten to Edward when I had you shielded at the flower shop, although I'd have expected you to fall under his control as soon as you were unshielded."

Jess sighed. "I know what it is—why I couldn't sense the pack. What I felt back at the flower shop. Edward kicked me out of the pack."

Lexi nodded. "Of course. It was the only way he could stop you from being taken over by the man."

The door to the study opened and Caleb walked in, followed by Edward and a couple of his pack.

"Ahh! Miss Braxton—or do you prefer 'Bianca' these days? I'm afraid you've missed a splendid wedding."

Lexi moved her hand to her unhealing scar.

"Edward, would you mind placing your knife at your throat? If I am harmed, please cut your own throat."

The shifter did as he was told, and she lowered her hand slowly.

The man walked closer to her and extended his hand—not touching, but close. Her gaze flicked to Edward and she ground her teeth. "I don't sense an affinity for any of the lower supernaturals. All I sense is your mage. My, you did get the short end of the stick, didn't you?" He looked at Scott. "My talented young nemesis. You've caused some inconvenience to me today." He touched the young man in the center of the forehead and he fell heavily to the floor. "I bet you don't know that one." Caleb chuckled as he made his way to a desk and picked some papers up.

"Come along, new Mrs. Ellis. Be a dear and sign your name on these papers."

Lexi watched as Kate entered the room. She leaned over the desk and signed where she was told to.

"There we are. Now, you've been a lot of trouble, haven't you, Mrs. Ellis? I think you should come with me. I have a friend who has...let's say, taken a shine to you and would very much like to meet you in the flesh."

Lexi shook with fury and wanted nothing more than to separate him from his head, but when she glanced at Edward, the blade bit into his skin.

Caleb laughed at her predicament. "Gentlemen, take care of our unwanted guests, please."

He laughed again, gestured with his arm, and created a whorl of black smoke—a portal. He took Kate by the arm, stepped through, and vanished.

Lexi stood protectively over Scott and prepared to face Edward and his two pack members. She tried to estimate their chances when the door opened and another twenty shifters streamed in.

Hastily, she glanced at Scott and wondered if she could simply catch hold of him and get enough magic to send them all to sleep at once. Her thought was interrupted by Jess.

"I challenge you as pack leader and alpha of the San Bernardino pack."

Edward blinked.

The conflict was very evident in his eyes. He'd been told to kill them but this was a challenge for alpha. It was in his DNA to not deny this.

The pack retreated and left the two challengers facing each other. She knew she could go for her katana now, but if Jess could win this fight, she might not have to kill Edward—and she really, *really* didn't want to kill him.

The pack began to file out of the study, and she was dragged along with them. The guests were all still in the ceremony room but most of them had collapsed.

Lexi caught up with Jess. "Can you win this? And can you do it without killing him?"

Edward glanced at the two of them. His eyes were like granite.

"I don't know." The woman looked at her and she saw the emotions that had been missing from Edward's eyes—regret, fear, and determination. Lexi dropped back as the current alpha and the contender led the group into the ballroom. Suddenly, she wasn't sure who would be alive at the end of this. She smoothed her hand over her dimensional pocket.

The pack surrounded the alpha and the beta, and they both shifted.

Edward snarled and snapped at the air immediately. He was a huge wolf, and Lexi knew he was fast and strong. Jess, small and wiry though her wolf-form was, had fought her way to beta, however. She imagined that had required prowess and guile on her part. The opponents stalked each other in circles, bared their teeth, and snarled continually.

Jess danced in and away, always angling toward Edward's injured leg, but he wouldn't let her near it. His hackles were raised and it was clear that even though he was under the sorcerer's influence, he wouldn't hold back. He had been given the order to kill them. Jess might actually be forced to kill him to stop him. Equally, if he came out of this mind-control to find he'd killed Jess, he would be heartbroken.

This might end badly.

The shifters surrounding the challengers were eerily quiet.

Jess was on her third taunt when Edward snapped. He gave a guttural snarl and surged into an attack, only to find her gone. Lexi had never seen a creature other than a vampire move that fast. The beta had flipped onto the larger wolf's back and she bit once into his shoulder.

He squealed and twisted toward her throat, but she evaded the attempt, leapt clear of him, and darted away. Once again, they circled each other. Edward shook out the pain from the bite and blood flew from his fur. Jess's ears drooped and she looked momentarily sad. He snarled wildly at her, and her ears pricked up again.

The beta attempted another feint, but he had expected it. He ran her down and bit savagely into her rump and she squealed.

Lexi turned cold, slid her hand into her pocket, and took hold of her katana.

It looked like Jess had made a costly mistake. Edward was on top of her, ready to rip into her again, until she took careful aim at his left back leg—his injured one. She realized that the smaller wolf hadn't made a mistake at all. She'd deliberately given him the opening to allow her to reach his injured knee. Her jaws closed on it, and his howl filled the air. Jess used his distraction and pain to put some distance between the two of them.

Edward tried to drag himself after her, but it was useless. She shifted again and the pack bowed to her as the new alpha. He shifted too, knowing he had lost and that the shifters were no longer his pack. Jess was their alpha, and Caleb did not control them.

Lexi raced to the study to find Scott still unconscious. She stroked her hand down the scar and said, "Awake."

He sat up, confused and alarmed.

"Morning, sleeping beauty."

"What happened?"

"Caleb."

He lay still for a moment to allow it all to come back to him.

"Come on. Edward's injured."

Scott stood and wobbled, so she put his arm around her shoulder and led him to the other room.

Edward was still on the floor when they returned to the ballroom.

Jess was in the hall, leaning against the wall to try to compensate for her injuries. "I never wanted to do that to him."

"Let me see what I can do." The young man put his hand on Jess and healed her.

"You won't be able to heal what I took away from him." The woman looked at the floor.

He walked to Edward. As the shifter opened his eyes, he stopped cautiously. "Do you still want to kill us?"

"No. I'm controlled by Jess now." He didn't sound defeated.

Scott put his hand on the other man and muttered a few words.

Edward stood and flexed his knee. "Holy shit! It's better than it's been for years. I could go another round with Jess."

Lexi looked at him

"Kidding. She's earned her place."

"But I didn't want it. I'm not ready for that kind of responsibility. I'm so sorry." Jess stood in the doorway.

"What do you think my intention was when I released you

from the pack? This was the best outcome I could hope for. And I'm not going anywhere. I'll be here to help you...boss." He smirked.

Lexi walked up to the two of them. "We need to get to that pit and stop Caleb."

"I don't think you'll do that." Stan entered with his much larger pack. There were at least thirty of them, and they began to shift.

"We don't have time for this shit." She yanked her katana out.

"You're right," the shifter agreed and strode past her toward Stanley.

"Stanley, I challenge you as alpha and leader of the Palm Springs pack."

His adversary shifted and leapt at him in wolf form in one fluid motion. Edward didn't even bother to shift. He delivered a mighty right hook to the side of his adversary's head and completely changed his trajectory. The wolf landed awkwardly and lay still.

His pack stood and shook their heads as though coming out of a deep sleep. They bent the knee to Edward.

Jess stared at Stanley's unconscious form as he shifted, then glanced at Edward. "So, what happened to 'I'm not going anywhere?'"

He shrugged. "I'll still be on the other end of the phone."

Scott looked around and moved to the door. "Where's Dolores?"

"I haven't seen her since Caleb—" The shifter stopped and realization dawned on his face.

"What?" Lexi felt Scott's heart hammering through their link, or maybe it was hers.

"I set the pack on Dick." Edward turned to his new pack while he retrieved his cell. "We're looking for a short woman with her hair up, dressed as a maid."

They began to flood out of the door, but one man turned. "How short?"

He shrugged. "Anywhere between half an inch and five feet." He turned to Lexi, and they brought each other up to date.

She didn't put her weapon away. "Right. We need to get after Caleb. By the time we get there, he'll have had nearly an hour's head start."

The shifter placed his hand on Scott's shoulder. "Can't you take us through a portal? Like Caleb's?"

The sorcerer shook his head. "His portals go through a low-level hell dimension. It's where those demons come from. I don't know how to make one safely. If I get it wrong, we'll be lost in there."

Edward shook his head. "Whatever's coming through that portal he's creating in the pit could well be through by the time we get there."

"Then it's a good thing you've got a short-cut," said Dolores from the doorway. "Sorry I had to step out. Betsy and Todd didn't get away as we'd hoped. I've left them getting medical attention in Fae."

"Are they okay?" Lexi gripped her blade tightly, expecting awful news.

"I doubt it. I think Betsy will have them all guzzling gin by the time I get back."

"I meant Betsy and Todd."

The woman patted her arm. "They will be. They're being helped."

Lexi turned to Edward and Jess. "Get your people together. We're going after him."

Dolores took Scott's hand. "Show me where we need to go."

Jess held her cell out. "Someone needs to help the witches in the flower shop. Now!"

CHAPTER TWENTY-THREE

Kira placed the new runes around the space while she chanted with the witches. Suddenly, the atmosphere in the room changed. She likened the feeling to a vacation she had taken when she had dived to the ocean floor. One by one, as they felt it, the witches stopped chanting.

Seconds later, the new rune splintered. She considered skipping out of the ritual ring to pick it up.

Demeter caught her hand tightly. "Something's changed. Don't break the circle."

As they waited in trepidation, the flowers in the tubs around them blackened and crumbled. A loud rumble issued and the floor in the back room buckled and began to fall away. The witches stared in horror at the creature that clambered out with its black eyes and many arms. It stood motionless as though assessing them.

Demeter faced it as it moved closer with an unnerving clicking sound. "Don't break the circle." She began to chant again, and the creature lunged forward with one of its sharp-taloned fingers. One of the witches wrenched her hands free and ran. The creature caught Demeter around the throat.

Kira was in shock and couldn't make her body move.

The door's right there. We should run.

The monster took a step closer, then froze and tilted its head downward. Her eyes followed its gaze. One of its feet was planted in the salt. It vibrated and a moment later, it burst and covered Demeter in ooze.

She caught Gaia's arm. "It's the salt."

They looked at the protective ring of salt. It was too close to afford them any protection, though, as the creatures could still reach them with swipes of their talons.

Kira took her cell out and sent a message to Jess.

A clicking sound drew their attention to the rear of the store, where more creatures now climbed out of the hole.

She stooped, snatched a handful of salt, and threw it at the nearest monster. The grains caught it squarely in the face and it exploded.

"Hey, it's better than slugs." She heard herself laugh with a little too much hilarity.

"Is this right? Aren't they the goddess' creatures too?" Freya asked. Everyone suspected she was still a Christian. She'd only joined the coven to embarrass her husband, a pastor who was screwing his secretary.

Demeter faced her. "Oh, fuck off, Carole."

Freya looked at her feet. "I see. Well. I mean, I thought we don't use our mundane names."

"I'm sorry, Freya." Their leader sighed. They were all terrified.

One woman raised a hand. "Couldn't we simply step out and lock the door?"

"Maybe there were only a couple of them," one of the ladies squeaked.

The clicking resumed, and a scramble for the salt on the floor ensued.

Kira put a pile of salt into Freya's hand. "Think of your husband and throw this."

The creatures retreated as the women scooped handfuls of salt from Gaia's bag and the poured circle. They scattered it across the floor to stop the creatures from creeping forward.

One of the witches laughed. "Ha! Now you're stuck."

The creatures stepped onto the wall, then the ceiling.

"Well, shit!" Kira looked hastily around her for a weapon, but all she could see were dead flowers.

The women were being herded against a side wall.

Her cell rang and she risked a glance at it.

Either get out or stand against the wall.

One of the creatures stood between them and the exit, and they were already pressed against the wall. She shrugged.

A hazy, swirling light appeared in the middle of the room and turned into an arched doorway.

"Holy Mary, Mother of God." Freya crossed herself.

Demeter pursed her lips and her gaze slid to the woman. "I knew it."

An object appeared out of the haze, landed, and rolled across the floor.

"Grenade!" Demeter dived on top of as many of her coven as she could.

No explosion followed, but Lexi burst through the fae door with her katana in one hand and a nerf gun in the other.

Scott appeared at her side. He turned to her and smiled. "Alexa, play 'Mr. Brightside' by The Killers."

A voice came from the object on the floor. "Here's 'Mr. Brightside' by The Killers." An incredibly loud noise issued from the speaker, and Demeter covered her ears "What the hell is that?"

They watched as the creatures covered their eyes, shook their heads, and stumbled into each other. One plummeted from the ceiling, landed on its back, and exploded in the salt.

Kira stood again. "I believe that's Mr. Brightside."

Lexi aimed the nerf gun and fired at a demon on the wall.

Several salt-covered sponge balls bounced off it, and a moment later, it popped in a spray of goop. Scott began to bring salt rocks into existence and slung them at the enemy. His partner moved to the back room and fired as she moved. After shooting a few more salted sponge bullets, she was out. She dropped the nerf gun and put her katana to use to skewer the creatures that writhed on the floor, incapacitated by the music.

She turned to Scott and grinned. "I like your music."

Dolores came through with bags of salt and passed them to the women. They dove into them without hesitation and hurled the contents everywhere.

When Lexi glanced over her shoulder, a demon dropped from the ceiling between the fae door and the witches. Demeter threw herself in front of the other witches as it lunged. A sharp pincer pierced her in the chest and she slid off it and fell, lifeless. The creature moved in to attack another witch. Opening its huge maw, it revealed row upon row of pointed teeth.

Freya snatched the salt lamp in Daisy's window display, stepped in front of it, and wedged the huge salt rock into the creature's mouth. "Take that, you cheating bastard."

It exploded, and the woman, now covered in goop, shouted, "Yes!"

Lexi refocused. The creatures continued to emerge from the hole. She picked up the Bluetooth speaker, held it out as she fought her way closer to the hole, and thrust her katana into their skulls when they appeared.

As she perched over the aperture, more of the floor fell away. She jumped back, but the chasm now separated her from the others. Pots of flowers slid along the floor as the back of the building lurched. More of the creatures spilled out.

"Lexi," Scott shouted.

She turned as a twenty-pound bag of salt appeared in the air over the breach in the floor. Reflexively and with no thought at all, she met it with her katana and sliced the bag open.

It released its contents and the majority of the salt went into the unnatural entrance. The top three demons burst, followed by a loud rumble.

Demon goop surged out like a geyser.

When it died down, she peered in to see that most of the demons had been destroyed. She put the speaker into her pocket, looked at Scott, shrugged, and jumped in.

"No!" he cried, but it was too late. She slid down the goop-filled tunnel.

It was about twenty feet long. Lexi glided through the foul-smelling gunk and killed the creatures methodically along the route. She emerged covered in slime, but it had been worth it for the fast descent. Scott's state when he climbed out of that tunnel would be a real reason to laugh in all this.

She now stood in what appeared to be a natural hollow in the wall of the pit. Her unhealing scar itched so badly, she wanted to rip her arm off. One wall of the little cave was covered in iridescent, undulating light. The dimensions were aligning, and she stood exactly where the demon would appear.

When she looked across the pit, the first person she saw was Scott. He and the witches had come through the fae door. Lexi looked at herself—she was covered in slime and he was not—and rolled her eyes.

The clicking in the cave was deafening. Demons scuttled frantically in every direction as shifters poured out of the fae door with axes and salt. Both packs fought the creatures with weapons. Some had shifted to distract the demons, but none of them dared bite them.

The brainwashed citizens in the pit attacked the shifters with shovels and picks. Scott had already begun to put them to sleep in an effort to keep them safe and out of the way. Dolores shrank any monster she could get close to and stamped on them.

Lexi didn't have to search to find Caleb. He stood facing her with Kate at his side. With the witches' protection broken, she was merely another victim of hypnosis and stared into space.

The air crackled, and a slow, nasty smile spread across the sorcerer's face.

She looked at the sea of demons between her and her enemy. A reckless voice in her head told her to simply attack and start slashing.

A sudden pain through the empathetic link made her look back quickly. The bride in her dirty wedding dress had struck Scott across the head with a shovel. He sent her to sleep but stumbled, his hand on the back of his head.

Lexi leaped to a ledge running along the side of the pit. She had to jump down a short distance later and plow through a few demons before she could climb again and finally return to her friend. When she reached him, she healed his head, then pulled the speaker out of her pocket. "What happened to the music?"

He held his phone up. "We're too far underground and my sounds are in the cloud."

"Can't you boost it with magic?"

"I don't think so." He tried to take the speaker from her hand.

"It's worth a try." She touched her hand to her scar and the device began to play the next song on his playlist.

The demons began to show signs of confusion again, but both wolf packs turned to Lexi as "Barbie Girl" rang out. She passed the speaker to Scott and disassociated herself from it. He face-palmed.

"Look at that. Even Caleb's horrified. You've embarrassed us in front of the bad guy." She shook her head.

"Well, it's doing the job and I like it." The words were barely out of his mouth when a man who had crept up behind them pushed him into the sea of demons below. While she knew he was most likely hypnotized, she punched him in the face. The speaker was crushed under the panicking demons and she honestly couldn't say she was disappointed. She moved to vault after Scott, but Dolores held her back. The creatures weren't hurting him. They were ferrying him to Caleb.

"Enough!" The sorcerer's voice echoed around the huge chamber and distressed the demons again.

Scott was dropped in front of him, and a monster placed its pincers around his neck.

Everything stopped.

The creatures had the shifters surrounded. Lexi realized that all the humans Scott had put to sleep were back on their feet and now stared disconcertingly at her.

Caleb gestured arrogantly, and Dolores's portal vanished. He turned his face to the cave. Lexi ran along the ledge, stopped when she was about level with him, and glanced at the hollow area. It was almost completely filled with iridescent light, and a figure moved slowly toward the front. The man grasped Kate by the back of her neck and shoved her to her knees. "A fitting welcome gift for my new friend."

The beast couldn't be seen clearly through the veil of the worlds, but Lexi could make out that it was at least ten feet tall. Its body glistened red as though it was covered in blood. It roared, and the black creatures throughout the cavern shrank away. Earth began to slide down the wall to the left. She wondered if the whole place might be about to collapse and her gaze returned to the demon.

As it moved closer to the front of the cave, she again tore her gaze away and looked at Scott. Since he lay face-down, she couldn't see him clearly but she saw Caleb. His face was a mask of terror. She smirked. It was small consolation that he'd clearly bitten off more than he could chew.

The demon reached the front and began to enter the human world.

CHAPTER TWENTY-FOUR

A guttural voice boomed, *"Why can I not enter?"*

Caleb looked at the creature in horror. "I don't understand. She signed the property over to me. You should be able to step through."

After a moment's silence, he clutched his head and screamed. "Azatoth—my Lord, please."

He twined his fingers in Kate's hair and pulled her up. "You signed the papers. It's mine."

She was unfocused but she answered truthfully. "It wasn't my property. I already sold it."

"What?" Caleb screeched. He looked from her to Azatoth and back again. He slapped her and screamed in her face, "To whom? Who owns it?"

More earth sifted beside the wall of the large area.

"Ah! That would be me."

Lexi spun to where Dick stood at the entrance to the pit with three shifters. Her jaw dropped.

"Close your mouth, dear. The wind might change and you'll be stuck like that." He winked at her, then looked at Caleb. "I swore I'd ruin you when I discovered what you did to Harv. I meant it."

"Get him," the sorcerer screamed, and a sea of black demons moved as one toward him.

The side of the cave that had first shown signs of the veil now looked like a normal cave wall. The dimensions were beginning to move out of alignment. Azatoth noticed too and howled in frustration.

"My Lord, I can still bring you over," Caleb assured him hurriedly. "I'll use my power—our power—to draw the edge of the veil out. It would only be a few feet."

Lexi felt the power of his magic. Fully unleashed, it was so much more than mere sorcery. The veil shifted and undulated, then began to move.

Azatoth took a step.

The earth sifted down the side of the underground space again.

She glanced at Scott again and knew she had to get him out of there. Perhaps she could drop while the monsters pursued Dick, who raced at vamp speed around the cave and dismembered the creatures around the shifters.

The huge demon took another step. She tried to gauge how far he was from the land owned by Caleb. It could be mere inches now.

Something touched her shoulder and she turned, ready to behead whatever it was. She gaped when she focused on Scott's face. She peered at the version who was on the ground in front of Caleb and in the grip of a demon, then back at the one who stood before her.

"Yeah, that won't last for long." He grinned.

Sure enough, the other Scott faded, and the demon holding him skittered around in search of him.

Lexi wanted to hug her friend. Instead, she clutched his arm. "I think we'll need a miracle."

He smiled and pointed upward. She grinned when she realized that the roof was covered in bags of salt. "Shall we make it rain?"

"Going somewhere?" Caleb asked. Scott and Lexi turned toward him.

Dick had been racing past the sorcerer, probably to free Kate, and his feet seemed frozen to the floor.

The sorcerer grinned, although his face was red and sweaty. "What do your friends call you? Dick? Well, I'm afraid your luck's run out, *Dick*."

The vampire punched him hard. The sound of his nose breaking echoed through the pit.

He took a handkerchief out and wiped his hand. "Only my friends call me Dick."

Lexi drew her hand down her scar. "Burst."

Salt rained on the creatures, and they began to explode randomly on every side.

Caleb jumped at the chaos, then sneered at Lexi. "No matter. You're too late." His breathing was labored and sweat ran down his temples. His gaze slid to the cave.

Azatoth had begun to emerge from the portal.

The points of two huge horns appeared, followed by a hooved foot covered in red slime. Its veiled doorway was narrow now, but it looked like the beast would make it through.

The sorcerer pulled Kate to her feet. "I think you should be awake to meet your new friend."

The woman shook her head, saw the creature standing before the ritual entrance, and screamed.

The side of the cave finally gave and a wolf with a metal collar around its neck burst through, howling and snarling. It collided with Azatoth, and both wolf and beast tumbled through the entrance of the portal. Everyone's eyes were glued to the shrinking veil, waiting to see if anything would emerge again. The length of chain from the wolf's collar which had dangled out of the mouth of the cave was cut off, and it dropped heavily to the ground.

"No!" Caleb screamed.

A new noise started to fill the space—the sound of chatter as people awoke from their state of hypnosis.

Dolores shouted, "Gas leak, this way to the exit," to anyone who would listen. Her new fae door looked like a set of double doors with an exit sign above it. Beyond it was the storage company's parking lot.

Lexi drew her katana and turned to finish Caleb but he had vanished.

Scott cast a spell on the room but there was no sign of residual magic. He wandered to the little cave, climbed up, looked around, and dropped again. "There's no sign of the demon or the shifter."

She looked at Dick. "You bought Kate's land?"

"When Betsy told me what Caleb had done, I wanted to kill him. Then I decided it might be better to stop him from getting what he seemed to want more than anything. I went to Kate, and she signed it over then and there. Of course, when I returned home, they caught me with one of those portals."

She raised her eyebrows. "Are shifters usually so trusting of vamps?"

Kate joined them. "We are when the vamp uses his own home as collateral."

The vampire chuckled. "Of course, we promised to swap again if we were still alive at the end of this. We're still doing that, right?"

The woman smiled. "I hear your place is really fancy." She shook her head. "Is it over?"

"By my calculations, it will be at least another thousand years before that dimension aligns with any location on Earth again," Dolores interjected.

"What about Caleb? Won't he be angry?" Kate looked nervous.

Scott looked around. "I'm surprised he had the energy to get himself out of here. He'll probably be depleted for months. Still, I'd rather know where he is."

"I'll work on that tomorrow. Let's get the hell out of here." Dolores looked at Lexi. "And you need a bath."

Lexi stood outside with Scott and Dick. "What's next for you?" she asked the vampire as he retrieved his cellphone.

"I need to make sure Betsy and Todd are all right when they return from Fae and sort out the paperwork with Kate to ensure I get my home back."

"Well, I guess it's goodbye, then." She extended her hand to him.

He stepped back. "I'd hug you but you don't smell very nice." He turned to Scott. "Did you show her yet?"

"Not yet, but I've got it here." Scott grinned. He took her hand and covered it with his own and she expected to see the little teardrop pendant appear. When he removed his hand, she gazed into her palm at the gold ring.

Her face lit up. "Is it mine?" She drew him into a hug and whispered, "Thank you." When she released him, her eyes glittered.

He blushed. "Look on the inside."

She turned it to the streetlight. Inside were two dates, May 16th, 1980, and September 23rd, 1990, and interlocking hearts.

Lexi looked at Scott. "I don't understand. The September date is my birthday, but what's the other date?"

"Those were there when I drew the gold from the net. I suspect they were always there but hidden by magic."

She gazed at the ring. "Bryan found it in Braxton's safe. It was in an envelope with my name on it."

"I'd guess it's probably your mother's wedding ring," Dick said and slid his cell phone into his pocket. "Well, Jesús isn't picking up. I'd better see what he's up to. Lexi, it's been...well, I'm not sure what it's been, but you saved my life and for that, I'm grateful."

"You're all right, Dick."

He turned to Scott. "You're a fine young man, Scott. I hope we meet again."

CHAPTER TWENTY-FIVE

T he vampire entered the house and called, "Jesús."

He dropped his keys in the dish and was immediately aware that something wasn't right.

When he entered the living area, he found Jesús gagged and bound in the Eames lounger with a box-cutter held at his throat.

"Hello, sir." The man with the blade was reverential.

He turned his back on the scene and walked to the kitchen where he took a glass and filled it from the refrigerator's blood cooler. He nodded and looked up. "Hello, Geoffrey."

The man watched him drink the blood. "What are you doing, drinking that stuff? You don't need that. You've got me. You don't need him, either."

Dick glanced at Jesús. His eyes were red and his breathing was labored. He'd probably cried so much his nose was blocked and he looked terrified.

The vampire returned his gaze to his unwanted visitor. "Really? My Givenchy scarf?"

"I'm sorry, sir. He wouldn't shut up."

For now, he needed the knife to move away from Jesús. "Geoffrey, what are you doing? I said you would be welcome here when you were healed, but you keep running away from the hospital."

"I couldn't bear to be away from you and they'll never let me leave. Not now."

He narrowed his eyes. "What have you done?"

"She was giving me pills—pills that would turn my blood bad. I had to make her stop."

A muffled squeak issued from Jesús.

Dick glanced at the trickle of blood on his houseboy's neck. "I see. And you thought getting blood all over my Eames lounger would encourage me to welcome you home?"

"I didn't think—"

"No, you didn't. Well, if you're back, you're back. I'll get changed. You would absolutely not believe what these stains are. I don't know if they'll ever come out." He washed the glass out and turned it upside-down on the drainer.

The two men both watched as he walked to the little bowl and lifted the keys out.

"You'll have to get yourself a key made." He threw the keys across the room to Geoffrey, who instinctively moved his hand to catch them. By the time they were in his hand, Dick was at his throat.

The vampire pulled the scarf from Jesús's mouth, used the box-cutter on the ties, and walked to the bar and poured them both a large drink.

CHAPTER TWENTY-SIX

Lexi and Scott were very pleased to be back in their piece-of-shit car and headed out of Palm Springs.

She looked at her companion, who grinned broadly as he drove. This was a real treat for him as she rarely let him take the wheel.

In all honesty, she didn't have the energy. Edward had invited them to stay the night and she'd been tempted. If they'd stayed, though, they'd have to get involved in the clean-up and that really wasn't her thing.

Relieved that she'd at least avoided that, she took the opportunity to close her eyes.

"Holy shit!" Scott swerved and the car spun, left the road, plowed through a fence, and impacted with a billboard.

Lexi put out her arms and was hauled against the seat by her seatbelt. "What the fuck? Are you okay?"

"I'm fine. I only—" He looked at the road over his shoulder, his expression dazed.

"Then what the fuck?" She leapt out of the car and walked to the front. "Well, this is going nowhere."

"I'm sorry. There was someone on the road."

"Really? Or did you nod off, you jackass?" She punched him in the arm.

"Could I offer you a ride somewhere?"

She turned to the familiar voice. "Dick?"

"Dude, was that you? Why were you standing in the middle of the road?" Scott leaned heavily on the hood and dragged his fingers over his scalp.

"I was worried you'd miss me." The vampire walked around the car.

Lexi folded her arms. "You're *lucky* we missed you. What are you doing here?"

He released a huge, dramatic sigh. "I am so over Palm Springs."

She raised an eyebrow. "What's up? Wouldn't Kate give you back your house?"

"Oh, we resolved that. Jesús will look after it for a while."

"I thought you were going to check on Betsy." Scott pulled his duffel out of the trunk.

"I'll write." Dick turned to Lexi. "Can I come along for the ride?"

Lexi narrowed her eyes. "You've already agreed on this with Dolores, haven't you?"

"Well…" He spread his arms and shrugged.

"We seem to be shit-out-of-luck in the engine department, anyway." She began to walk toward his day car.

The three of them climbed in and the vampire locked the doors. "So, where are we heading?"

"New Orleans." She smirked.

He looked in the rearview mirror. "Wait, what? No. It's too humid. I'll die."

Scott raised a brow and smirked. "You're already dead."

"You know what I mean." He rolled his eyes.

"It's your own fault. You gave me the clue." Lexi held the photograph up.

"Well, shit. Buckle up. Do you want the radio on, or should I simply ask Alexa to play something?"

CHAPTER TWENTY-SEVEN

Scott lay across the back seat with his hands over his ears. "We've been driving for days. I can't listen to this noise anymore."

Dick glanced into the rearview mirror. "It's been three hours, you insufferable child. My car, my rules—and take your feet off the window. People will think there's a monkey in the car."

Lexi snorted and turned to face the young sorceror. "I quite like it. I've never really listened to old music before."

The vampire slid his gaze to her. "It's not old, it's classic."

Scott moved his feet, sat, and rested his chin on the back of her seat. "It's so disturbing I can't even meditate." He slumped in his seat. "I'll go into my dimensional pocket to—"

Dick's cellphone rang. He passed it to Lexi and she answered it. "Hi, Dolores, how's it going?"

"It's going remarkably well." The fae sounded pleased. "Caleb has surfaced. He's in Mexico."

"You're kidding!" Lexi had thought he would never be seen again.

"Right, where can I turn?" Dick had heard Dolores clearly.

"What? What's happening?" Scott straightened again.

The vampire glanced at him. "Caleb's in Mexico." He raised his voice and added, "Where in Mexico, Dolores?"

"Cabo San Lucas," she continued. "He appears to be on vacation. I have to say I'm a little surprised. There's a large community of duende in the area. How he thought he'd fly under the radar there is beyond me. He checked into the resort this morning."

Dick's face lit up. "Cabo? I adore Cabo. And I don't need to turn around. It occurs to me that I have an old friend with a private plane based in Phoenix."

Two days later, Lexi gazed out of the window of their suite onto the pool area in the resort hotel.

Upon their arrival, Dick had connected with the duende who had first seen Caleb and recognized him from pictures Dolores had distributed through her large network. Once in their room, they didn't risk leaving it and monitored his movements through the strange young duende.

They waited for their opportunity to eliminate him.

Lexi spoke to Dick as she watched the people at the poolside. "I still can't believe you called Betsy."

Scott nodded. "I can't believe she hopped on a plane and flew down here."

The vampire's voice came from the body bag. "She has as much if not more right to be here as the rest of us. Although I'd have preferred it if she watched from the window. I had forgotten how strong-willed she can be." He paused. "What are you doing?"

"Nothing." Scott continued to point his finger at the bag and he smiled as little diamantes appeared where he indicated.

"I don't see why we couldn't do this at night so I could do it. I should be the one doing this—to his face." The vampire sounded sullen.

She watched Caleb through the scope as she spoke. "You know why. He comes out to sunbathe at the pool for an hour a day. It's the only time he's accessible. Anyway, you *will* be doing it."

He ignored that and continued to complain. "I can't believe I'm back in Cabo. I haven't been here since I was alive. This whole burning-in-the-sun thing is such an inconvenience."

Scott looked astonished. "Really? I think I could fix that."

"I doubt it." Dick sighed. "I think I'd have heard about that by now."

Lexi glanced at her friend. They both shrugged. *Why not?*

"It's kind of against the rules to even try something like that," the young man continued, "but since we're fugitives, I'll see what I can do."

"Are you shitting me?" The vampire sounded indignant.

"Shh! It's going down." Caleb sat in his usual lounger, reading his newspaper. Lexi's gaze followed a beautiful young server who carried a tray. She approached from behind and to his side, put the drink down, and turned to walk away.

Unfortunately, she turned at the sound of a click.

Caleb, still reading his newspaper, had produced a fifty-peso note and held it up between two fingers. The young woman's gaze shifted uncertainly to Lexi's window.

"Shit!" She shook her head to indicate that the woman should get out of there.

Dick half-sat in the bag. "What's going on?"

"He's trying to tip her." She couldn't keep the disappointment out of her voice.

Scott stood to look out of the window. "If she takes that note, he'll sense the magic."

Her gaze remained focused on the scene through the scope. "If she doesn't take the tip, he'll know something's wrong."

The server looked at the other guests around the pool, then glanced at the window. She raised her hand to a thin chain around her neck and pulled.

As it broke, so did the spell. Had anyone been looking, they would have seen the beautiful young woman instantly turn into a little old lady.

Betsy leaned forward and snagged the note from Caleb's fingers. "*Gracias.*"

She walked as far as the bar, then turned to watch.

"Is she inside?" Dick asked.

Lexi shook her head. "No, she's at the bar, ordering a drink."

"What if he sees her? We shouldn't have involved her." The vampire wriggled so much inside the bag that she was tempted to tell Scott to sit on him.

"It was your idea." She rolled her eyes.

Caleb put his newspaper down and picked the glass up. She focused on his lips as he muttered a word. He seemed satisfied that the drink was safe, glanced at the little pot of olives and cocktail sticks, and smiled. With a practiced movement, he snagged an olive and dropped it into the drink before he knocked it back.

"I'm glad she's here. I'd never have thought to put it in the olives." She shrugged.

The sorcerer sat bolt upright, instantly aware that something wasn't right. He looked around and his jaw dropped at the sight of Betsy seated at the poolside bar with a glass of gin. She toasted him with a broad smile.

He muttered a word at the woman, then muttered again. He seemed to have discovered that his magic wasn't working.

"What's happening?" Dick punched the bag from the inside.

Lexi took the shot. The gun was shielded by magic so no one

heard it. The bullet was a Scott special, a combination of tech and magic, and it found Caleb's heart without breaking his skin.

She addressed the body bag. "It's done. Over to you."

The sorcerer clutched his chest. It was clear he knew something was coming.

Dick paused for a moment before he said, "Stop."

His heart stopped and he sagged onto the lounger, dead.

Lexi stared at the ocean from a little table on the promenade.

Betsy placed a hand on her arm. "Where will you go now?"

"We only got as far as Phoenix when the call came. I guess we'll go back to pick up the car and continue to New Orleans. How about you?"

"I'll return to the house. Dolores will contact me about visiting Todd in Fae. It'll take some time for him to heal."

Dick turned to the older woman. "What's the point in knocking around that big place alone? Why don't you come to New Orleans with us?"

"Dick, I'm eighty years old. I'm too old to be gallivanting around the country fighting monsters."

Scott stood, removed the chain from his pocket, and placed it on the table in front of Betsy. "You don't have to be too old to do anything."

She picked it up with two fingers and dangled it in the air in front of her face. "I'll admit it was good to move around without arthritis pain."

"Here it comes." Lexi sat up excitedly.

The vampire passed Marcel to Betsy. "If this doesn't work—"

"Dude, have some faith." Scott clapped him on the back and sat.

He turned to the young man. "I'm sitting here about to face

the sun. I think I'm showing an extraordinary level of faith in you, Scott."

Dick faced the ocean and saw his first sunrise in over seventy years. A tear rolled down his face in a moment so magical that nothing could spoil it.

"Okay, I got one," Scott began. "A vampire walks into a shifter bar…"

THE BOUND LEGACY

The story continues with book two, THE BOUND LEGACY, available now at Amazon and Kindle Unlimited.

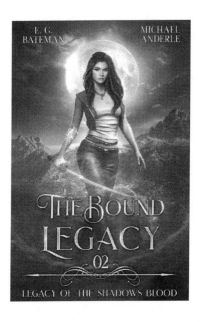

AUTHOR NOTES - E.G. BATEMAN
APRIL 8, 2020

Once upon a time, I went to Bali. And that's where my life began.

There were many reasons to go; the awesome people, the incredible conference sessions, and *holy shit, it's Bali!* But I went there with one primary goal. And the day I pushed a few chapters of something I'd been working on into Michael Anderle's hand, that goal was achieved. It could have gone horribly wrong. I knew he didn't usually accept unsolicited manuscripts at big conferences like Vegas, but Bali was an intimate gathering. I hoped the fact I'd thrown my life savings into an event that had been designed for authors way more successful than I was, would show I was serious. It was a massive gamble.

The whole experience was mortifying. After a conference session, I found him chatting with the exceptionally talented, Ell Leigh Clarke. I stood there with the chapters shaking a little in my hand. People were filing out of the room and I kind of assumed these two would stop talking and move like everyone else. Nope. Pretty soon, there were three people in the room, two of them who were (it was now abundantly clear) having a MEET-ING, and me, standing 2ft away, watching like it was the centre court at Wimbledon.

I know what you're thinking. *Elaine, why didn't you just turn and leave?* I know, I was being all kinds of rude. But there comes a point when turning and walking away (through the large, echoing room) looks as weird as staying put. Also, I might never get the nerve to do it again. Also, I don't think my feet would move.

So, there I stood, thinking, *come on Michael, just flick your eyes in my direction and I'll shove these pages at you and run.*

Nope!

Finally, the meeting was over and Michael addressed the elephant in the room, me. I was surprised he didn't call me out for being so rude. But he was very kind, he took the sheets, and I bolted.

I was mortified by the barefaced cheek I'd shown. For the next day or so, I actively *hid* from Michael, to the point that I actually waded, fully clothed through the swimming pool to avoid passing him on a walkway. Okay, only up to my knees, but still. Then, I got a grip of myself. I knew he wasn't going to read it until after Bali, so I stopped hiding and enjoyed the conference, the socializing, and the sun.

After two weeks of fearing I'd just blown the bank on a pipe dream, I got the call.

Forming the characters and bouncing dialogue around with Michael has been a hoot. I fell in love with Lexi the moment I visualised her clinically decapitating a vampire with her thighs (*sorry, Dick*). I love them all, and hope that you will come to love them too.

Elaine

AUTHOR NOTES - MICHAEL ANDERLE
APRIL 13, 2020

THANK YOU for reading our story!

We have a few of these planned, but we don't know if we should continue writing and publishing without your input.

Options include leaving a review, reaching out on Facebook to let us know, and smoke signals.

Frankly, smoke signals might get misconstrued as low-hanging clouds, so you might want to nix that idea...

SERIOUSLY?

I don't remember the part of Elaine's story in Bali nearly like she did. Also, I thought I DID read what you gave me to read (your other story) while in Bali, and you were right.

I read it because you spent that much effort to get the stuff into my hands.

I don't do Vegas like that because it is MEANT to be an all-inclusive event that just about anyone can get to (or as close as we can make it.)

So, feeling a bit of guilt that she did all she could to make her dream happen, of course I would read it.

And yes, Ellie and I argue like that because we are friends and she has problems. I'm the normal one, *I promise.*

Me normal, her not. Not her, me.

Her problems start and end with "she's British," and there are a whole lot of funny other reasons in the middle of that British sandwich explanation.

But, this isn't about ELC. This is about Elaine.

One thing that hit me in the gut with Elaine was her super funny dialogue. Her challenge was fitting that dialogue into a story.

Bali was something like January 4th, 2019.

Elaine and I started discussing a collaboration and just having conversations on writing in general on January 16th, 2019. (I had stayed over on that side of the world for extra days. I don't think we hit the shores of the US again until about the very end of January.)

Then, Elaine went "all-in" and took time off work to finish her trilogy. I warned her that writing as your only occupation is very hard for those not accustomed to having no rules.

Elaine didn't believe me.

Here are a few snippets from our conversations. Note the dates.

February 4th, 2019

Elaine 10:55 AM

Cool, me too. Maybe catch up there. (*London Book Fair – Mike.*)

10:59

You were dead right about people not working not being efficient writers. I'm on kind of a sabbatical. Today was the first writing day. Anyhoo, turns out The Marvelous Mrs. Maisel is really good.

michael 1:37 PM

HAHAHAHAHAH

February 5th, 2019

<u>Elaine</u> 6:17 PM
No Netflix today. Netflix is the work of Satan.
<u>michael</u> 11:53 PM
Yeah, better figure this stuff out!

February 6th, 2019
<u>Elaine</u> 4:12 AM
You're not wrong! Yesterday went better without the Netflix! I've been in organizing mode. I've finally listed out my characters (which I should have done from the beginning) and found a couple I'd forgotten that I can add to the current book. I'm surprised by how many I've killed. It's like SIMS all over again.

Thanks to the advice of Grace Snoke I've now got a wiki to list the characters for the readers (and me!). I'm glad I've taken the time to work on this.

This series has plot twists so I don't want to disappoint the readers who will be expecting to be surprised in the last book. But while books with twists are great to read, they're a time-consuming pain in the arse to write.
<u>michael</u> 8:41 AM
THIS !! >>>> "But while books with twists are great to read, they're a time-consuming, pain in the arse to write."

Pain or not, Elaine worked hard, and I hope you enjoyed the fruits of her talent & labor!

Remind me next time to plug in the parts that started THIS book. ;-)

Mike's Diary: "Sometimes life just *is*."
So, my company is testing new software to allow us a virtual experience while we work. As of now (4/13/2020), it is performing better than I could have hoped in bringing those who collaborate with LMBPN together, no matter the location or time of day (or night.)

This same software, I hope, will allow us to create virtual meetings with fans, and (I'm trying, but I'm not sure the company behind the software will make it affordable) I want to create a place for fans to get together and create all sorts of fun stuff with LMBPN.

And frankly just have a place to hang a while.

If you would like to know more (and are on Facebook) join us on the Kurtherian Gambit Facebook Group For Fans and Authors

Link: https://www.facebook.com/profile.php?id=127989844503323&ref=br_rs

I hope to have something up to start testing this in the next week or two. We will start with small groups, and possibly move up from there.

Clean is the New Dream

My office isn't messy… exactly. It is lived-in *chic*.

Honestly, a whole *lot* of the lived-in part. (If you add chic to the end of any descriptor, you immediately sound artsy. No, really, try it.

"That's ugly."

"No, that's ugly-*chic*."

"That man-cave crap has got to go."

"No, that's man-cave *chic*. It stays."

"That's hideous."

"No, that's hideous—"

"If you end that with 'chic,' I will shove my cottony house slippers so far up your ass you will be burping tiny clouds."

"Right. So, what now? I lost my train of thought with that visual."

(You thought 'Hideous *chic*, and that would have worked, #AmIRight?)

I will have to take another set of boxes to the storage room tomorrow after our meetings, and maybe then I'll have a bit of "clean" in my office. Judith cleaned the living room and Kitchen (both places she works from) yesterday, and believe it or not, I am a bit #Jealous of her clean areas.

(Don't worry, I'm having trouble believing it too.)

I'm So Going to Regret This.

So, I have the new 2020 iPad (#SupportApple and #ItsGoodTo-HaveAppleEmployeesWithDiscountsAsFriends along with #SupportFriendsByBuyingApple), but I don't like using it just as it is.

I want either a Smart Keyboard Folio or the new More Magic Keyboard for the iPad, or maybe something clamshell (but won't that effectively make it a Mac?).

Have I mentioned I'm seriously impatient? I work six often seven days a week (#ThankGodILoveWhatIDo), and when it comes to my technology, I splurge on myself. It's the one thing I can point to my wife and say 'it's a write-off' and 'Don't harsh my (writing) buzz, woman.'

(Actually, only one of those responses works on Judith. #ThankGodAppleDoesn'tRefreshOften and #IReallyDoWait-2YearsBetweeniPhonesNow.)

I swear Apple better not upgrade their keyboard on the larger MacBooks in 2021, or I might have to try therapy to hold-back on an upgrade (yes, I have the 2016 MacBook 16".) If therapy is more expensive than my purchase, doesn't that make it smarter just to purchase the product?

I think it does.

Are you paying attention, Steve? (#StephenCampbellNeedsa-NewMacbook13Pro)

Anyway. My iPad is sitting in its box unopened because I don't have a keyboard for it. I can't get the Magic Keyboard until May at this point, or maybe later. Since I suffer from #ImpatienceIsAThing, I am looking to see if anything cool is out for my iPad that includes a touchpad for mousing around.

You know, if—and this is for the benefit of my fans who

might wish to know—I buy a clamshell with touchpad and report that information back here in a future *Author Note*, that's research and something I can write off on taxes, right?

So, I might sacrifice a larger credit card bill on the altar of #DoingItForTheFans.

If you happen to write a review for any of our books, maybe drop a line in the review "I Support Mike and his Magic Keyboard!" (Or, if you hate Apple products, feel free to suggest I buy other technology. Especially really *REALLY* expensive hardware that I can point to and show my wife how frugal' I was with the purchases I have already made or might <snicker> make soon.

Ad Aeternitatem,

Michael Anderle

THE FUGITIVE LEGACY

Sign up for E.G. Bateman's email list and receive your free copy of *The Fugitive Legacy,* the exciting prequel to the Legacy of the Shadow's Blood series.

With faulty powers and a vampire attack, can Lexi do what's right?

Lexi has worked extra hard to compensate for her faulty paranormal abilities and prove she deserves her place among the supernatural protectors, Kindred.

The aftermath of a vampire attack leaves her questioning her loyalties.

Can she hide her secret? Or will she be forced to flee from the only family she has ever known?

But Kindred don't just let you leave...

Get your free copy here.

CONNECT WITH THE AUTHORS

Connect with E.G. Bateman

Website: www.egbatemanwrites.com

Facebook: https://www.facebook.com/egbatemanwrites/

Instagram: https://www.instagram.com/egbatemanwrites/

Twitter: https://twitter.com/EGBateman

Sign up for E.G. Bateman's newsletter and receive The Fugitive Legacy!

Connect with Michael Anderle

Website: http://lmbpn.com

Email List: http://lmbpn.com/email/

Michael's Social Media

https://www.facebook.com/LMBPNPublishing

https://twitter.com/lmbpn

https://www.instagram.com/lmbpn_publishing/

https://www.bookbub.com/authors/michael-anderle